NO MORTAL REASON

NO MORTAL REASON

A Diana Spaulding Mystery

KATHY LYNN EMERSON

PEMBERLEY PRESS
CORONA DEL MAR

Published by
P E M B E R L E Y P R E S S
P O Box 1027
Corona del Mar, CA 92625
www.pemberleypress.com

A member of The Authors Studio
www.theauthorsstudio.org

Cover art by Linda Weatherly
Cover design by Kat & Dog Studios

ISBN13 978-0-9771913-4-5
LCCN 2007000048

Library of Congress Cataloging-in-Publication Data

Emerson, Kathy Lynn.
  No mortal reason : a Diana Spaulding mystery / Kathy Lynn Emerson.
    p. cm.
  ISBN 978-0-9771913-4-5 (pbk. : alk. paper)
  1. Spaulding, Diana (Fictitious character)—Fiction. 2. Women journalists—
Fiction. 3. New York (State)—Fiction. 4. Hotels—Fiction. 5. Uncles—
Death—Fiction. 6. Historical fiction. gsafd I. Title.
  PS3555.M414D43 2004
  813'.54—dc22
                                    2007000048

CHAPTER ONE

ഇൗ

May, 1888

Diana Spaulding peered through the grime-streaked glass of the train window at rolling green countryside. Dotted with small farmsteads and numerous apple orchards, the landscape should have been a soothing sight. Even under overcast skies, it possessed the kind of pastoral beauty that appealed to artists and poets.

Diana was too nervous to appreciate it.

After they'd switched from the New York Central Railway to the Ontario & Western line at Oneida, the morning had passed with excruciating slowness. Their train had stopped at every tiny depot along the way—Fish's Eddy, Cook's Falls, Livingston Manor—all small, rural places Diana had never heard of. Now that she thought about it, she did not recall having seen a single factory since leaving Buffalo. She was out of her element here and she knew it.

"Lih-ber-tee! Liberty, New York, next stop!"

At the conductor's call, Diana felt her already straight back go stiff as a ramrod. Her right hand clasped hard around the handle of the crocodile skin gripsack beside her on the plush seat of the parlor car. Only the feel of the carved wood biting into her palm brought her to her senses. With an effort, she loosened her grip and ordered herself to relax, but the silent command had little effect on the knot of tension between her shoulder blades.

"Regretting your decision?" Ben Northcote asked. He sat opposite her in one of the car's reclining chairs, watching her face with an intensity that further unnerved her.

"Which one?" she asked with an attempt at lightness.

Just now it seemed the height of foolishness to have postponed their wedding. Ben had wanted to marry her before they'd left Denver, and Diana's mother had thought it would be a great treat to hold the ceremony in one of the parlors at the Elmira Hotel. That suggestion alone had made Diana reconsider. In the end, they'd decided to return to Ben's home in Maine before finding a preacher. To do otherwise would have left Maggie, the formidable and somewhat eccentric Northcote matriarch, out of their plans.

Now, however, Diana worried that her single state might complicate their stay in Sullivan County. She had no idea how the locals felt about the propriety of a widow traveling with a bachelor, even one she planned to marry the following month. A proper sort of female would have taken the precaution of hiring a companion or, at the least, a maid. Diana hadn't bothered with either. Then again, she hadn't thought of herself as truly "proper" since she'd run away from the Young Ladies' Seminary of San Francisco at the tender age of eighteen.

"It isn't too late to change your mind," Ben said.

"We're getting married in Maine on the thirtieth of June and that's that," Diana said in a firm voice.

A wry smile kicked up the corners of Ben's mobile mouth. His neatly-trimmed, midnight-colored beard and mustache twitched and the amber flecks in his dark eyes twinkled. "I'm glad to hear it, but I meant it's not too late to change your mind about getting off this train at the next stop."

"Oh." She felt hot color rush into her face and ducked her

head, pretending to smooth out the wrinkles in the newly-purchased, dark gray traveling dress she wore. "I confess I *am* nervous about meeting my uncles. What if they are cut from the same cloth as their sister? It's likely, you know. And no one can hold a grudge like my mother."

"If you're convinced that this newly discovered family of yours won't want to claim you, then stay on the train. New York is a few hours away. We'll stop long enough to collect the trunk and boxes you left at Mrs. Curran's boarding house and be on our way back to Maine before you know it."

Diana permitted herself a wistful sigh but shook her head. As soon as she'd realized that her relatives lived only one hundred and twenty-five miles northwest of New York City, she'd known she'd have to visit Lenape Springs. It had not required much of a detour to do so, just the selection of a different railway line between Buffalo and Weehawken, the terminal from which ferries conveyed train passengers the rest of the way to Manhattan.

"My life would have been much simpler," Diana murmured, "if Mother had never bothered to correct my mistaken belief that she was an only child."

It had been a shock to learn that Elmira Grant Torrence had been cast off by her family for marrying Diana's father, just as Elmira and William Torrence had later disowned Diana for her runaway marriage to Evan Spaulding. The recent end to Diana's estrangement from her mother had been, in many ways, a mixed blessing. Elmira Torrence was a cold, selfish woman, incapable of showing affection, let alone love. While it was true that she'd insisted on buying her daughter a new wardrobe—her trousseau, she'd said—before Diana and Ben left Denver, Diana knew that her mother's generosity came from guilt, not fondness.

As for the information about the Grants of Lenape Springs, she'd tossed that out with a careless laugh when Diana had remarked that she hoped her mother would come East for the wedding, since Diana had no other kin to invite.

"You've got a passel of kinfolk," her mother had informed her, and had proceeded to reel off the names of all five of her brothers and sisters.

Another small sigh escaped Diana as the train slowed on a long curve. She didn't see anything ahead that looked like a railroad station, which made her wonder just how tiny a village this Liberty, New York might be. She knew little more about it than that it was the nearest the O&W Railroad came to Lenape Springs.

"I should have written first," Diana fretted.

"We've been all through that," Ben reminded her. "We'll arrive as paying guests. That assures us of a welcome." He'd made all the arrangements by telegram before they'd left Colorado.

They'd been traveling for days, giving them ample opportunity to speculate about the welcome they might receive. Diana's mother had not been able to tell them much except that her two older brothers, Myron and Howard, still operated the hotel their father had owned before them. Elmira Grant Torrence had left her childhood home thirty-three years ago and had never looked back. Truth be told, if she hadn't become reacquainted with another former Lenape Springs resident, Ed Leeves, after moving to Denver, she wouldn't have been able to tell Diana even that much about her family.

"My married name will mean nothing to the Grants." Diana squinted at the high point of land beyond the train window. There appeared to be a large building at the very top.

"Do you want me to play Devil's advocate? Anonymity is to your advantage, or so you've been telling me for more than a week now. It will allow you to decide whether or not to introduce yourself as Elmira Grant's daughter after you meet them. You can get to know them first, let them get to know you, and then—"

"—reveal my deceit?"

"If it troubles you that much, tell them who you are at once." A hint of irritation crept into Ben's resonant baritone. Even his equable temperament had its limits.

Diana repressed a third sigh. She couldn't blame him for being impatient with her. They'd had this conversation before, and more than once. It wasn't like her to be so indecisive, but in this case she could not seem to settle on what was best to do.

"We will go ahead as planned," she mumbled. "I've come this far. I will at least satisfy my curiosity. If they appear unlikely to welcome their sister's daughter back into the fold, we will simply depart with no one the wiser."

"Do you want this?" Ben asked. While she'd dithered, he'd been collecting the books and newspapers with which they'd passed their time during the long journey. He held out a week-old copy of the *Independent Intelligencer,* the New York City newspaper for which Diana had once written a theatrical gossip column called "Today's Tidbits." More recently she had reported on crime, both in New York City and in Denver, and written a few pieces about her travels.

With a sound like the groan of a dying elephant, the steam engine's air brakes brought the train to a stop at the station. Diana hastily stuffed the newspaper into the capacious tweed bag she carried slung over her shoulder.

They were the only passengers to disembark at Liberty on this early Friday afternoon in the middle of May, although several men wearing suits and carrying sample cases waited on the platform to board. The station agent emerged from a modest frame structure that looked more like a freight house than a passenger depot, gave Diana a genial nod, and headed towards the baggage car. The depot was small enough that the man who staffed the ticket office also served as baggage master.

Diana's mother had showered her with so many gifts that she'd had to purchase two trunks to transport them all. When Ben went to reclaim these large pieces of baggage, she took charge of the pile of smaller ones—her tweed bag and gripsack, the hat box, two large Gladstone bags, one for each of them, and Ben's doctor's bag.

While she waited, she surveyed her surroundings. Except for

the large white water tank to her left, she couldn't see much. The depot blocked her view on one side, the train on the other.

Diana was glad of the warmth of her wool traveling dress. Now and then a feeble ray of sunshine penetrated otherwise gray skies, but the air stayed chilly. A stiff breeze stirred the hem of her skirt and made the crimson feather on her smart new hat dip and sway. As the train departed, the wind abruptly increased to gale force. Diana squeezed her eyes shut as a gritty haze billowed back to engulf her. So much for the O&W's claim that anthracite coal-burning engines produced neither cinders nor dust!

When the air cleared and the last of the dark green passenger cars disappeared en route to points south, Diana could at last see what lay on the other side of the tracks. Just across from the passenger depot was the real freight house. A coal yard was situated adjacent to it. On her right and a short distance up a hill were a few scattered structures, but not enough to be the center of town. The only vehicular traffic was a single wagon slowly making its way towards the depot.

Diana had to walk to the edge of the platform and look downhill to find the village of Liberty. From that vantage point, her view encompassed a good number of houses and several churches. The high, white steeple of one of them dominated the scene. Beyond rose a line of hills. They were scarcely mountains compared to those she'd just left behind in Colorado, but she had looked at a map. It had told her that both Liberty and Lenape Springs were situated in the foothills of the Catskills. If this had been a clear day, she suspected she might have seen a few peaks in that direction.

The wagon, a weathered buckboard, arrived at the depot. Apparently it was the house rig because the words HOTEL GRANT were emblazoned on signs attached to each side. The driver, a thin, stoop-shouldered man of indeterminate age, ignored Diana and spoke to Ben. "You Dr. Northcote?"

"Yes, that's right," Ben said. "How far is it to the Hotel Grant?"

"Five miles." The words were clipped and he scowled at the

two heavy trunks on the platform. "Won't need fripperies. Lenape Springs don't go in for fancy dress."

The sound of a muffled chuckle made Diana turn. The station agent stood a little behind her. "Don't mind him," he said. "That's just his way. Floyd Lyseth hasn't had a good word to say about anything since his daughter ran away with a peddler ten years back."

Diana wasn't sure how to respond to this confidence, but she was struck by the fact that, just lately, she heard stories about runaway marriages everywhere she went. Perhaps she was simply more attuned to such tales. She recalled something her friend Rowena had written to her a few years earlier. When Rowena had first learned she was to have a child, she claimed to have seen babies everywhere she looked, when previously, or so Rowena swore, she could go months at a stretch without so much as a glimpse of anyone under the age of ten.

"Come to think of it," the talkative station agent continued, unconcerned that Diana had made no reply, "Lyseth wasn't exactly a ray of sunshine before young Elly took off."

"Does he work at the Hotel Grant?" Diana asked.

The station agent nodded. "He's the handyman, driver, bell boy—whatever needs doing, Lyseth does it. Even came into town here and helped out with replacing the station roof when Myron Grant told him to." He indicated the simple frame structure beside them. "Sure feels good to have something solid over our heads again. The old roof blew right off during the blizzard in March. Highest winds we've ever had in these parts. Took the chimney off that house over there, too." He pointed to a nearby home.

"How terrifying for those inside," Diana murmured. She'd had her own frightening experiences during that particular storm.

They exchanged the look of fellow survivors.

"Coldest winter anyone around here can remember. Should have expected something like that. March twelfth it was, and we had snow drifts twelve feet deep. There's *still* snow on the ground some places." He pointed towards a nearby wooded area. "Got a snowbank about two feet deep right over there."

"How long was the O&W tied up?"

"Six days."

"The storm paralyzed most of New York and New England for the better part of a week."

"Diana?" Ben called, preventing her from sharing her own blizzard story. The buckboard was loaded and wanted only her presence to leave for the hotel.

Bidding goodbye to the friendly station agent, Diana hurried towards the wagon. She reached it in time to hear Ben ask their driver a question about the waters that had given Lenape Springs its name.

Floyd Lyseth looked as if he'd bitten into a sour apple. "There's just the one and that spring's been nothin' but trouble. Can't see no mortal reason for them to go addin' on to the hotel. Fine just the way she was. Outsiders comin' in are goin' to bring nothin' but trouble."

Diana hid a smile. The station agent was right. The man was a real curmudgeon.

Barely waiting until his passengers were settled on the hard wooden seats behind him, Lyseth took up the reins and urged the horses forward along the hard-packed dirt street that ran parallel to the railroad tracks. They were soon out of the village and heading west over an uneven road made worse by recent rains. Diana clung to Ben's arm for balance and was glad she had him there to support her when they turned north onto an even more deeply rutted country lane. The land rose all around them and, in common with the hilltop she'd noticed from the train as it entered Liberty, one directly ahead also had a large building at its crest.

Slowed by mud and mire and by the narrow road's many twists and turns and ups and downs, it seemed to take eons to reach Lenape Springs, though in reality considerably less than an hour passed. At the end of the journey, Diana found herself in a pretty little hamlet situated in a pleasant valley. A hotel was the first building they came to, but it was not their destination. A sign proclaimed that it was the Lenape Springs Villa. Down a side road to the right, Diana caught sight of a mill. As the wagon continued along the main street, they passed two stores, a post office, and a church on one side of the road, and a livery stable and blacksmith shop on the other, all interspersed with a sprinkling of houses. A wooded stretch of perhaps a quarter mile in length separated the last of these from the entrance to the hotel grounds, a long drive that curved gradually upward.

"Hotel Grant," their taciturn driver announced when he brought the wagon to a stop. Those were the first words he'd spoken since leaving the depot at Liberty.

For a long moment, Diana simply sat and stared. It was the building she'd seen earlier from a distance, but that glimpse of a far-off hilltop had given her no hint of what to expect. She'd never seen anything quite like the structure in front of her.

What was still recognizable as a two-story farmhouse was at the core of the hotel, but various additions had been made to it. There was a three-story section that, by itself, might have seemed a natural extension . . . if someone had not added another wing with two five-story towers. Just visible over the mansard roof of the three-story section were the tops of several lower towers at the back of the hotel. A wide veranda, intended to provide guests with a place to socialize in the fresh air, wrapped around as much of the structure as Diana could see. Parts of it appeared to have been built recently and were still unpainted.

"Expanding, are they?" Ben asked.

Diana could hear no hammering or sawing, and no workmen were in sight, but she thought she heard a distant shriek—the kind of noise a board made when it was ripped free of its fellows.

Lyseth's answer was muffled by the heavy trunk he'd just hoisted onto his shoulders. "Tryin' again. Didn't learn their lesson the first time."

That sounded ominous, Diana thought, exchanging a concerned glance with Ben. She wondered what had happened "the first time" the hotel had been renovated. Then again, judging by the hodgepodge of styles the structure boasted, the "lesson" might have been that the Grants should have employed the services of an architect before expanding.

With a grunt, Lyseth steadied his burden and led the way towards wide steps cut into the terrace. Halfway there, he stopped dead as a goat appeared out of nowhere to block his way.

"Confounded nuisance!" Lyseth stamped his feet, hoping to drive the animal away, but it stood its ground and bleated at him. When Lyseth took a step forward, it lowered its head as if it meant to charge.

"That's some guard dog you've got." Diana heard the amusement in Ben's deep voice. She had to stifle a giggle herself.

"Get out of the way, Tremont," Lyseth bellowed, his face going very red as he kicked a rock in the goat's direction.

Tremont bleated again and backed off far enough for Lyseth to reach the steps. Ben hustled Diana after their driver, but the goat seemed to have no interest in butting anyone else. Diana had the feeling this was a long-standing feud between man and beast, and wondered if there might be a piece for the newspaper in it. Then she put the idea aside to think about later, for they had entered the hotel.

Diana's feet sank into soft, deep carpet. Even on this overcast day, enormous windows provided plenty of illumination and her gaze was drawn first to the huge fireplace directly ahead of her. Situated against the far wall, across an expanse of open space, it dominated the lobby.

Diana frowned. It was cold in the cavernous room, but no one had lit a fire. She thought that strange but had too many other things on her mind to dwell on the oddity of it. She took note of the elevator to one side of the hearth and the grand staircase curving upward on the other. Then her focus shifted to the ornately carved mahogany check-in desk that stood near the stairs.

A large, leather-bound guest register sat open on the counter. Pen and ink waited beside it, but nowhere was there any sign of a desk clerk or any other member of the hotel staff. When Diana looked around, she realized that Floyd Lyseth had also disappeared, taking her trunk with him.

"Did we imagine him?" she whispered.

"Probably," Ben said. "If Mother were here, she'd be sure the place is haunted."

"How very peculiar that no one is here to greet us. They obviously expected us today." Unless, of course, Floyd Lyseth *was* a ghost."

A little hand-lettered sign beside a brass bell said "Ring for Service." Tentatively, Diana did so.

Before the last echo of the ding died away, a young woman threw open the pocket doors of the room directly opposite the check-in desk and scurried towards them, hastily wiping her hands on the sides of her well-worn, white lawn apron. The garment had definitely seen better days. It had probably started life as part of a parlor maid's uniform, starched and pressed, its bib and shoulder straps embroidered and in pristine condition. Years of use had yellowed the fabric and left it torn in two or three places.

"Forgive my appearance!" The young woman sounded a trifle breathless. "We knew you were coming. I just lost track of the time." As she ducked behind the check-in desk, she whipped off the apron to reveal a serviceable red calico frock with a narrow white collar and plain, wrist-length sleeves. She wore neither corset nor bustle, which Diana supposed was only common sense since she'd plainly been cleaning in the other room.

Diana shifted her attention to the woman's face. Was she a cousin? She had red highlights in her light brown hair. Diana's hair was also reddish-brown. Beyond that, and the fact that they both had blue eyes, there did not seem to be much resemblance. Diana was of medium height and build. She had a slightly square face with wide-spaced eyes and fair skin—a gardenia-petal complexion, so Ben liked to say—and a small nose. The desk clerk was shorter than Diana and possessed of a noble nose and a generous bosom. She was a bit too thin elsewhere. Her face was very pink. Either she was flustered by their sudden arrival or she'd recently spent too much time in the sun without the protection of a hat.

Embarrassed, Diana decided, thinking of the apron, though she had no reason to be. No sensible woman would do housework in her best clothing.

As Floyd Lyseth had done, the young woman ignored Diana and addressed Ben. "Welcome to the Hotel Grant. You must be Dr. Northcote. Uncle Myron is real anxious to meet you. At least he is if you're a medical doctor."

"Is he ill?"

"Uncle Myron?" Cornflower-blue eyes widened at the very idea. "He's never been sick a day in his life. We're all healthy here in Lenape Springs. It's the water, you know."

"Why does he want to meet me, then?"

"Oh, he hopes you'll endorse the wondrous properties of Lenape Springs water. I'm sure you will, once you've tried it for yourself."

"I came to fish," Ben said, clinging to the fiction he'd decided upon during their train journey.

Diana used one silk-gloved hand to hide a smile. She'd once heard Ben wax caustic over an advertisement for a popular spa that claimed its medicinal springs could cure anything from dyspepsia to torpid liver. He would never agree to give Myron Grant the testimonial he wanted, but for the present, because of her, he could not come right out and refuse.

"I hope you'll forgive the confusion," the young woman continued, apparently satisfied that Ben would change his mind about the endorsement. "We expect to be finished with all the construction before the season starts."

"The season?" The term confused Diana.

Ben seemed to understand the young woman's meaning but still looked surprised. "Are you open only for the high season? A friend told me this was a fine area for fishing and advised me to visit before the flies get bad. May fifteenth to June fifteenth, he said. Or wait until the fall."

"We do get some fishermen, and a few families come to the area in mid-June, but for the most part we only take guests from July 10 until September 10, just like the other summer hotels and boarding houses in Sullivan County. Some folks come and stay six or eight weeks, whole families sometimes, except that the husbands can only come up from the city to join them for the weekends."

"Do I gather that your family owns this hotel?" Diana asked, seizing the opportunity to find out more about the desk clerk. "Your uncle, you said?"

"Uncle Myron. Yes."

"Myron Grant?"

"Yes. My name is Mercy Grant. I'm in charge of the desk and I grow all the flowers we use to decorate the public rooms."

Which meant, Diana concluded, that she must be the daughter of the younger of the two Grant brothers, Howard. Diana's mother had given them the names of all five of her siblings—Myron, Sally Ann, Luella, Ida May, and Howard. Mercy Grant's father was some five years older than his sister Elmira, which meant he must be in his late fifties. Mercy herself didn't look a day over eighteen.

While Diana had been questioning her newfound cousin, Ben had signed the register. He cleared his throat to get their attention and the desk clerk at once remembered her duties.

"I hope you will find your accommodations comfortable," she said, pausing briefly at a key rack before she came out from behind the check-in desk. "Your rooms are in the north tower. I'll show you the way. It's a bit of a maze through the corridors. Your luggage will be brought up, if it hasn't already been delivered. Do you need help with your unpacking? We haven't any chambermaids on staff at the moment, but I'd be happy to—"

"That won't be necessary," Diana interrupted. She wished her cousin would stop talking for a moment. She had the feeling she'd just missed something of significance. No chambermaids? That seemed a bit odd, even if the hotel wasn't open. Did Mercy do *all* the housework herself?

Ben caught Diana's arm as Mercy rushed ahead of them towards the elevator. His eyes stayed on the other woman until he was sure she was too far ahead of them to overhear. Then he bent close to Diana's ear and whispered, "Don't make a scene. I have my reasons."

She stopped in her tracks, realizing at that moment what it really was that had seemed wrong to her. Ben had signed the register. She had not. And Mercy had taken only one room key from the key rack behind the check-in desk.

A none-too-gentle tug from Ben got her moving again. "Come along, *Mrs. Northcote.*"

Diana obeyed, but only because she did not wish to embarrass herself. How *could* he? This was a disaster. By signing the register as Mr. and Mrs. Benjamin Northcote he had put her in an untenable position. If her family ever found out they had shared a room in the hotel without benefit of clergy, they'd be outraged and horrified—as they should be!

"All the tower suites have a spectacular view," Mercy said when they got into the elevator. She gave Ben a bright smile as she set it in motion. "You and your wife can enjoy a splendid vista of mountains and treetops from your very own private balcony."

Ben's hand tightened in warning on Diana's arm, but he needn't have worried. She was not going to denounce him in front of her new-found cousin. She'd keep her thoughts to herself until they were alone.

Emotions warred within her, perilously close to the surface. Her cheeks felt quite warm and a tight knot had formed in her chest. Beside her, Ben seemed unconcerned. He even chuckled at some remark Mercy made.

Diana felt a bleakness descend upon her as she listened. Did

Ben Northcote understand her so little? Did he not realize the enormity of what he had done? She had thought that if she decided to tell the Grants who she was, she might also invite them to the wedding. That would be impossible now. And to think, only a short time ago she'd been worried that they might question her character just because she'd made a train journey unchaperoned in a gentleman's company!

Oblivious to the brewing storm, Mercy Grant sang the praises of the newly installed hydraulic elevator all the way to the third floor. At the end of a long passageway and up a flight of stairs, they came to the top of the north tower.

As promised, the parlor of the suite offered a panoramic view of the Catskill Mountains. Furnished in Eastlake style, with a lovely red rose Brussels carpet, it also boasted a fireplace, this one supplied with kindling and firewood ready to be lit.

"The bedroom is in here," Mercy said, opening a door to reveal a sinfully large, comfortable-looking bed. "Oh, good. Your trunks and boxes have already been brought up." She indicated a second door. "And this is the private bath. Tub and water closet."

Diana said nothing. The suite was lovely. Perfect. And all wrong. If there had been a second bedroom, perhaps they might have brazened it out, but the only other place to sleep was a sofa much too short to accommodate someone of Ben's height.

"Is there anything else I can—?"

This time it was Ben who cut Mercy off. "I believe a bit of rest is called for after our long journey."

His firm, almost brusque manner put an end to the young woman's chatter. After pointing out the annunciator, which could be used to communicate with the check-in desk, Mercy took her leave.

Dead quiet reigned in the parlor after she'd gone. Ben waited for Diana to speak first. Diana wanted him to explain himself without being asked.

After a moment, he knelt by the hearth and struck match to

kindling. It *was* cold in the room and she appreciated his thoughtfulness, but she was far from ready to forgive his high-handed behavior.

Diana had been deceived too often in the past by those she should have been able to depend upon. The possibility that she had been wrong to put her faith in Ben Northcote not only shook her self-confidence, it sent a stab of fear deep into her heart. If she couldn't rely on him, that meant she might *never* be able to trust her own judgment again.

"When I booked this suite," Ben said quietly, "I still hoped you'd agree to wed before we left Denver."

"You should have changed the reservation when we decided to wait."

"I was wrong not to. I admit it." He flashed a charming smile over his shoulder before he went back to poking at the fledgling fire. "But it is too late to make other arrangements now."

She made a sound of exasperation. "Do you care nothing for my reputation?" Her late husband had not, but Diana had thought better of Ben.

"The Grants need never know we aren't married yet." Satisfied with his efforts, Ben rose from the hearth to face her. "I *am* thinking of your reputation, Diana. If we'd arrived together and taken separate rooms, your family would have been convinced you were a woman of loose morals."

"Only if you'd been caught sneaking into my room," she muttered.

His indulgent chuckle grated on already raw nerves. "Perhaps it would have been you caught sneaking into mine." He reached for her but she evaded his grasp and backed away, one arm extended to fend him off.

"This is not a matter for levity."

"Nor is it cause for harsh words between us. I do not want to quarrel with you, Diana." Hands on hips, he stood with feet wide apart and surveyed the room. "This is not the first time we've shared a suite in a hotel. It did not trouble you overmuch on the last occasion, and back then there was, as yet, no talk of marriage. The only difference I can see now is that this hotel is owned by someone you may—or may not—want to acknowledge as kin."

"Reminding me of my weakness where you are concerned is not the way to make amends. And this isn't just about deceiving my family. You deceived *me*, Ben. All the way east, we talked about how the use of my married name would hide my connection to the Grants until I was ready to reveal that I was Elmira Grant's daughter. *I* meant I'd be known as Mrs. Spaulding, a respectable widow. You intended from the beginning that I should be introduced to them as Mrs. Northcote."

He didn't deny her charge. He didn't even try to claim he'd meant to tell her what he'd done but that the time had never seemed right. The truth, she suspected, was that he'd not had any intention of taking separate rooms here, married or not. He'd wanted her close at hand. That a part of her wanted that, too, did nothing to diminish her feeling that he'd taken away her right to choose.

"Diana, I didn't mean to upset you."

"We . . . are . . . not . . . married." She enunciated each word clearly. "You cannot arbitrarily make decisions for me." But he *would* be able to after they were wed. Husbands gained a totally unwarranted measure of control over their wives as soon as they repeated their vows. She'd learned that lesson well during her years with Evan Spaulding. It did not bode well for their life together if Ben developed the habit of making decisions for her without bothering to consult her wishes.

"I have no desire to dictate to you," Ben insisted. "I only want to take care of you. To protect you."

She could feel the intensity of his gaze and hear the sincerity in his voice.

"I've come too close to losing you too many times. Is it so wrong to wish to keep you close until we're safely back home?"

"So you deceived me for my own good?" Diana deplored the

hitch in her voice. She would *not* cry.

"Perhaps this will appease you." Ben produced a small box from the pocket of his trousers. "I bought it a few days after I first asked you to marry me."

Helpless to stop the anticipatory flutter of her heart, Diana stepped closer. He opened the box, revealing a gold wedding band studded with small colorful gemstones.

"Tourmaline," he said. "From mines in Paris."

"Paris, France?"

"Paris, Maine. Take off your glove."

She obeyed, too choked with emotion to speak. The wedding ring he'd chosen reminded her of all that was good between them. He was not Evan. She knew that. He hadn't changed the reservation, true, but she'd been so indecisive about coming to the Hotel Grant that he'd probably expected her to decide against the visit altogether and stay on the train.

"It is the most beautiful ring I've ever seen," Diana whispered.

The stones fascinated her. The gems varied from opaque to transparent, and their vibrant shades of blue, red, and green sparkled even in the watery afternoon sunlight of this overcast day. The center stone was multicolored, with a green outer layer surrounding a pink core.

"Wear it now," Ben urged. "It will give credence to our charade."

Diana felt as if she'd been hit in the face with a bucket of cold water. The joy went out of her heart, leaving a deep, empty space behind. She lifted her gaze from the ring to Ben's face and had all she could do not to slap him.

He took in her expression and frowned in confusion. "Diana, I love you."

"And you think that makes everything all right?" Evan had claimed to love her too. That hadn't stopped him from repeatedly betraying her trust.

"I think your usual common sense has deserted you." He sounded testy, as if her attitude was the one that was unreasonable.

"Wear the ring." Without a by-your-leave, he shoved it onto her finger.

Tears pricked the back of Diana's eyes. She pulled away from Ben, hiding her face.

"I wish to be alone."

If he stayed much longer, they'd both say things they'd regret, things they might not be able to take back.

"I'm not moving into another room."

"That's not what I meant," Diana said wearily, sinking into a chair upholstered in cream-colored brocade. "I didn't suppose you would go, even if I became hysterical and demanded it. And you know full well I don't want to call that kind of attention to myself."

"What *did* you mean, then?"

"That I need a bit of privacy. To think. To get over being so . . . annoyed with you." How could he not understand? Having him place this ring on her finger during the wedding ceremony would have made her the happiest of women. To wear it now was wrong.

"All right," he said, using an oh-so-reasonable tone of voice that she found most provoking. "Perhaps I'll go for a walk."

"An excellent idea," Diana muttered, clinging to the remnants of her self-control by a thread. "Here's a better one. See that mountain?" She indicated the view from the balcony. "Go climb it!"

CHAPTER TWO

ಚಿಂಡ

The lobby was once again deserted by the time Ben passed through it. Out of curiosity, and to keep himself from dwelling on the mistake he'd made by not warning Diana that he meant to register them as husband and wife, he stopped to look through the open pocket doors of the room Miss Grant had come out of earlier.

It was a large parlor, and she had obviously been hard at work washing windows and polishing woodwork. Unfortunately, neither ammonia nor lemon-scented wax could quite hide an underlying mustiness. The stain on a patch of wallpaper below a bank of windows plainly showed where there had been a leak. Upon closer inspection, Ben saw that the black walnut chairs were of good-quality but sadly dilapidated and that the carpet at the center of the room was not only threadbare, but moth-eaten.

A pity, he thought. It looked as if Hotel Grant had fallen on hard times. On the other hand, given the external repairs he'd seen on the way in and the newly installed elevator, perhaps their fortunes had recently taken a turn for the better.

Passing through an outer door, he stepped out onto the veranda and headed for the east end of the wide, wrap-around porch. The boardwalk he'd noticed earlier led into the trees. Little oil lamps, spaced out like street lights along one side, indicated that it was also meant to be used for promenades after dark.

Once he was in the woods, Ben felt a sense of peace descend upon him. Vibrant greens engulfed him, even though, here and there in shady spots, he occasionally glimpsed the rusty remnants of the winter's heavy snows.

He walked slowly, enjoying the way the boardwalk meandered through a series of pleasant groves. One, bordered by a profusion of laurel bushes, contained a small model of a Greek temple, another a grouping of cast-iron planters in the shape of Grecian urns, and a third, though hardly by design, a pair of fallen trees. He did not venture close enough to identify the species, but as he walked he picked out chestnut, black walnut, and butternut trees, as well as hickory, hemlock, black cherry, and birch.

Ben paused at a lookout to study the view. At a distance stood a building that had been designed to resemble an Egyptian obelisk. His best guess was that it was a water tower, since it was situated on a high point of land. It was at that moment that Ben realized the rushing noise he heard in the background was the sound water made flowing over rock. Continuing along the boardwalk, he soon reached the secluded glade through which the brook in question bubbled.

The boardwalk ended there, somewhat abruptly. Lumber lay piled along both banks of the stream, obviously intended for use in building a spring house. At present, however, the "fountain" consisted of a large wooden tub sitting in the stream bed and connected to a fissure in a nearby outcropping of rock by a length of pipe.

Curious, Ben stepped closer, avoiding muddy spots, and bent over the contraption. A quarter of the top of the tub was hinged, so that it could be flipped back to allow access to the water below. It was securely shut and fastened with a large padlock to discourage further investigation.

"You looking to take the waters?"

Ben turned slowly in the direction of the raspy voice and found a square-built, florid-faced individual regarding him with suspicion. Deeply incised wrinkles around the man's eyes and his iron gray hair suggested he'd seen at least six decades come and go. He was dressed like a farmer or workman in an open-necked white shirt and blue denim trousers held up by braces, but he had a proprietary attitude. Ben had little doubt who he was.

"Just curious," he said. "I'm a guest here. My name is Benjamin Northcote."

An eager look replaced the wariness in the pale, deep-set eyes. "Dr. Northcote!" The man splashed through the water from the other side of the brook, his feet protected by rubber boots, and scrambled up the near bank to stick out a slightly grimy hand with fingers the size of sausages. "Good to meet you. I'm Myron Grant."

As they shook, Ben studied Grant more closely. In spite of the Scots surname, the Grants were clearly descended from the colonists who'd populated this area when it was still known as New Netherlands. He reminded Ben of the fat Dutch burghers he'd seen portrayed in late Renaissance paintings.

Pulling a key from the deep front pockets of his trousers, Grant bent to open the padlock and fling back the top of the tub. "I know it don't look like much yet, but it's an improvement over what used to be here. In my pa's time, there was just an old barrel with the staves open and this stream here was surrounded by trees, stumps, and logs. Folks had to walk along a log to reach the fountain. First thing we did was put in a shower bath, over there in those bushes, but the ladies don't like being out in the open like that, so we got plans to build a regular bathhouse, like the ones they got over to England. Real fancy."

Ben bent close enough to see—and smell—the steady stream of malodorous water running out of the end of the pipe into the open brook below. A ladle hung from the inside of the lid.

"Won't be long before we'll have a dipper boy working here, all ready to ladle up half pint tumblers of mineral water." Grant stuck the ladle under the flow of water, filled it, and offered it to Ben. "We're going to build a nice pavilion here, with a railing so the customers don't get too close. Seen one of them at Saratoga Springs. You ever been there?"

"Yes. Some years back." At Saratoga, known as "the queen of the spas," there were more than twenty mineral springs and at least as many grand hotels.

"I mean to charge five cents a dipper and maybe I'll bottle some to sell, if I can get the right kind of endorsements."

Reluctantly, trying not to show any reaction to the smell of the stuff, Ben took the ladle. "Have you had a chemical analysis done of the water?"

Beaming, Grant rattled off the components as if he'd memorized them, as most likely he had: "Chloride of sodium, chloride of potassium, bicarbonate of soda, bicarbonate of ammonia, bicarbonate of magnesia, bicarbonate of iron, nitrate of potassa, alumina, sulphate of soda, sulphate of magnesia, sulphate of potassa, carbonate of lithia, organic matters, and carbonate of acid gas."

He gave no proportions and Ben did not bother to ask for them. He had no intention of lending his name to any quack claim that drinking the foul-smelling stuff trickling out of this rusty pipe was a cure-all. Neither did he mean to taste it himself. The moment Grant turned his back to secure the lid on the tub, Ben flung the contents of the ladle into the bushes.

"Don't forget this," he said, handing back the empty dipper.

Oblivious to Ben's deceit, Grant replaced it and the padlock and continued his spiel. "Lenape Springs water gives relief in cases of kidney disease, dyspepsia, and impure blood. It will cure skin diseases, nervous debility, headache, loss of appetite, bladder and kidney stones, Bright's disease of the kidneys, salt rheum, and liver complaint, and it's been found useful by patients with rheumatism, dropsy, scrofula humors, and male weakness."

"Impressive."

"Ain't it? Just what a high-class clientele wants in a summer watering hole. I've been working on the advertising pamphlet." He gave Ben a sly look. "Letters from satisfied guests are easy to produce, but testimonials from medical men are harder to come by. What would you say to the whole week here free for you and the missus?"

"I'd say I couldn't take advantage of you that way. I'd have to witness the effectiveness of your waters before I could claim they'll help sufferers, and at present there are no patients to observe."

"Huh," Grant grunted. "An honest physician. Just my luck."

"I could vouch for the quality of the air," Ben offered. "This is an ideal location to bring those who suffer from lung disorders."

As he'd anticipated, Myron Grant bristled at the suggestion. "No consumptives! We don't want their kind here. No, sir, I aim to attract only the best sort of people. Folks who don't really have much wrong with them, but are willing to pay to cure what little is. I'll do it, too."

He started walking back towards the hotel and Ben accompanied him, frankly curious to hear what the old man would say next. Ben could think of a half dozen reasons why Grant's plans were impractical, but there was a bizarre fascination in listening to him elaborate on this pipe dream.

As they walked, taking their time, Grant pointed out such sights as the gas plant, the old barn they'd converted into a laundry, and the new artesian well. By the time they came out into the open again, the sky was no longer overcast. They had a clear view to the southeast.

"See there?" Grant waved a hand towards a distant hilltop. "That's the Walnut Mountain House. Built two years back just off the road between Liberty and Jeffersonville. This time last year, they started taking reservations. Within a week, forty guests from New York City had already engaged rooms for the summer."

"I can see why this area would be a popular destination for

people who live in Manhattan. It's only a short trip by train. Five hours?"

"About that. And Hotel Grant has been here a lot longer than that place. Got a reputation, so to speak. And we've got the spring."

"Just the one?" Ben asked. It was a reasonable question. The town was named Lenape Springs, after all. The Lenape, Ben recalled, were an Indian tribe.

Grant's glower returned. "Got other springs around." He made a vague gesture in the direction of the village. "But our spring is the only one with healing properties. The others are just plain water."

They resumed walking with Grant leading the way past the front of the hotel and out along the curved drive that led to the road. Wooded areas were interspersed with fields. One boasted a scarecrow.

"See that swampy area?" Grant indicated a patch of ground overgrown with rhododendron and laurel. "By high season, that'll all be cleared out and we'll have put in a small pond for boats. My niece says we should have geese, too. We can use the feathers for pillows." He gave an indulgent chuckle.

"A practical girl."

"About some things."

"Your niece—that would be the desk clerk?"

"That's right. She's my brother Howd's girl." He shook his head. "Talk your ear off, that one, and go all the way around Robin Hood's barn before she'll get to the point. And stories! That girl's got a head full of romantic twaddle. Still, she's a first rate manager. Keeps the records just as good as a real accountant."

Unable to think of an adequate rejoinder to these observations, Ben changed the subject. "You say you have a brother. Does he work at the hotel?"

Grant snorted. "Howd? Not so's you'd notice. Only interested in art." He gave the word a highfalutin sound.

"Ah. I sympathize. I also have a brother who's an artist."

"What's he paint?" They ambled back towards the hotel as they talked.

"Landscapes. Some figures." Grant didn't need to know about Aaron's predilection for putting naked mermaids in his paintings.

"Howd does water colors of critters. Mostly birds." Contempt crept into his tone. "Lives in a camp in the woods half the time so he can be close to nature. Lot of nonsense, I say. He's got no notion of how to get on in the real world."

Ben paused to regard the front facade of Hotel Grant. "You've done a good bit of remodeling here in recent days."

"We commenced the repairs and expansion last fall, as soon as the season was over, and started up again this spring. Put on a new roof. Extended the veranda to two hundred and forty-four feet. *And* got a plate glass window for the dining room—have you seen it? The dining room's a hundred feet long now, twice the size it used to be, and there's a separate room for guests' servants and children to eat in. The bedrooms have all been refurbished and bath tubs and water closets added to all the suites. We have room for a hundred and fifty guests now, but when I'm done we'll be able to accommodate twice that."

Tremont the goat wandered across the lawn, stopping here and there to eat grass. That was her function, Ben imagined, recalling that Lyseth, for all his apparent dislike of the creature, had been careful not to hurt her.

"Picture the place with a fresh coat of white paint," Grant said, "and the veranda furnished with wicker chairs—I've got eighty of them on order. You know how folks like to sit out on a veranda. See and be seen."

Remembering the crowded verandas of various hotels he'd stayed at during his travels, Ben nodded, but Grant didn't give him a chance to get a word in edgeways.

"Entertaining the guests is important. We put in a dance floor during the winter, too, and a billiard room. Still a lot to do yet, though. I'm thinking of adding tennis courts and a place to play croquet. Fancy folk like those."

"No bowling alley?" Ben inquired when Grant finally paused to take a breath.

The reaction was unexpected. Grant exploded with laughter. "Suppose there should be," he said, wiping tears from his eyes. "This is mighty close to Rip Van Winkle country, you know. According to the old stories, thunder is the sound of a ghostly game of nine-pins."

"I was thinking ten-pins myself," Ben said, which set Grant off again.

It could work, Ben supposed, as the other man chortled. He'd heard there were several flourishing, self-contained hotels in Maine and New Hampshire. He'd been considering taking Diana to one of them on their wedding journey.

"There's one thing besides the spring that'll have them flocking to Lenape Springs," Grant said, recapturing Ben's attention. "I mean to built a racecourse."

Ben hastily revised his opinion of Grant's chances of success.

"Dirt track, oval in shape." Grant indicated an area off to the west and sketched the shape with his hands. "I'll fence it in, put up a grandstand and some board-and-batten barns to house horses, trainers, and hands."

"And the bookies?" Ben asked, watching two red squirrels dash across the empty meadow that was currently all that was visible in that direction. "Where will you put them?"

"Out of sight of my neighbors," Grant said with a chuckle.

"They don't approve of gambling?" Ben was not surprised. All small towns had much in common, which was why successful self-contained, rural hotels did not build race tracks.

"Some folks don't approve of anything. The other hotel in town, it's a temperance house. Ever since Lida Rose Leeves married that Free Methodist preacher, entertainment at the Lenape Springs Villa consists of daily blessings, prayer meetings, sermons, and psalm singing."

Lida Rose Leeves, Ben assumed, was the sister of Elmira Grant Torrence's friend Ed Leeves. He wondered if Lida Rose and her husband knew what Leeves did for a living.

"Some folks can abide trotting but think flat racing's the work of the devil. And steeple chasing, well, that's something else again. I'll have all three."

From the way Myron Grant gazed at the hotel and its environs, Ben supposed he was visualizing them as they would be when all his grandiose schemes came to fruition. Ben saw only what was there. It wasn't Howard Grant who had an unrealistic view of the world, he thought. It was his older brother. Myron Grant wasn't going to be content to build a self-contained resort, which might have a prayer of success. He really thought he could turn Lenape Springs into a second Saratoga!

৪৩৫৫

When she'd finished unpacking and changed into a plain but comfortable dress of dark blue cashmere and a pair of kid walking boots, Diana felt much more settled in her mind. She was still disappointed in Ben, but she was willing now to give him the benefit of the doubt. She had been put in mortal danger twice in the short time they'd known each other. His concern for her safety and his desire to stay close to her to protect her were wrongheaded but understandable.

She paused as she left the suite for the dimly-lit corridor. Given that they seemed to be the hotel's only guests, she had to admit that she'd not have relished staying in a room at any distance from Ben. The stillness of the place had a decidedly eerie quality.

With more haste than grace, Diana made her way to the elevator, only to find that it had returned to the ground floor. Just as well, she decided, and went in search of the nearest stairwell. Every elevator she'd ever been in had been staffed by an operator. She had never paid much attention to what made it go up and down, or even to how to open the door once it came to a halt.

A short time later, having descended a narrow flight of steps, Diana emerged into a passage that did not look at all familiar to her. She looked both ways and listened. A faint clacking sound came from her right, so she turned in that direction. After a moment, she reached an open door. The brass plate set into the wall next to it said "Casino."

The word made Diana frown. In her vocabulary, casinos were places where people went to gamble. Her husband had died in one, shot by an angry poker player who'd accused him of cheating at cards. But she could already see into the room. There were no roulette wheels, no tables for cards, no Heironymous bowls for dice. It contained nothing but a few chairs and two billiard tables. A young man in shirt sleeves was practicing shots at the one nearest the door.

"Well, hello there," he said when he noticed her. His voice was warm with approval.

Diana felt heat rush into her cheeks. His stare was very bold, but then she supposed that any woman who ventured into a hotel's billiard room should expect a stranger to think the worst of her. "I beg your pardon," she said, hastily retreating along the corridor. "I lost my way."

"Wait, wait! Don't let me frighten you off!" He crossed to her in three long strides and caught her arm. "This place is a tomb. You mustn't deprive me of the only delightful sight I've seen in weeks."

She glared at his offending hand and he hastily removed it. Then, a twinkle in his eyes, he sketched a courtly bow and humbly begged her forgiveness.

Diana peered more closely at him. He had hair the color of cornsilk, bright blue eyes . . . and Mercy Grant's nose. It looked better on him. Was he a relative? Except for the nose, she saw no other similarities to herself or her mother or Cousin Mercy. He had a slender but solid build and was taller than Diana, but not so tall as Ben. As to age, she'd guess he was a few years older than her own twenty-three.

"Who are you?" she asked.

"My name is Sebastian Ellington."

That meant nothing to Diana, and there was something about him that made her wary. Sweet talk only aroused suspicion when a man was so quick to lay his hands on a woman he'd just met.

"Are you a guest here?" she asked.

He grinned at the suggestion. "I'm the youngest son of the oldest sister of the owner of this place. You can imagine how far down the pecking order that puts me. Still, if you've come to apply for a job, I can put in a good word for you with Uncle Myron. He pays $2.50 a week for waitresses and provides lodging. You'd be seeing a lot of me if you worked here."

The simplicity of her attire, Diana supposed, had given him the mistaken notion that she was seeking employment. Or had it? Dark blue cashmere was something a housekeeper might wear. A local farm girl looking for her first position would be more likely to have clothing made of serge.

The corner of Cousin Sebastian's mouth twitched.

"I think you know perfectly well who I am, Mr. Ellington," she said in a repressive tone. He really was much too forward.

"But I did not anticipate that some stuffy old medical man would have such a young and lovely wife. Please, tell me you're his daughter."

For a moment Diana had forgotten that they all thought she and Ben were married. It gave her a jolt to hear herself referred to as his wife.

"You are! You *are* his daughter! My prayers have been answered."

"Stop your foolishness." The admonition came out more sharply than she'd intended. She drew herself up straighter. "I am Mrs. Benjamin Northcote."

He reacted to her bold lie by catching her hand and carrying it to his lips. "It is a great pleasure to make your acquaintance," he assured her. "I am your humble servant."

She jerked her hand free. He was incorrigible. It was as if the discovery she was married made him more determined to charm her.

"You said you were lost," he continued. "Where do you wish to be?"

Diana hesitated. "I was hoping for . . . tea, perhaps?" It was too early for supper, but she knew many of the larger hotels offered a late afternoon repast for guests. It had been a long time since the sandwiches she and Ben had consumed on the train.

"Let's see what we can find," he said, reaching for her arm. When she eluded his grasp, he turned the movement into a sweeping gesture that indicated she should follow him.

They went back the way she had come, Sebastian a few steps ahead, pointing to closed doors along the way. "Gentlemen's room. Ladies' parlor." Diana caught a glimpse of the huge fireplace and the check-in desk as he whisked her past an arched opening on their right. "And this is a reception room." It was long and narrow and dust motes danced in the light coming in through the windows. At the far end was another passage with doors opening off both sides. "Children's and nurses' ordinary," he said, indicating the first. "The rest are private dining rooms. And this—" he flung open double doors with a flourish— "is the newly enlarged dining room."

It was huge.

It was also empty.

"Come on," he urged, picking up the pace. "The kitchen's on the far side."

To Diana's relief, this proved to be true. In one small, suspicious part of her mind she had been entertaining the possibility that her too-eager escort might be luring her into some private lair where he could attempt further liberties. She'd been prepared to scream very loudly—and kick him in the privates—if it became necessary.

As Diana entered the room, Cousin Mercy had just taken the

kettle off the stove. "Almost ready, Pa," she said to the man seated at the table, and poured hot water into a teapot. Without looking towards the door, she asked, "Do you want a cup, Sebastian? It's chamomile today."

"Yes, I do. And so does the lovely Mrs. Northcote."

Startled, Mercy almost dropped the kettle. "Ma'am, you shouldn't be back here. Guests—"

"Are not permitted to eat?" Diana interrupted, her gaze focused on a plate of sandwiches and another overflowing with freshly baked cookies.

"I . . . that is, I did not think . . . I do apologize, Mrs. Northcote. I should have offered to bring something up to your suite."

Diana hesitated, then decided she'd already broken the rules and might as well continue as she'd begun. "I am not accustomed to being treated like royalty," she told her cousin. "I know some might think it a terrible breach of etiquette, but I will feel much more comfortable, Mercy, if you will call me Diana."

This suggestion seemed to fluster Mercy even more, and caused her to slop hot water onto a sketch pad that had been left on the table.

The man she'd called "Pa," her father, Howard Grant, moved swiftly to remove it from danger before it was completely ruined. "Only damaged the first few pages," he said, examining them. "Do you want to save them?"

Mercy glanced at the sheets, now detached. "Those are the sketches I did of Mrs. Saugus. They aren't very good." After blotting up the excess moisture with a towel, she tossed them into the kindling box.

"I don't know the lady," Diana said, "but your portraits seem quite fine to me." They showed a woman with a hard face and curly hair, wearing an elaborate hat.

"My daughter is modest."

Mercy blushed. "You're the artist in the family, Pa. I just dabble."

"But you've a gift for faces, and I have not. I specialize in birds," he explained in an aside to Diana.

"You should do a sketch of Diana, Mercy," said Sebastian, who apparently did not share his cousin's hesitation to abandon the more appropriate form of address. "She's far better looking than Belle Saugus, and far more pleasant, too."

Oh, gracious, Diana thought. *I hope I have not encouraged him to be even more forward.*

Warily she settled herself in the chair Sebastian held out for her and accepted Mercy's offer of tea. She had just selected a molasses cookie when she realized that Howard Grant was staring at her.

"You remind me of someone," he said bluntly.

Diana's mouth went dry. She did not bear a strong physical resemblance to her mother, but she might well share some small but telling trait with the younger version of Elmira that Uncle Howard remembered. What if he guessed who she was?

After a moment he shook his head. "I'm sure I've seen you before. Can't put my finger on where, but it'll come to me. I've got a real good memory for details."

₭ℂℜ

The more Myron talked about his big plans, the more convinced Ben became that the older man had set impossible goals. He seemed to have no concept of the problems he'd face. Staff? Oh, they'd come from surrounding towns. But no Irish nor Jews need apply. He wasn't sure about coloreds.

Noises indicative of demolition had been issuing from the far side of the hotel for some time when Grant decided he needed to check on the workmen. "I've been itching to get at the west wing ever since we started renovations," he said as he headed off in that direction.

Ben debated whether to follow him or go check on Diana. In the end, he did neither. The clop and rattle of an approaching horse and buggy halted Myron Grant's progress. He returned to

Ben's side, a forbidding scowl darkening his features.

"Didn't figure he'd be back till dark," Grant muttered under his breath.

A surrey pulled by a little Morgan made its way to the front of the hotel and came to a stop. The words CASTINE LIVERY STABLE, LENAPE SPRINGS, N.Y. identified it as a hired vehicle. The driver, a dapper fellow whose blue and brown checked serge Norfolk jacket, deerskin driving gloves, and beaver hat marked him as something of a dandy, took one look at Grant's face and frowned.

Fine lines fanned out from eyes the color and hardness of sapphires. They narrowed as he canted his head to listen. Ben knew the exact moment when he realized that the sound he heard was a board being torn loose. He tossed the reins aside and sprang down from the seat.

"What the hell's going on here?" he demanded. "We've got more important things to do than mess with that burnt-out wing."

Grant approached the surrey, tipping his broad-brimmed straw hat to the other occupant of the conveyance. "Afternoon, Mrs. Saugus. Hope you and your husband had a pleasant outing."

She regarded him with a cold, hazel-eyed stare. She was fashionably dressed but, like her husband, had chosen excessively bold colors and patterns. Her hat was a bright confection of magenta velvet and purple taffeta ribbons.

Beneath the curved brim, her face seemed unremarkable, save for the fact that she wore makeup. This obvious attempt to hide her age also concealed any emotion she might feel. She did not respond to Grant's greeting and, after one covert survey of Ben through lowered lashes, she shifted her gaze to the mitt-encased hands she held primly folded in her lap.

"Damn it, Grant!" Saugus raged. "We're on a tight schedule here."

In his agitation, he all but jumped up and down, and the jerky movements sent his hat tumbling to the ground. Beneath, his hair was as black as Ben's, but the color had a flatness to it that suggested the shade came out of a dye bottle. Saugus's bushy mustache and side-whiskers contained a liberal sprinkling of gray.

Another glance at Mrs. Saugus told Ben that her hair, what little of it showed beneath that triumph of the milliner's art, had probably once been bright red. Now it had faded to a muted echo of its former glory.

"One afternoon's work won't make much difference," Grant argued, "and I was sick to death of that eyesore."

"What eyesore? It was all grown over. Even had a couple of bushes on top of it. Flowers on 'em, too. No one would have looked twice at it. No one would have known there was ever another wing there if you'd just left it alone."

"Well, it's too late now." Grant's belligerence rapidly turned into anger. With his bulk, he dwarfed the smaller-boned man. "And just so you know, I aim to rebuild that wing. We're going to need the space once Lenape Springs water catches on with the posh set."

The horse shifted nervously in its traces as voices got louder.

"You damned fool!" Saugus shouted, undaunted by the fact that a giant loomed over him. "There are more important things than—"

"Good afternoon," Ben interrupted, hoping to prevent fisticuffs. He stepped closer to the surrey, keeping a weather eye on the horse in case it decided to bolt. "I'm Dr. Northcote. Mr. Grant has just been showing me the spring with the idea that I might endorse its healing properties."

Saugus's change in attitude was instantaneous. He slapped Ben on the shoulder as if he were an old and dear friend. "Excellent fellow! I am Norman T. Saugus, Mr. Grant's financial backer. I'm putting together a joint stock company to expand the hotel and turn it into a first class spa. That's my wife," he added, glancing briefly back towards the surrey.

"Are you staying here also?" Ben asked. He'd assumed from

Mercy's remarks, that there were no other guests at the hotel.

"Yes, indeed. Beautiful place, isn't it?"

"Very."

Since Saugus made no move to assist his wife, Ben circled the surrey and offered her his arm. As soon as he did so, Saugus turned his attention back to Myron Grant. "Those men can put in another hour painting before they leave for the day," he declared.

With Mrs. Saugus safely on the ground, Ben glanced at the sky. It had been nearing mid-afternoon before he and Diana had arrived at the hotel, and he'd been talking to Grant for some time. Dusk could not be far off.

Grant started to sputter an objection, then abruptly fell silent. A puzzled expression crossed his face as he turned to look towards the construction site. The sounds of demolition had ceased.

Before any of them had time to do more than wonder why, one of the workmen rounded the veranda at a fast clip. When he caught sight of Grant and Saugus, he changed course, veering away from the front entrance and heading towards the little group beside the surrey.

The man stumbled to a halt, his face sheet white. "Found a body," he stammered. "Dead." He swallowed hard. "Murdered."

For a moment, no one spoke.

"Show me," Ben said. "I'm one of the city coroners back home," he added when Saugus started to protest.

"This has to be a case of injury, not death," Grant said. *"Murdered?* Nonsense. There must have been an accident. Someone fell."

"What happened?" Ben asked the workman as they hurried towards the partially demolished west wing.

"Don't know. Looks like someone landed a hit on the head, then just left the body where it fell. Covered it over with dirt."

Buried in a shallow grave? That didn't sound good.

On Myron Grant's orders, the workmen had ripped out underbrush and large sections of the fire-scarred flooring they'd found beneath. Debris was scattered everywhere.

"We pulled up a piece of warped flooring and there it was," the workman said, pointing.

Under the floor? Ben barely had time to process this new information before he knelt by the irregular opening into the earth. The smells of dampness and sweat and another, slightly musty odor reached him, but there was none of the stench of recent death. He understood why as soon as he saw the body.

The remains were skeletal.

"Someone fetch a lantern," he instructed.

"Not built atop a sacred Indian burial ground, are ya, Grant?" Saugus, coming up beside Ben, with Grant right behind him, tried to sound convivial but failed miserably. He glanced into the hole once, then avoided looking that way again.

Without waiting for more light, Ben dropped through the opening, angling himself so that he did not block the sun. Low in the sky, its beams slanted into the depths, giving him just enough illumination to verify the workman's claim. The skull had a crack in it. The body appeared to have been shoved into this space after death. It lay at an awkward angle, the head twisted sideways, giving him a clear view of the damage.

A few remnants of clothing clung to the bones, but most had rotted away. Here and there dirt covered the remains, although it did not look as if there had been any attempt at burial. With scientific detachment, Ben examined the size and shape of the pelvis and concluded that the cadaver was that of a woman. More than that he could not judge, not even how long she had lain here.

By the time Ben hauled himself back out of the hole, the number of spectators had increased. Mrs. Saugus stood off on her own, abandoned, the blank expression on her face even more obvious than before. At the opposite side of the work area, probably closer to a back door, stood a little group consisting of two men he did not recognize and two women—Diana and Miss Grant. Even at this distance, Ben could see the concern etched on Diana's countenance.

His attention shifted to her male companions. He'd never seen either man before, but the older of the two had to be Myron Grant's younger brother, Howard. If not for the greater number of lines inscribed in Myron's face by age, they might have been mistaken for twins.

Hesitantly, Howd Grant left the others where they were and approached the work site. He knelt as Ben had done and stared through the opening. At first, he showed no reaction. Then, as his gaze roamed over the skeletal remains, his face suddenly lost all trace of color. He gripped the edge of the fire-blackened flooring so tightly that his knuckles showed white and he had to clear his throat before he could speak. Even then it came out as a harsh croak.

"I know who she is."

"Impossible." Like Norman Saugus, Myron Grant avoided looking into the hole after the first glimpse of what it contained. "You can't tell anything from bones."

"I can. It's Elly. Elly Lyseth." Howd Grant heaved himself awkwardly to his feet.

"This can't be Elly," his brother insisted. "She packed up all her belongings and left town. Everybody in Lenape Springs knows that."

"Apparently everyone's been wrong." The younger Grant brother sounded angry now, and his hands had curled into fists at his sides.

"Sometime before the fire destroyed this wing of the hotel, someone stowed this body in the crawlspace under the floor," Ben said. "It might never have been found if Mr. Grant hadn't insisted on clearing away the debris." He kept his eyes on Diana's Uncle Howard. "How can you be so sure of your identification?"

With a hand that trembled, Howd Grant pointed into the hole. Ben's exit from that cramped space had dislodged some of the dirt covering the remains. The setting sun now picked out the glint of gold. A heart-shaped pendant lay tangled in the neck bones. "That was Elly's."

"How do you *know* that?" Myron Grant's voice went up an octave as he glared at his younger brother. "That could be *any* locket. That could be any *body.*"

His expression forlorn, Howard Grant bowed his head. "I know because I gave it to her . . . just before she disappeared."

CHAPTER THREE

⊰⊱

Diana stood frozen between Mercy and Sebastian, an unpleasant queasiness clawing at the pit of her stomach. When a workman had burst into the kitchen a few minutes earlier, babbling about murder, she had been certain he was mistaken . . . or mad. This was a *respectable* hotel. Now her mind was awhirl with confusion and concern.

There *was* a body beneath what had once been the west wing of the building and her newfound uncle had just confessed to a connection with it. Uncertain what to do or say, Diana glanced at Mercy and Sebastian. They were her cousins, but they didn't know that. She was an outsider, scarcely in a position to ask questions, or even offer comfort.

Fortunately for Diana, Sebastian also seemed to be at a loss for information. "Who's Elly?" he demanded.

Mercy's face had lost all its color when her father had made his startling announcement. It rushed back, turning her cheeks scarlet. Her voice shook when she replied. "Elly was Floyd and Celia Lyseth's daughter. She ran away years ago. I was still a small child. I barely remember her."

Something the station agent in Liberty had said came back to

Diana then. He'd told her that Floyd Lyseth's daughter had run away with a peddler.

Apparently, she had not. She'd been right here all along. Diana's skin crawled at the thought.

She did not for a moment consider approaching the cluster of men peering into the gaping hole in the flooring. She'd been involved in murders before—both reporting on them and solving them—but she'd never had to view a victim's remains and she had no desire to get any closer to this corpse, even if it was an old one. She frowned at the thought. By now, she supposed, there would be nothing left of it but dried bones. Still too grisly, she decided.

For the first time, she wondered how Ben stood it. He was a coroner as well as a physician. Not only did he have to see dead bodies, he had to perform autopsies on some of them. She shuddered at the very idea.

As if he felt her gaze upon him, Ben looked up. At once, annoyed at her own squeamishness, Diana held herself a little straighter. She forced a smile for him but was relieved when he returned to an exchange of words with her Uncle Howd and two men she had not yet met.

They spoke too softly for those at any distance to hear, but Diana could see them clearly. The man Uncle Howd had called Myron, an older, slightly heavier version of Howd, was the oldest Grant brother and her other uncle. He betrayed his exasperation by hands that were in constant motion when he talked. Finally losing patience, he knelt by the opening and, a moment later, eased himself down through it.

"Don't disturb anything," Ben called after him.

Less than a minute later, Uncle Myron emerged. He held a necklace in one hand. The length of delicate gold chain was recognizable even at a distance.

"Oh, Pa," Cousin Mercy wailed. "How could you?"

Startled, Diana shifted her attention to the young woman. Cousin Mercy seemed to have no qualms about getting close to the remains. She'd almost reached the site when her uncle held up his find. Now she sprinted across the short distance remaining and seized the prize from his hand. It was plain to Diana that she'd already recognized it, but for a moment Mercy just stared at the object she held, an expression of shocked disbelief on her face. When she turned on her father, her scowl was ferocious and her voice razor-sharp.

"This was my mother's locket! How could you give it to someone else?"

In silent appeal, Uncle Howd reached out to her, but Cousin Mercy backed away, evading his touch. She would have stalked off the construction site, taking the necklace with her, if Ben had not caught her elbow.

He spoke softly to her as he gently pried the bit of jewelry from her clenched fist. By then, Diana had moved near enough to hear what he said.

"That's evidence, Miss Grant. You need to leave it here."

"Evidence of what? An old man's foolishness? A father's betrayal?" Her voice became more shrill with every word.

One of the anonymous workmen answered her. "That's evidence of murder, that is. Them bones didn't get there by themselves." He looked at Howd Grant when he said it, suspicion writ large on his bovine countenance.

This was not good, Diana thought, taking another step towards her cousin. Not good at all. At best, her new-found family was about to face an uncomfortable inquisition from the authorities and a lot of unwelcome publicity. At worst, her Uncle Howd might be arrested for murder.

"Damn," Sebastian muttered.

Diana had forgotten all about him, but he was still at her side. She thought at first that he'd sworn because he'd come to the same conclusion she had, but his attention was focused on two women who had just rounded the corner from the back of the hotel and were fast approaching the group around the hole.

"I beg your pardon, Diana," Sebastian said. "That was no language to use in front of a lady, but here's more trouble coming. Can you keep Mercy away from Mrs. Lyseth? I'd better go find her husband."

Although Diana did not entirely understand why Mercy and the victim's mother *needed* to be kept apart, she saw the sense in locating the dead woman's father without delay. Besides, she was glad of something useful to do. "Which one is Mrs. Lyseth?"

"She's the younger of the two. The other is my aunt, Tressa Ellington. She's my father's oldest sister and housekeeper here."

The two women were dressed nearly alike, one in brown and biscuit plaid, the other in gray. Both wore white lawn caps that nearly covered their hair, but there the similarity stopped. One moved with a determined, ground-eating stride across the grass. As she came closer, Diana saw that in spite of long skirts and tight corseting, this exertion didn't even have her breathing hard. The other woman had to struggle to keep up. She was a pear-shaped individual, not as tall as her companion, but considerably stouter. Her face might have been pretty once. Now any beauty was over-shadowed by bags under the eyes and a wobbly double chin. She was puffing and panting as she scurried across the lawn.

Four men caught up with the two women just as Diana intercepted them. They were, Diana supposed, the neighbors. Word of the grim discovery had doubtless already spread throughout Lenape Springs.

Diana approached the taller of the two women. She had the sort of bone structure that made it difficult to guess her age, but the few salt-and-pepper curls that did show beneath the frilled edge of her cap suggested that she was older than her energetic movements would indicate. "Mrs. Ellington?"

She'd guessed right. Tressa Ellington nodded. "What have they found?"

Diana led her a little aside, glad to see that one of the newcomers, a man with a beard like a thicket, dressed in a black, shad-bellied coat and wearing a broad-brimmed, well-crowned black hat, had engaged Mrs. Lyseth's attention. In a whisper, she repeated what little she knew.

"They're certain of the identification?"

"Mr. Grant is. Mr. Howard Grant."

"Well, he'd know."

The situation had already been chaotic. It descended into bedlam as soon as Mrs. Ellington informed Mrs. Lyseth that her daughter's remains had been discovered. The dead girl's mother let out a screech that would have done a banshee proud.

Another of the new arrivals, a gaunt young man with lank brown hair, rushed to Mercy's side and, without a by-your-leave, embraced her.

"Oh, Luke!" she wailed, burying her head on his shoulder. "It is too dreadful for words!"

The bearded man caught Mrs. Lyseth by the shoulders and began to pray in a loud voice.

He was a minister, Diana belatedly realized, and berated herself for not knowing that at once from his attire. Unfortunately, his efforts did not seem to calm Mrs. Lyseth in the least. She slapped at his hands. He gave her a shake and began to lecture her on Christian humility.

By then, the other two men had joined Ben and the workmen. One took exception to Ben's refusal to let anyone else examine the remains. He objected in such strong terms that Diana's attention was diverted from Mrs. Lyseth.

Off to one side, her uncles exchanged soft but obviously heated words. Out of the corner of her eye, she caught sight of the flashily-dressed stranger who'd been with them when she'd arrived. Seizing his chance, he'd slipped away from the others. It was plain he did not want to attract attention to himself as he went. He looked back over his shoulder, then increased his speed when he got close to the corner of the veranda. A woman, who had apparently been standing unnoticed on the sidelines from the beginning, eased out of the shade of an elm tree and followed him at a leisurely pace.

Diana wondered briefly who they were, but she was soon distracted by the more dramatic scenes being played out all around her. Sebastian had asked her to keep Cousin Mercy and Mrs. Lyseth apart. She supposed she could best accomplish that task by taking Mercy inside. It appeared, however, that this Luke, whoever he was, had prior claim. When Diana looked around for them she discovered that the young man held her cousin nestled in his arms, stroking her back as she sobbed her heart out. Their ease with each other spoke of long intimacy, perhaps even an engagement.

A prolonged wail of distress had Diana's head snapping around to stare at Mrs. Lyseth. She was batting at the preacher's hands, which still clasped her shoulders. Diana moved towards them, unsure what she could do to help the woman, but knowing that she must try. She came to an abrupt halt when she reached a point close enough to hear what they were saying to each other.

"Damned forever!" Mrs. Lyseth wailed. The expression on her face was one of ecstasy.

"You know where the fault lies. This town has been perverted into an unsunk Sodom!"

"Glory! Glory! Glory!" She wasn't fighting his hold. She was in the throes of religious fervor.

Diana backed hastily away. Her interference would not be welcome, nor did she wish to draw the preacher's attention to herself.

She'd encountered religious zealots before, men who tried to frighten their congregations into abandoning everything that brought joy or pleasure. They forbade such innocent pastimes as singing and dancing. Games were an anathema, especially card games. And they denounced as sinful all reading material save the Bible and forbade attendance at theatrical productions. Diana could imagine what the reaction would be should Mrs. Lyseth and her minister learn that "Mrs. Northcote" had once traveled with a troupe of thespians and now earned her living writing articles for a newspaper.

After a moment's hesitation, Diana turned back towards the construction site. She didn't have to look at the body. She'd go only as far as the edge of the old flooring.

The fellow who'd been arguing with Ben had apparently given up his effort to get a look at the remains. He was no longer anywhere in sight. His companion had moved off, as well. Diana was halfway to her goal when she saw this second man give a start. He'd spotted Luke and Mercy.

"Unhand that girl!" he bellowed, waving heavily muscled arms in a shooing motion.

"Father—" the younger man protested.

"You heard me. Get your hands off her. And you, missy, keep your claws out of my boy."

Mercy looked as if she wanted to make a sharp retort, but she apparently thought better of it. Instead, with an anguished look at Luke, who was being hustled away by his father, she fled towards the nearest entrance to the hotel, right past Sebastian and Floyd Lyseth.

"Is that my Elly down there?" Lyseth demanded.

Reluctantly, Myron Grant nodded. Along with Howd, Mrs. Lyseth, the preacher, Tressa Ellington, Sebastian, and the workmen, Diana watched in silence as Lyseth stomped up to the hole and peered down into it. Someone had lit a lantern and lowered it so that he could see what lay beneath the old flooring.

"Can't tell nothin' from that." With a snort, Lyseth left the scene, ignoring everyone, even his wife.

The preacher stepped up, as if to take his place, but Myron Grant blocked his way.

"I've sent for the coroner," the preacher said. He sounded almost gleeful about it.

"I would have done that myself, Riker," Uncle Myron said in an irritable voice. "Buckley's a good man. He'll sort this out."

"How long will it take the coroner to get here?" Ben asked.

"He's got to come from Liberty. Probably be a couple of hours."

"Until he arrives, no one else must disturb the remains." Ben gave brisk orders to two of the workmen. They didn't look pleased to be posted as guards, but they didn't argue with him.

He had an air of command, and a charisma that most people responded to. Diana felt a sense of pride as she watched him. Ben might have a few faults, but his good points far outweighed them.

He could even deal with people like Pastor Riker. After a brief exchange of words, he asked the preacher to escort Mrs. Lyseth home. Diana could almost feel Ben exerting the force of his personality to persuade the other man to cooperate without further argument. To everyone's surprise but hers, Riker agreed to the suggestion, although he couldn't resist a parting shot at Diana's uncles.

"The keeping of summer boarders is a snare of the devil," he intoned. "Unless you keep a temperance house, even good Christians stray. Here's just more proof that such sinfulness leads men to desecrate the Sabbath, play cards, drink liquor, commit adultery, and contaminate the local young people."

That said, he led the grieving mother away. Except for the two guards Ben had posted, everyone else left, too, and Ben was free to join Diana.

She shivered when he took her arm. For the first time she became aware that the sun had set. Within a quarter hour, full darkness would descend.

"Was it really murder?" she asked.

"It looks that way," he said.

Ben was concerned about Diana. She seemed more shaken by the afternoon's events than he would have expected. He could not imagine that she'd already formed an attachment to members of her family. She'd barely met them. In fact, she'd yet to be introduced to her uncle Myron.

A woman intercepted them as they entered the lobby. "Dr. Northcote? I'm Mrs. Ellington, the housekeeper. I'm sorry, but the main dining room is not yet ready to serve meals in. We haven't the staff for one thing. I can provide you with a set meal—nothing fancy, mind you—at a set time, in one of the private dining rooms, but you'll need to tell me when you want to eat."

He was pleased to be offered food at all, given the circumstances. "An hour?" he suggested. Diana must be starving. It had been a long time since what had passed for luncheon on the train. Perhaps that was why she'd reacted so strongly to their disconcerting discovery.

In the privacy of the elevator, which he was able to operate after a brief study of the controls—pulling the cable down started the car moving up—Diana finally spoke.

"If we've walked straight into an old murder, then my family is right in the middle of it."

"They're going to have a difficult time," he agreed. The unease he felt concerning the afternoon's events increased.

"I'd like to help them somehow," Diana said, "but I'm an outsider. I have no inkling what connections exist among these people. It's a small community. For all we know, Elly Lyseth's death is part of some feud that goes back for generations, and I don't even want to think about what the good pastor may do to stir things up."

"The situation is confusing right now," Ben agreed as he brought the elevator to a smooth stop. He took her arm to walk to their suite. Diana seemed to have forgiven him for registering them as husband and wife, but he was not such a fool as to broach that subject. "It is impossible to think clearly on an empty stomach," he said instead. "After we have that set meal, we'll talk."

In the suite, he saw at a glance that his forgiveness was still in doubt. Diana had not unpacked for him. His Gladstone bag sat beside the sofa. A pillow and blanket had been stacked next to it.

When she went into the other room and closed the door, Ben hurriedly changed his shirt, collar, and cravat, and brushed his hair. His coat and trousers could have used a good brushing, too, but he did not have a great many clothes with him and it did not seem necessary to put on the Prince Albert he wore as formal evening dress. He assumed the vest and coat he'd been wearing, then sat down in one of the parlor's comfortable armchairs to wait for Diana to reappear.

Contrary to what he'd told her, he already had a very clear notion of what they should do. This was not a propitious time for a family reunion. Moreover, he had sensed dangerous undercurrents in Lenape Springs. As Diana's future husband, it was his responsibility to keep her from getting caught in a riptide. As soon as possible, he intended that they leave this place.

Ben and Diana had only just stepped out of the elevator into the lobby when Miss Grant intercepted them. "The coroner's here," she announced.

"He made good time."

"Pastor Riker sent for him even before he came here to view what the workmen found. He delights in making trouble for us. And Mr. Buckley has a good horse. He wants to talk to you, Dr. Northcote, in the family parlor. I'll show you the way."

"I'll come with you," Diana offered.

"He just wants Dr. Northcote." Miss Grant's earlier anger at her father seemed to have faded to a simmering irritation directed at the world in general. The look she sent Diana was unfriendly in the extreme.

"I'll wait for you in the dining room," Diana said, accepting the inevitable. They both knew it would be a waste of energy to protest such an edict, but she did not yield without a grimace. She hated to be left out of anything, even a situation likely to distress her.

Ben lifted her hand to his lips. "Eat something. As one who knows you well, I predict it is only a matter of minutes before your stomach begins to growl. Loudly."

This indelicate remark had Miss Grant goggling at them, but Diana only smiled and sent him on his way. What he'd said to her was nothing less than the truth. It also called up pleasant memories between them.

After calling out, "Doctor's here," Miss Grant left him at the parlor door.

Ben pushed it open and went in. It appeared that the coroner, a thin, bespectacled man of about Ben's own years, was just finishing up his interview with the Grant brothers. Howd Grant, ill-at-ease and fidgeting, stood by a window. Myron Grant, once again scowling fiercely, sat facing Mr. Buckley, both of them in balloon-back chairs.

There was only time for a brief survey of the room itself. Under other circumstances, Ben would have remarked upon the quality of the many water colors of birds that decorated the parlor, but this did not seem an appropriate time for compliments.

"So," Mr. Buckley said, his sharp voice demanding Ben's full attention. "I'm told you are a doctor." He waved Ben into a matching chair.

Ben acknowledged that he was, indeed, a physician. He turned the chair around and sat with his arms folded on the curve of the wood. Face to face with his inquisitor, he waited for the coroner's next question. He did not intend to volunteer anything. He was familiar with the procedure followed by Maine's coroners but uncertain what subtle variations existed here in New York. Until he knew more, caution seemed wise.

"Your training?"

The question surprised Ben. He hadn't expected his credentials to be challenged. "I received my medical degree from Bowdoin College and have practiced in Bangor, Maine since then." He hesitated, then added, "I've been one of that city's coroners for the last two years."

Buckley looked unimpressed but nodded as he made a note to himself. "Having you on the spot will save me calling in another physician," he announced.

That answered one question, Ben thought. New York coroners did not necessarily have medical training. They didn't in Maine either, though many of those holding the position were doctors. It made the job simpler all around.

"What did you observe when you first examined the bones?" Buckley asked.

"The remains had been there for some time. They were the bones of a woman. The skull was fractured."

Buckley looked up from his notes. "You are succinct."

"I prefer not to speculate."

"You have no opinion about the cause of death?"

"A blow to the head."

"Was Miss Lyseth murdered?"

"The injury to her skull could have been the result of a fall— an accident."

"But you don't think so?"

"I don't know," Ben repeated, although he had to admit he had few doubts. Why cover up an accident? She'd clearly been stuffed into that space to hide her. If the fire that had destroyed that wing of the hotel had occurred shortly thereafter . . .

Ben's ruminations were interrupted by the arrival of Mrs. Ellington. Everyone stood when she entered the parlor.

"Six potential jurors have shown up," she announced. "I've put them in the casino."

Only the smallest twitch at the corner of Buckley's mouth betrayed him, but Ben was relieved to see this evidence that the man had a sense of humor. He disliked dealing with people who saw only grimness and despair. Men of sour disposition, in Ben's experience, were less likely to be open minded in considering evidence.

"Do you mean to have the inquest here?" Myron Grant demanded when his housekeeper had left. He sounded affronted.

"Would you prefer we adjourn to the Lenape Springs Villa after viewing the remains? Yes, we'll hold it here, if I can find enough qualified jurors."

"Everyone will turn out," Howd predicted. "It's a small town."

"Exactly the problem," Mr. Buckley grumbled, glancing at the cuckoo clock to check the time.

Ben was surprised to discover only fifteen minutes had passed since he'd left Diana.

"I cannot summon any person related to the deceased," Buckley continued, "nor any person related to anyone suspected of causing her death." He gave Howd Grant a pointed look. "Nor anyone who is known to be prejudiced for or against a suspect. The process could take days."

Ben cleared his throat. "I don't believe you *have* a suspect, Mr. Buckley. That means only Miss Lyseth's relations need be eliminated from consideration."

"Did you see this locket Mr. Howard Grant has identified as belonging to Miss Lyseth?" He held it up so that the gaslight caught the delicately etched design on the little heart.

Ben acknowledged that he had, but felt compelled to add, "I also saw Mr. Howard Grant's face when he recognized it. He was surprised by the discovery of the bones but, more than that, he was shocked to discover that the bones were Elly Lyseth's."

"All that time," Howd whispered in a broken voice, "she was right here and we never knew."

Buckley ignored him, addressing Ben. "You're prepared to say that before the inquest?"

"I am."

"How is it you come to be here off-season, Dr. Northcote?"

Although the abrupt question caught him off guard, Ben thought before he answered. "Mrs. . . . Northcote wished to come here. She became curious about the place after it was mentioned to her by an acquaintance."

"Who?"

He hesitated, then decided he might as well test the waters. "A Mrs. Torrence. She—"

But before he could get any further, Myron Grant's roar silenced him. "Elmira! Is it *Elmira* Torrence you mean?" At Ben's nod, Grant's skin mottled. "How dare Elmira even *mention* this hotel after what she did?"

Not only was his face livid, but his hands had curled into fists at his sides. Fury made him almost incoherent as he continued to rage against the sister he hadn't seen in over thirty years.

Ben caught only bits and pieces of the muttered invective, but that was enough to tell him that Diana's mother had never been forgiven for running out on her brothers after their father's death.

"Tell them, Howd," Grant sputtered. "She had no business taking off with that no-account Liberty boy."

Ben's eyes narrowed. William Torrence had come from Liberty? He was certain Diana did not know that her father's family was also from this area. Her mother had only told them about the Grants.

"She was the youngest sister," Howd Grant said, "the one who stayed to take care of Father after the other girls married. It was understood that she'd go on taking care of Myron and me after Father died." He still sounded distracted by thoughts of Elly Lyseth's death, but was considerably calmer than his brother when talking about their sister.

"She had no business—"

"—wanting a life of her own?" Ben interrupted.

Myron's reply was cut off by the coroner clearing his throat. "If you'll come with me, Dr. Northcote, I'll see if we have enough jurors for the inquest. I won't need you two," he added, giving the Grant brothers a pointed stare.

ℰ℧ℭℛ

The flashily-dressed man Diana had seen leaving the scene of the crime was named Norman T. Saugus. The woman was his wife, Belle. She had changed into a low-cut evening dress and carried a patchouli-scented shawl.

In the small, private dining room, Diana could not avoid coming to their attention. Once they introduced themselves, it would have been churlish to refuse when they insisted she join them at their table. Five minutes in their company, however, was long enough to make Diana grateful they'd been almost through with their meal before she'd arrived.

Hurry, Ben, she thought as she forced yet another smile. Until Ben finished talking to the coroner and came to her rescue, she was trapped. Norman Saugus fancied himself a raconteur. In truth, he was nothing but a braggart, and a boring one, at that.

"I don't anticipate any problems running telegraph line to Lenape Springs," Saugus informed her, leaning close enough so she could smell the musky hair oil he used. "We could do it in just a day or two. Get a couple of farm boys to tie a rag on the hind wheel of a wagon and count the revolutions to measure the distance from one pole location to another. Then a bit of digging." He chuckled. "I've done it before. Had a little trouble then with the right of way, but I took care of it."

"Oh, this is a delightful story," Mrs. Saugus said, with what struck Diana as an excess of enthusiasm. She beamed encouragingly at her husband, but something seemed false about her smile. As for Saugus, Diana couldn't help but feel that his patter was the build-up to a sales pitch, though she couldn't imagine what he might hope to convince her to buy.

"One of the farmers decided he wasn't going to let us put any poles on his property."

Saugus shifted his chair a little closer to Diana. She inched away, put off by hair oil too liberally applied and by the man himself. He didn't seem to notice her retreat.

"The farmer owned both sides of the road, so there wasn't anywhere else for us to go, so we went ahead and dug two holes in his roadside. Well, what did he do but send his wife and daughter out to squat down over those holes so we couldn't put the poles in!"

Saugus chuckled and finished the last dregs of coffee in his cup. Mrs. Saugus laughed merrily. Diana managed not to cringe. The woman's behavior made her increasingly uncomfortable. It was as if she had undertaken the role of supportive wife but couldn't manage it without overacting.

"We were at a standoff for quite some time, but then the old farmer made a mistake. He shoved one of my workmen, and I had him arrested for assault. While he was in jail, my men dug two extra holes—those women were still covering up the first two— and set two poles and strung a wire from one new pole to the other. When he got free, the farmer threatened to chop them both down, but by that time I had a lawyer to sic on him. In the end, he decided not to get his fingers burned."

"You seem to be involved in all kinds of projects, Mr. Saugus," Diana said politely.

"That's how I make my money. Invest in a good thing and rake in the profits when it succeeds."

"And you think the Hotel Grant will succeed?"

"Going to be another Saratoga Springs."

Since she could not imagine such a thing, or think of any sensible comment to make, Diana was relieved to have Ben arrive at that moment. In short order, Mr. and Mrs. Saugus had gone, and Mrs. Ellington had brought Ben and Diana their meal. It was, as Diana had expected, a simple supper consisting of two chops, a baked potato, and a "slip on"— hot mince pie.

"What do you know about Norman T. Saugus?" Diana asked Ben.

"Not much. I gather he's a speculator investing in your uncle's hotel."

Diana repeated what Saugus had said, then added, "I've never been to Saratoga Springs, but isn't it, er, much *bigger* than this?"

"*Much* bigger. Your uncle might succeed in making the Hotel Grant into a successful resort along the lines of some in the Adirondacks and the White Mountains. He could enlarge it to perhaps twice its present size. But to hope for more seems extraordinarily foolish. Saratoga Springs took decades to grow into what it is today, and that was with the support of the entire community. Hotel builders came in from outside. A number of them. Such a project couldn't possibly be financed by one man, no matter how wealthy."

"I don't believe Mr. Saugus is a rich entrepreneur. And I didn't much care for him."

"What do you make of his wife?"

"She doesn't like him much, either." Diana sighed and picked up her fork. "I wonder if I might have become the same sort of sycophant if Evan had lived?"

"Never."

His certainty pleased Diana even as the sharp tone made her wince. She hadn't meant to mention Evan's name. She knew how much Ben hated to be reminded that she'd been married before. That they both knew Evan had been a liar and a cheat did not make matters any easier.

In a way, she'd rubbed salt in a wound by making Ben wait for her answer to his marriage proposal. He was nothing like Evan, as she'd repeatedly assured him, but she'd taken her time about saying yes because she had wanted to make sure she did not make the same mistake twice. Impulsiveness was one of her worst failings, and that first time she'd leapt into marriage without regard for the consequences.

Mrs. Ellington appeared at Diana's elbow with a pot of fresh coffee. "Thank you for your help with the coroner," she said to Ben.

"I only told him what I observed," he said modestly.

"Was she there?" Diana asked when Mrs. Ellington left them alone once more.

"Only for a moment." He took a sip of the coffee. "I wonder how she knew that I spoke up in your Uncle Howd's defense."

"I can guess. It isn't difficult to eavesdrop if one knows the proper places to conceal one's self, and a housekeeper is in the perfect position to learn where those are. What else might she have overheard?"

Diana listened intently to Ben's account of the interview with the coroner and the inquest that had followed immediately after. "It didn't take long for the jurors, biased or not, to reach a verdict. Once they decided that the manner of death was unknown, there was nothing more for them to do."

"But her death was caused by a blow to the head. You *do* know that?"

"Yes, but not whether that blow was the result of accident, murder, manslaughter, excusable homicide, or justifiable homicide. Since it seems unlikely, after all this time, that anyone will be able to determine which it was, the matter will likely be dropped."

"That seems rather cavalier."

"Would you prefer your uncle to be arrested? Howard Grant is the only obvious suspect, because of the locket."

They ate in silence for a few minutes while she pondered what he'd said. When she looked at Ben again, she was surprised to find a frown on his handsome face. "Did something else happen?" she asked.

"You know me too well," he complained. "While we were still in the family parlor, Mr. Buckley asked me why I came to the Hotel Grant. I decided to try the truth. I said that you were acquainted with a Mrs. Torrence and that she told you about the hotel. Your Uncle Myron knew at once who I meant. He hasn't forgiven her, Diana. He was all but foaming at the mouth when he said her name."

A deep sense of disappointment settled over her. "I hoped he'd be willing to let bygones be bygones."

"It was clear to me, from Myron Grant's reaction, that he isn't about to be reasonable. I don't think he'll look kindly on anyone who is related to her." Ben reached across the table to enfold her hand in his. "I'd like you to consider leaving tomorrow, without telling them who you really are."

She freed her fingers and used both hands to rub her temples. "I admit that the thought of revealing my true identity does not seem very appealing right now. No one's likely to kill any fatted calves on my behalf." She'd always thought the story of the prodigal son should be taken with a grain of salt. "On the other hand, how can I live with myself if I skulk away at the first sign of trouble? We've only just arrived, Ben."

"But surely there's no need to stay longer?"

"Perhaps not." If he was right about Uncle Myron's attitude, there'd be no point in ever telling him who she was. Elmira Torrence's daughter would not be welcome here under any circumstances. She sighed. "I'm too tired to think any more about this tonight."

At once he was solicitous. "You've had a long day, all that travel topped off by an excess of drama. What you need is a good night's rest."

What she needed, Diana thought, was to be wrapped in Ben's arms and cuddled. At the mere thought, she felt warmth climb into her cheeks. If they spent the night together, she would not be worrying over what to do. She knew from experience that he could banish all such irrelevant thoughts from her mind.

Ben appeared to be brooding as they walked along the upstairs hallway towards their suite. Was he thinking the same thing she was? That they should have found a preacher before they'd left Denver.

Once inside the parlor, he seemed about to say something, then tilted his head, listening. "Do you hear that?" he whispered.

From directly below them came the sound of raised voices. A man and a woman were quarreling in loud and passionate tones.

"Saugus and his wife?" Diana guessed.

"There are no other guests in the hotel," Ben reminded her.

Diana could catch only a few words, but those she overheard were enough to give her pause. She heard "that girl" and "scoundrel" and "crimes" from Belle Saugus and, in her husband's deeper tones, "whore," then "stage," and finally, "murderer."

CHAPTER FOUR

ಶಿಲೇಶ

As if to make up for the deficiencies of supper the night before, breakfast was on a scale with what the fully-operational Hotel Grant would provide when renovations were complete. As soon as Ben entered the private dining room, Mrs. Ellington left a table by the window, where she'd been going over what appeared to be an account book, and asked him if he would like hot cereal, fried lake fish, steak, a cutlet or chop, an omelet, cold roast beef, or cold ham.

"Steak," Ben said.

"Choices for a side dish are French fried potatoes, any of six kinds of bread, or griddle cakes with syrup."

"Surprise me," Ben told her.

The beverage selection was also wide ranging, everything from coffee, chocolate, and herbal teas to a variety of breakfast wines. Ben was in no doubt there. "Coffee. And keep refilling it."

It was not until he'd polished off two cups and most of the steak and potatoes that he realized Mrs. Ellington was hovering. "The food is excellent," he told her, and gave her the smile Diana assured him could melt the hardest female heart.

Tressa Ellington blushed like a schoolgirl. "Is there something else I can get for you, doctor?"

"You could sit down and have a cup of coffee yourself," he suggested.

Her eyes widened at the suggestion, but after a glance around the empty dining room, she shrugged. "No reason not to, I guess. And one good one to agree. Thank you, Dr. Northcote."

"Meaning you hope to convince me to endorse the medicinal waters of the spring?"

"I was thinking rather of the healthful menu we offer."

"It *is* excellent food," Ben acknowledged.

About the spring he said nothing. There was an added advantage to his plan to take Diana away from Lenape Springs. With a little luck, they would be gone by late afternoon . . . before he was obliged to sample so much as a single glass of Myron Grant's vile, sulphur-laced water.

Mrs. Ellington sipped at her coffee. She seemed about to ask a question when something she saw through the window behind him made her stiffen.

Ben turned to look. Sebastian Ellington stood on one of the gravel-paved paths that crisscrossed the lawn, arms waving as he exchanged words with the black-clad, bearded preacher Ben had seen the previous day. "I perceive that the good reverend does not approve of hotels and boarding houses."

"Jonas Riker is nothing but a hypocrite!"

When Ben's arched brow encouraged her to explain, Mrs. Ellington took another sip of coffee, then wrapped both hands around the cup, as if she sought to absorb its warmth.

"It all started last spring, just over a year ago, when some preachers got together and held a camp meeting near the schoolhouse in Liberty Falls. Everybody went. Well, what else is there to do for entertainment? You never saw such shouting and carrying on! Maybelle Potter, she fell right down in the middle of the aisle, overcome by the Spirit, and lay like a dead woman for a good ten minutes. Then, just when everyone figured she'd gone to her reward, up she jumped and began to testify what the Lord had done for her and hollering 'Glory! Glory! Glory!' until she went hoarse." Mrs. Ellington gulped more coffee, apparently parched herself, then went on in a cynical voice. "By the time it was over, there were two miraculous cures and a whole passel of folks had seen the error of their ways."

"Including Mrs. Lyseth?"

"Oh, she'd already seen the light. The prize that day was Lida Rose Leeves. She was particular affected by one of the preachers." She inclined her head toward the window. "They say when he gets going the tears pour down his cheeks and drip right onto the floor. Lots of passion, if you know what I mean. Anyway, Jonas Riker up and married Lida Rose, and that made him the owner of the Lenape Springs Villa."

"I'm surprised he didn't close the place down."

"Might as well have." She gave another snort and swallowed the remaining coffee in one gulp. "Temperance house! What's the world coming to when you can't get wine with a meal at a hotel?"

"Is Riker the preacher at the church here in Lenape Springs?"

"Not much choice about that. He's the one who built it. It was ready in time to hold quarterly meeting in last December. Free Methodist, they call it, but he goes well beyond any Free Methodists I've ever heard tell of."

Ben was not much of a churchgoer. Sunday was a busy day for a physician and he generally used that excuse to avoid services. But even a man with as little interest in religion as Ben Northcote knew something of the controversy that had split apart the Methodist community. Methodist Episcopal churches, especially in larger cities, charged parishioners for their pews. What had started as a splinter group, the so-called Nazarites, preached that salvation was free and so were the pews.

Yes, Riker was a Nazarite, Ben thought. That hat he was wearing was called a "helmet of salvation," the style of coat a "robe of righteousness."

"He's planning another camp meeting," Mrs. Ellington said. "I heard all about it from Celia, who had it from Lida Rose. He thinks folks will come in from all over the state, even if they have to walk the whole five miles from the depot in Liberty to the Lenape Springs Villa." She shook her head. "Folks will stay in Riker's hotel as well as in tents, and they mean to put up one large tent with seats for the services and another for meals. I hear they'll be charging $3.50 for meals for the week." This seemed to amuse her, though whether it was because the price was too high or too low, Ben could not tell.

He considered what he knew of camp meetings and revivals. As he understood it, they could last a weekend or a week. The folks who came to hear the preaching camped out in big tents—separate accommodations for men and women, of course. Those who attended were encouraged to "testify," to repent in public for any sins they might have committed and to recount those sins in considerable detail. There was usually a lot of shouting and singing, too, and sometimes speaking in tongues.

And sometimes the preachers running the show were confidence men, only after what they could get in the collection plate.

"Can I bring you anything else?" Mrs. Ellington asked, seeing that Ben had finished his meal.

"Thank you, no. I believe I will take a walk into Lenape Springs."

"Looks like rain," Mrs. Ellington warned, indicating the overcast sky.

"I won't melt," Ben assured her, but he was grateful that Sebastian Ellington and the preacher had disappeared from view. He hadn't minded Mrs. Ellington's company but he had no desire to engage in further conversation. Nor did he wish to be delayed in completing his errands.

His first stop was the post office. It was the smallest building in town, tucked in next to the general store. There was barely room to turn around once Ben was inside the tiny foyer. All the space was on the other side of the counter, where the postmaster was busily sorting letters.

He accepted Ben's contribution and read the address with interest. "Maine, eh? That where you're from?"

Ben agreed that it was. He had written one of his less informative letters home, since he didn't know for certain what to give his mother and brother as a date for his return.

"Is there a telegraph office nearby?" Ben's brother, Aaron, was still recovering from serious injuries received some seven weeks earlier. It had been several days since Ben had been in touch with the doctor tending him in Ben's absence.

"Nearest one is in Liberty," the postmaster told him.

"What if a telegram comes there for me?"

"That they send a boy to deliver. Hired a new lad this spring from over to Liberty Falls. Call him Scorcher. Fastest thing on two wheels. With that bicycle of his he can make the three-and-a-half mile trip from Liberty to his pa's farm in Liberty Falls in eleven minutes flat."

"That's the second time this morning someone's mentioned Liberty Falls to me. Is it far from here?"

The postmaster, who introduced himself as Osmer Nicholls, produced from behind the counter a large book bound in dark green. The words "Sullivan County Atlas" were lettered on the front.

"This here's a map of the town of Liberty," Nicholls said.

It included a number of villages, among them Liberty, Liberty Falls, and Lenape Springs. Ben saw at once that numerous roads connected them. A boy on a bike who knew his way could indeed make excellent time.

"There's Gil Tanner's place. That's Scorcher's pa." The postmaster jabbed a finger at the name. Like many such local atlases, the detailed maps included the names of property owners.

"And the telegraph office?" Ben asked.

Nicholls turned the page to a larger map that showed just the village of Liberty. The railroad depot, freight house, and Wales Coal Yard were clearly marked, allowing Ben to orient himself.

"Telegraph office is here," Nicholls said, tapping the spot with his index finger. "It's not Western Union. It'll cost you an extra ten cents a message if it has to be sent along their lines."

Ben mumbled something appropriate in reply, but his attention had been diverted. Near the center of town, on a side street, he'd spotted the name "I. Torrence," inscribed beside a small square meant to represent a house.

Curious, Ben turned to the back pages of the atlas, where businesses were listed. Under "Town of Liberty" he found the villages of Liberty, Liberty Falls, Parksville—actually Parksvllie, due to a typographical error—Glen Cove, Stevensville, Lenape Springs, and Robertsonville. It did not take him long to read through all the names in Liberty village. There were no Torrences, although he could not help but notice in passing that a Mrs. Phebe Low, M.D. was listed. Her entry read: "Chronic diseases a specialty."

"This atlas is almost twenty years old," Nicholls said, sliding the book away from him and closing it. "Anyone in particular you're looking for?"

Ben hesitated. If he pursued the matter of Diana's father's family, they'd have to delay leaving the area. He hadn't mentioned them to her last night—a deliberate oversight on his part—but now a guilty conscience pricked him. Should he try to find out more about them before they left? On the other hand, he had no reason to think the Torrences would be any more forgiving than the Grants. Everything Ben had ever heard about Diana's father indicated he'd been even more intractable than her mother.

He took his leave of the post office without making further inquiries.

Ben's second stop was the combination blacksmith shop and livery stable across the road from the church. He recognized the blacksmith instantly. He'd seen him first as the disapproving father of the young man who'd tried to comfort Mercy Grant the day before, and later as a juror at the coroner's inquest. His name, Ben recalled, was Erastus Castine.

His agitated friend, the one Ben hadn't allowed to climb down into the hole with the remains, had also been on the coroner's jury. George Prinney had turned out to be the owner of the local mill.

"I'd like to rent that surrey Mr. Saugus had out yesterday," Ben announced. If he could persuade Diana to leave this afternoon, he didn't want to be dependent upon Floyd Lyseth to drive them to the depot.

Wiping his hands on a leather apron, Castine pasted a smile on his face. "Dr. Northcote. Happy to oblige. That is, I am if you promise to do a better job of returning it than Mr. Saugus did. Old Jessie had to bring the surrey back on her own the last time I leased it out."

Ben belatedly remembered that Saugus had abandoned the rig in front of the hotel when word had come of the discovery of Elly Lyseth's bones. "Good thing the horse knows its way."

"Last time I'll do business with Norman Saugus," Castine vowed as he got out the paperwork for the rental. "I don't hold with neglecting animals, and I should have remembered he wasn't reliable."

"Sounds like you've known him awhile." In spite of his desire to leave Lenape Springs as soon as possible, Ben found he was curious about Saugus. The quarrel he and Diana had overheard the previous evening suggested that the entrepreneur, at least, thought Elly Lyseth had been murdered.

"He was the one who talked Myron Grant into trying to enlarge the spring," Castine said. "That was the *last* time he got big ideas about that hotel. Wanted to increase the flow. Ended up losing the source."

"Obviously he located it again." Ben read over the agreement Castine handed him and signed on the bottom line.

"So he says. *Says* he saw bubbles of gas rising in the stream that showed him where to find the source of the fountain in the underlying rocks, but some say that so-called spring ain't worth a plugged nickel."

"How so? I've seen it. And smelled it. The sulphur—"

Castine guffawed. "Salted. Leastways, that's what some folks say. Grant salted it. Oh, there was a spring. Once. Didn't smell that bad, though. Story is, he made a pond in the brook, put in four barrels of sulphur, and claimed he had a spring again. Payment in advance if you please." He pointed to the sum written on the rental agreement.

Ben discounted the tale of the salted spring. Even four barrels of sulphur wouldn't last long in running water. But he was unable to stop himself from asking, "What do folks say he means to do with this medicinal water of his?"

Castine shrugged. "*Some* say he means to sell baths to the city people for twenty-five cents a go."

After that remarkable statement, Ben concluded his business at the livery stable in short order, but his hope of a quick escape was dashed by the blacksmith's curiosity.

"How come Coroner Buckley had you tell us about poor Elly's remains instead of calling in the local sawbones?" Castine asked.

"I was on the spot," Ben said. "I'm a guest at the hotel."

"Not the first time you've done it."

"No. I'm a city coroner back home."

The blacksmith waited.

"Bangor, Maine."

"You're a long ways from there."

Ben acknowledged that he was.

"You think she mighta been murdered?"

"As I said at the inquest, I don't know what happened."

"You must have a theory."

"Do you?" Ben shot back.

"Well, there's some say somebody musta done her in. Otherwise, we'd have found her ten years ago."

"There was a fire at about the same time."

"That was a couple of days after Elly . . . disappeared. What was she doing *under* the floor? That's what I want to know. Not like she would have crawled under the building if she was just hurt from a fall. No, sir. She was hiding from whoever hit her, that's what . . . some folks say."

"I doubt we'll ever know what really happened," Ben said, striding purposefully towards the door. "That's why your verdict was the only one possible. Good day to you, Mr. Castine."

"Leaves a lot of unanswered questions," Castine called after him.

So it did, Ben thought as he headed back to the hotel, but it was not his job to find the answers and he was glad of it. He had to admit to being intrigued by the case, and he agreed with Castine that Elly Lyseth probably *had* been murdered, but the last thing he wanted right now was to get involved in tracking down a killer.

It was almost eleven in the morning before Diana finished her breakfast and began to wonder where Ben was. She found her cousin Mercy behind the check-in desk, perched on a stool and copying addresses out of the hotel register.

The young woman's appearance presented a striking contrast to the way she had looked the previous day. Gone was the faded calico frock. In its place was a silk dress in a pretty leaf-brown shade. It had a moderate bustle and a high-collared black velvet jacket. Very suitable for meeting the public, Diana thought. In addition, her face looked freshly steamed and every brass hairpin was precisely in its place in her neat chignon, although she'd deliberately left a few curls loose at her nape to soften the line.

Diana was tempted to ask Cousin Mercy if she was expecting a visit from her young swain, but instead inquired whether she had seen Dr. Northcote recently. Diana could not quite bring herself to refer to him as "my husband," and for once blessed society's tendency towards formality. Calling him by his title spared her blushes.

"He went for a walk," Mercy informed her. "Aunt Tressa said he left right after he had breakfast."

Since her cousin seemed less hostile this morning, Diana abandoned her plan to go looking for Ben in favor of lingering in the lobby. She needed a neutral topic, something to ease them gradually into a more personal discussion. She was very curious about her long-lost relatives.

"Lenape Springs is a pretty little place," she ventured. "Is the whole area like this? I'm afraid I don't know very much about this part of the state."

"Are you interested in the history or the geography?" Mercy seemed willing to put her pen aside. From the way she rubbed her wrist, Diana suspected she'd been at her task for some time.

"Both, I suppose, but your question suggests that the Grant family has been in these parts a long while. Is that so?"

"Ever since the first Dutch settlers came to what was then New Netherlands." Pride filled Mercy's voice.

Diana feigned puzzlement. "Is Grant a Dutch name?"

"The Grants came from Scotland to the Connecticut Colony, then moved west. The first Mercy Grant and her twin brother, Justice, had a wonderful adventure in the process. I'll tell you about it some time if you like. You probably won't believe it, of course. Unless you accept that it is possible to read another person's thoughts."

"The twins had some kind of telepathy?"

"That's how the story goes."

"And you're descended from Justice Grant?"

"From both of them, in matter of fact. The first Justice's great grandson married one of Mercy's great granddaughters."

Fascinated, and perfectly willing to accept that such things were possible, Diana asked, "Did you inherit their ability to communicate without words?"

Mercy's enthusiasm diminished visibly. "I wish I had. It would make getting through to certain thickheaded folk so much easier."

"What about other members of this generation of your family?"

"Not that I know of. But then, none of them are twins. Perhaps that's a necessary prerequisite. But you were wanting to know about the area. Do you plan to hike? Climb? Go birdwatching? If it's the latter, you should talk to my father. He's been studying the local birdlife for years and has painted most of the critters." This morning Mercy seemed to have put her anger with her father behind her and mellowed towards the rest of the world as well.

"Is your father an artist?" Diana asked.

"A naturalist," she corrected. The pride was back in her voice, but this time it was tinged with a trace of embarrassment.

"I don't mean to pry," Diana began, though of course she did, "but I can't help but be curious about yesterday's, er, discovery. Will there be any . . . repercussions?"

Mercy waved her concern aside. "It's nothing to us. Just some girl who used to work here years ago. I barely remember her. I was only a child of eight at the time."

Eight-year-olds noticed a good deal, in Diana's experience, but she didn't say so.

"I wasn't even aware that my father had spoken more than a word in passing to Elly Lyseth. He doesn't usually pay much attention to other people. Just birds. Probably took pity on her. Who wouldn't when she had a father like Floyd Lyseth?"

Diana frowned, remembering Mercy's outburst the previous day. Was she telling the truth? Or did she know more than she was saying about Elly Lyseth's murder?

Diana tried to refrain from picking apart Mercy's statements but could not quell her suspicions. In recent months she'd covered too many crime stories for the *Independent Intelligencer,* not to mention having two close personal encounters with murderers.

Something did not seem quite right about her cousin's reaction to the discovery of Elly Lyseth's bones.

Diana knew she should mind her own business, but this matter involved her mother's family. It *was* her business. It made no difference that they didn't know she was kin. Diana knew.

"Is your mother still living?" she asked abruptly.

"She died when I was born. Pa and Uncle Myron raised me."

That accounted for the deep affection Diana had sensed between Mercy and her father. It also meant that Howd had been a widower ten years ago, free to court Elly Lyseth if he chose. The heart shape of the locket he'd identified seemed to indicate a romantic connection between them.

What did all that mean? Diana was trying to think of a subtle way to find out more when a gangly lad of fourteen or fifteen ambled into the lobby.

"Mornin', Miss Grant." he called out. "You got a Mrs. Spaulding staying here? She's got a telegram."

"Spaulding? You sure about that name, Scorcher?"

Diana hastily stepped forward to claim the message. "That's for me. I'm sorry for the confusion."

Heart pounding, she thought quickly, aware that how she phrased her next words could make the difference between keeping her reputation and being found out. She'd known pretending to be married to Ben was a bad idea, but men never gave a thought to the trouble a careless lie could cause!

"When I met Dr. Northcote I'd been a widow for some time," she said, her words running together in her rush to get them out. "Many of my acquaintances are still unaware that I changed my mind about marrying again."

"You're a newlywed, then?" A dreamy look came into Mercy's eyes.

Diana hoped her blush would suffice for an answer because she preferred not to lie outright. She opened the telegram, giving herself a small paper cut in her haste. In truth, only three people knew she was here—her mother in Colorado, Ben's mother in Maine, and Diana's editor in Manhattan.

The telegram had been sent by the latter. After one quick glance at its contents, Diana excused herself and went back to the tower suite. She was still clutching the telegram, trying to decide what to do, when Ben returned.

"Did you have an interesting morning?" she asked him.

"Informative. I've arranged for a rig from the livery stable. If it's agreeable to you, we can leave here after luncheon and be in New York City by—"

"I can't leave now!"

"Diana, you must see that this is not a good time for a family reunion. Your uncle is in the midst of a business venture that is likely to fail. He has no support from the town. Indeed, there seems to be active opposition to his plans. You don't want to be caught in the middle of that. And then there's this matter of the body. There can't help but be trouble over it. This town is too small for there not to be. What possible reason could you have for wanting to stay when you have the option of coming back later, after things settle down?"

"Horatio Foxe wants a story on Elly Lyseth's murder."

Ben looked as if he'd just had a door slammed in his face. "There's no proof it was—"

"Her death, then, and finding her remains."

"How did he hear about that? And so fast? Did you—?"

"No, I did not!"

"Well, then?"

She shrugged. "He's been following reports of a murder that took place in this area last October. At a guess, his contact at the county jail sent him word of our discovery. I'd honestly forgotten all about Foxe's interest in the 'Sailor Jack' story until this telegram arrived."

She handed the slip of paper to Ben with an apologetic look and watched his face while he read it. He was displeased by her decision. Worse, she was not certain he believed her explanation.

"I expect that Mr. Buckley notified the sheriff before coming out here last night," Diana said. "It wouldn't take long to send a telegram from Liberty to the county seat in Monticello or from Monticello to Manhattan or from Manhattan back to Liberty and on to me."

"Why can't Foxe's contact in Monticello handle this?"

"Because whoever his source of information is, that person is not a journalist. Most likely it's one of the jailers, or perhaps someone in the county clerk's office. No one in a position to write about Elly Lyseth. He needs me for that." She put one hand on Ben's forearm and smiled up at him, but got only a glare in return.

"And Foxe knew you were here because . . . ?"

"I wrote to him before we left Denver. When we stopped in New York on our way to Maine, I'd planned to have a final interview with him."

"In which you were going to resign?"

"Well . . . no." She looked out at the view of the mountains. The sky was overcast again. Threatening clouds took away any sense of peace the vista might have offered. "I'd intended to talk to him about writing more travel articles, and perhaps a few interviews with some of your state's summer residents. I understand there are a good many wealthy businessmen who own property on the coast of Maine."

Ben caught her chin with both hands and gently tilted her face upwards until she had to meet his eyes. "Diana, you know you don't need to worry about making your own living any more. We'll be married in a matter of weeks, after which I'll provide for you for the rest of your life. That's what husbands do."

Sincerity radiated from him, but what she saw in his expression was a mixture of love and frustration. "Not all husbands. Besides, I want to work."

Diana loved Ben Northcote, but she needed to keep a small bit of independence . . . and control of her own income. Until now, she hadn't thought Ben had any real objection to having a wife who worked, except for wishing that she'd chosen some other employer.

"Perhaps you could write for the *Whig and Courier*," Ben suggested, naming one of Bangor, Maine's newspapers.

"I already have an assignment," she said in the gentlest voice she could manage.

"Let it go, Diana. Tell Foxe to send someone else to cover the story."

"How can I?" She slipped free of his loose embrace and began to pace. "You know there's something wrong about that girl's death. She was murdered, Ben. That it happened ten years ago shouldn't matter. She deserves justice."

"That it happened ten years ago makes it impossible to find her killer." He reached for her but she eluded his clutches.

"Not necessarily. This is a small town. People stay put. And if any do leave, their neighbors know about it."

"Do you hear yourself? You aren't a detective, Diana. You wrote articles about crime while you were in New York. You interviewed a few police officers. That doesn't qualify you to investigate a murder."

She whirled to face him, temper flaring. "I have, in my bumbling way, managed to bring one or two criminals to justice!" Really! The man was insufferable when he got on his high horse.

"And you almost got yourself killed doing it," Ben shot back.

Hands on hips, she glared at him. "I'm still here. I prevailed."

He glared back, but he kept his distance. "It was a near thing. Twice now, I've almost lost you. Do you think I'll allow you to put yourself at risk like that again? I love you, Diana," he shouted. "For your own good, we must leave here."

Allow her? The rest of what he'd said made no impression once she heard those words. How dare he speak to her as if she were his to control? She was not his child. Or his dog. *Or* his wife.

"I've made my decision!" she shouted back, so furious she could hardly see straight. "With you or without you, I'm staying right here until I know who killed that poor innocent girl!"

CHAPTER FIVE

❧❦❧

When Diana swept out of the room without speaking another word, Ben started to chase after her, then thought better of it. They both needed time to calm down.

He could feel the pulse in his neck throbbing, always a bad sign. He took deep breaths, but that didn't seem to help. She was comparing him to Evan Spaulding again. Nothing annoyed him quite so much. But the real irony of the situation was that, this time, it was his own fault. He knew better than to issue commands around Diana. Ben flung himself into a chair and let his head fall back against the antimacassar.

Spaulding had been arbitrary and controlling. At least, Ben thought, he didn't share the cad's other faults. Spaulding had been an actor—irresponsible, self-centered, and difficult to live with. He'd thought nothing of taking Diana into the worst sort of neighborhood. Not only had she accompanied him on tour, staying in cheap hotels and spending endless hours on trains, but on occasion he'd dragged her with him into gambling dens. That he'd died in one, to Ben's mind, had been poetic justice.

But Spaulding had left behind a legacy. His behavior towards his wife had made Diana slow to trust another man. His weakness of character had obliged her to become strong and, after his death, self-sufficient. Unlike most women, she didn't think she *needed* a husband, but Ben had thought he'd convinced her she *wanted* one.

He lifted the telegram he still held and stared at it. He could do nothing about Evan Spaulding. The man was already dead. Horatio Foxe was another matter entirely.

At their last meeting, Foxe had been all too willing to help Ben's cause, but he'd had an ulterior motive. It was always the headlines with Foxe, and the more scandal-filled the better. Now that Ben thought about it, he was not really surprised that the Manhattan editor kept track of murders all over New York state. Anything to sell more newspapers than his rivals at the *Times* and *Tribune* and *World*.

Diana readily acknowledged that she'd more than repaid Foxe for all he'd done for her—giving her a job after Spaulding's death, for one thing—but Ben knew she still felt a certain obligation to honor his requests. It was a matter of friendship, he supposed, and of loyalty, both admirable qualities. Foxe's sister, Rowena, had been Diana's closest friend at school. Diana had thought of Foxe as a surrogate brother before she'd gone to work for him.

Ben sat forward, resting his elbows on his knees, and let his hands dangle loosely between them. The telegram, now sadly crumpled, fell to the carpet, For a time, he stared, unseeing, at the pattern of roses on the rug, wondering if Diana would ever be free of her sense of obligation to Horatio Foxe. In a marriage, the wife was supposed to obey her husband in all things. It was right there in the wedding vows. What a pity he could not simply forbid her all further contact with her editor.

Abashed by the thought, Ben straightened abruptly. It was a good thing he hadn't put those feelings into words while Diana was still in the room. And if his mother ever found out he'd entertained such a notion, even for a moment, she'd have his guts for garters. That was the low phrase Maggie Northcote would use, too, Ben thought. She delighted in trying to shock people.

Ben rubbed the bridge of his nose, struggling to see the situation from Diana's point of view. She obviously thought he'd overreacted to her acceptance of the assignment. He had to admit that there did not appear to be any physical danger to her here in Lenape Springs. He wanted to take her away as much to avoid an ugly scene with Myron Grant as to protect her from harm. It would be only a matter of time before Grant found out who she was. Diana was a terrible liar.

Ben's hands clenched into fists, but he was angry at himself, not Diana. He was the one who'd forced her to complicate her lie. Every argument he'd used to convince her they should pose as husband and wife was still valid, but he could see now that he'd made a mistake by not consulting her first. He hadn't had the right to make that decision for her.

He hadn't really consulted her about leaving here, either. Oh, he'd mentioned the possibility last night, but the plan had been to discuss the matter this morning. He'd jumped the gun, assuming she'd see things his way. And when she'd sprung Horatio Foxe on him, he'd overreacted. His strident opposition to Diana's plans had left her no room for compromise. Every word he'd spoken had made her even more stubbornly determined to go her own way. Worse, by now she had probably convinced herself that he'd be just as undesirable a husband as the man she'd eloped with all those years ago.

Don't think about Spaulding!

Aware that his strong feelings about Diana's late husband always muddled his thinking, and knowing that he'd be unable to escape them if he sat there brooding, Ben rose and left the suite. It was time to find Diana—time to grovel, if necessary.

If she was determined to solve Elly Lyseth's murder and give Foxe his story, then he would help her. His offer of support would prove to her that he could tolerate her job. And working with her would make it possible to protect her. It would keep him constantly by her side. He only hoped that, this time, she wouldn't get too close to the truth for a killer's comfort and put herself in mortal danger.

A few minutes later, Ben found Diana in the small writing room off the lobby. She was seated at a ladies' desk, bent over a piece of writing. Ben was certain she heard him come in, but she did not look up. She appeared to be making a list.

"Suspects?" he asked.

"Yes." She still sounded annoyed.

"May I see what you have so far?"

"Why?"

"Because I want to help."

"You're staying?"

"There was never any question of my leaving alone. We're in this together, Diana. The investigation of the murder *and* the rest of our lives."

Although she continued to avoid his eyes, she had to clear her throat before she could speak. He took heart from the notion that she was momentarily overwhelmed by gentler emotions . . . but he didn't press his luck by saying anything more.

"I'm working on the assumption that Elly was involved in a secret romance with Howd," she said, recovering.

"No one seems to have known he gave her that locket." Ben came farther into the room, closing the door behind him, and settled into a chair by the window. "And it was heart-shaped."

"Did you see what was inside it?"

"I didn't get the opportunity. The coroner has it now."

"I want to keep an open mind, but all that secrecy is a motive of sorts. Perhaps she became too demanding and he killed her rather than marry her. Or, there could have been an accident during a lovers' spat." She looked directly at Ben at last. "Do you think he killed her?"

"I'm relatively certain he didn't. He was shocked to recognize the locket. Still, that might simply have been surprise that the bones were found at all. If he set the fire to hide his crime, he probably thought there'd be nothing left."

"When did the fire break out?"

"Apparently it was a few days later. It's the fact that there was a fire at all that makes the whole affair so suspicious."

"You think it was set to get rid of the body?" An eager light in her eyes, she awaited his opinion, appreciative of his expertise in such matters.

What a way to woo a woman, Ben thought. But he was willing to do whatever worked. "It was a miscalculation if it was. Heat and flames rise. The floor was scorched but intact. And the body, further protected by the damp ground, wasn't damaged in the blaze. It was pure chance that she wasn't found back then."

"Deliberately setting a fire doesn't make much sense. The entire hotel might have burned to the ground. Howd wouldn't do that to his own family. Perhaps it was sheer coincidence. And an accident."

"You don't want Howd Grant to be guilty."

"I like him, "Diana said. "So do you."

"I've barely met the man," Ben objected. "Neither of us knows much about him. Or about anyone here."

She wasn't listening. "Howd knew Elly had the locket," she mused, "and that it might be recognized. If he killed her, he'd have taken it away with him."

"Murderers aren't always logical, Diana. A man doesn't think very clearly right after he's killed someone."

"What if Howd didn't realize she was wearing the necklace? It could have been hidden by her clothing."

"Keep Howd on your list," Ben advised, "if only so you can prove him innocent. Who else have you considered?"

"Elly Lyseth's parents," Diana said promptly. "Perhaps she provoked her mother to a fit of rage because she tried to leave town. Or maybe they found out about her secret romance with Howd."

"You're suggesting her death was not murder, but rather due to an accident during a quarrel?"

"Why not? You said yourself that it was possible Elly fell and struck her head."

"Yes, but if that were the case, why hide the body? People die from accidental falls all the time. Husbands whose wives tumble down the stairs and parents who strike their children too hard aren't usually hanged for it."

Diana's brow furrowed. "I can imagine hiding the body in a moment of panic. I wonder—did Mrs. Lyseth get religion before or after her daughter disappeared?"

"I don't know, but it was years later before Pastor Riker came on the scene." A pity, he thought. The preacher would have made an excellent suspect.

Diana penciled a note to herself. "I will find out. As for Floyd Lyseth, we already know he is no prize."

"Being ill-natured doesn't make a man a murderer, Diana." He was too far away to see what she had written. Rising, he went to stand beside her, one hand on her shoulder.

"I suppose not. And, as you say, he'd have no need to hide the body if her death occurred by accident during a quarrel."

Suspect number four on Diana's list was Myron Grant. Would he have killed to protect his younger sibling? He might have. Ben knew he'd go to great lengths for his own brother, Aaron.

"Keep him on the list?" Diana asked, correctly reading his expression.

"Keep him on."

"And fifth," Diana continued, adding one more name, "is Cousin Mercy."

"She was just a child ten years ago," Ben objected.

"And she'd had her father's full attention all her life. What if she resented Elly Lyseth for taking him away from her? She'd have wanted to prevent them from marrying. I think it unlikely she'd resort to murder at such a tender age, or have the strength to kill a grown woman, but you never know. For the moment, she too must remain a suspect."

"Any others?" His wandering fingers found a knot of tension at the base of Diana's neck.

"I'm sure there must be more," Diana murmured, letting her head fall forward as he began to massage the spot with his thumbs, "but I don't know enough yet to add other names. It would have to be someone who was here in Lenape Springs ten years ago."

"Saugus and his wife were." As Ben gently kneaded Diana's neck and shoulders, he told her what he'd learned in town.

"I wonder if Saugus might have come back because he'd heard about plans to enlarge the hotel." She sounded more relaxed, but her thoughts were still fixed on murder. "If he knew where the body was, he'd want to make sure it wasn't found."

"Saugus apparently objected to Grant's plans to rebuild the west wing. That is suspicious, I suppose, but only if he had reason to kill Elly Lyseth in the first place."

"Maybe Howd wasn't the only one courting her."

"Saugus was married, Diana." He lifted his hands from her shoulders. His thumbs had given out.

Diana didn't seem to notice. "Then there's Mrs. Saugus. Belle. I suppose she might have been jealous, if she thought the girl was carrying on with her husband."

"You're grasping at straws," Ben warned.

"What about the quarrel we overheard last night?"

"They were discussing the discovery of the remains, just as we were."

"Discussing? Shouting at each other, you mean. And Saugus called someone a whore. Elly Lyseth, do you think?"

Ben considered her reasoning, then shook his head. "You haven't enough to go on."

"It's early days yet." She tapped the end of her pencil against her teeth. "The fire *has* to be connected, even if it did occur a few days later. We need to know more about everything that happened back then. Elly's life. Howd's. The hotel."

"For a newspaper story?"

His sarcasm earned him a glare. "For myself. For my _family_."

Ben told himself to behave. She believed what she said and she needed to find the truth, even if her quest led her straight into trouble. Just as he needed to stay by her side, helping her . . . keeping her safe from harm.

"Why don't you divide up your list?" he suggested. "We can each talk to half the people on it."

"An excellent idea." She took another sheet of paper, pondering a moment before she wrote three names on one half and four on the other. Then she tore the paper neatly in two and handed the top section to him.

She'd given him Myron Grant, Floyd Lyseth, and Norman Saugus. She'd kept the women . . . and Howd . . . for herself.

"Any questions?" A slightly outthrust jaw warned him not to challenge his assignment.

"Not a one," he lied.

☙❧

After luncheon, dressed in somber hues, Diana made her way to the little house occupied by Floyd and Celia Lyseth. "Mrs. Lyseth?" Diana inquired when the woman opened the door. There was no doubt it was she, although she looked years older than she had the previous day. "I have come to tell you how sorry I am for your loss."

Celia Lyseth stayed where she was, firmly blocking the entrance. Behind her Diana caught a glimpse of a cluttered hallway and the stairs leading to the second floor. "I don't know you," she said after she'd examined Diana from head to toe. "Who are you?"

"My name is Diana Sp— Northcote." Diana felt warmth rushing into her face but soldiered on. "I am a guest at the Hotel Grant."

"Oh," said Celia Lyseth. "Doctor's wife."

"May I come in?"

"Why?"

For a moment Diana could only blink at her. Was such rudeness common among country folk? That she was herself being rude and intrusive was beside the point. Whether it was regarded as an act of charity or a neighborly gesture, a formal condolence call on a bereaved family was an acceptable social practice.

"I . . . I just thought you might want company in your . . . time of sorrow."

"Pastor'll be by to pray with me later." Diana got the message. Mrs. Lyseth didn't want anyone else consoling her, certainly not a stranger.

"If there's anything you need, I—"

"I have the Lord." She started to close the door, then added in a grudging voice, "Funeral's after church services tomorrow if you're of a mind to attend."

Diana stared at the wooden panels for a long moment before retreating from the Lyseths' tiny front stoop. Such odd behavior, but did it mean anything? Elly had disappeared ten years ago. Perhaps her parents had done their grieving then.

Diana had walked to the Lyseth house from the hotel, a matter of perhaps a half mile. On her way back, she spotted Belle Saugus inside the village's general store. Taking advantage of the opportunity, she went in.

The place smelled wonderful. The agreeable fumes of freshly roasted coffee almost blocked the heavy, less amenable odor from the wet spot under the kerosene barrel. Pails filled with fine-cut, aromatic tobacco and the scents emanating from a half dozen gleaming glass jars atop the counter added to the pleasant atmosphere.

Mrs. Saugus didn't notice Diana at first, being intent on the selection of teas. It was sold from tea chests, in the original straw matting. Chinese characters decorated the sides of the containers, which sat in a row on the floor.

The proprietress, a robust countrywoman wearing blue-tinted glasses, the sleeves of her calico dress rolled up to her elbows, was wrestling an empty barrel through the back door. "Never fails," she grumbled. "Not another soul in sight when I start a job and the moment I'm in the midst of it, the whole world wants service."

"Don't bother about me," Diana hastily assured her. "I'll just look around till you're free."

"Good morning, Mrs. Northcote," Belle said.

"Mrs. Saugus." Diana pretended to be interested in a container of Towle's Log Cabin maple syrup. "How clever," she murmured. "The tin is shaped like a log cabin."

It was an inane thing to say, but she could hardly come right out and ask Belle Saugus if she'd killed Elly Lyseth. She turned to the dry goods counter opposite the one with the glass jars. A row of upholstered cast iron stools for ladies had been arranged in front of it and on top was a dispenser cabinet for thread. It was shaped like a great cylinder and whirled around to show off all the gauges and colors of Merrick's Six Cord Soft Finish Spool Cotton.

"Now then," said the shopkeeper, dusting her hands as she returned to the store. "What can I get for you, ma'am? The only thing we're out of at the moment is whiskey."

That was what had been in the empty barrel, Diana supposed. There were a great many barrels in the store, large ones for beer and vinegar and smaller ones to hold pickles, sugar, and crackers. Through the open door to the back room, she could see a great hogshead of molasses in a sturdy frame and a large cask marked "beef in brine." A smaller cask carried the label "pickled mackerel."

"We've an iced meat box for fresh meats, too," the shopkeeper said, seeing the direction of Diana's gaze.

Diana turned back to the counter that ran the length of the store. On top were the showcases for candy, cigars, and cutlery. The store cheese sat under glass. Behind the counter were shelves full of light groceries, chewing gum, and patent medicines.

Once more drawn to the gleaming glass jars, Diana studied a selection of corn kisses, Gibraltars, cinnamon red hots, lemon gumdrops, Zanzibars, and conversation candy—small, crisp candies made of sugar and flour that contained little slips of tinted paper printed with rhymes and sentiments.

"I've a craving for gumdrops," Diana said.

"Anything else?" The woman measured them out into a cone of paper and crimped the top to keep it closed. "I've raisins. Fruits both dried and fresh. Cheese, perhaps?"

"Thank you, no. Just gumdrops."

"And anything else for you, ma'am?" she asked Belle Saugus. Diana saw there was a parcel already on the counter, wrapped in heavy paper and tied up with string.

"Is this all you have for store tea?"

"Straight from China, that is."

Belle looked doubtful, but indicated she would take some. "I suppose anything is better than homemade brews. Mrs. Ellington offers nothing but sage, sassafras, and crop-vine teas."

"Makes them from her own yarbs," the shopkeeper agreed. "Healthier than drinking water from that spring if you ask me."

"You don't approve of taking the waters?" Diana asked. "I'm sorry. I didn't catch your name."

The woman grinned at her. "That's because I didn't throw it. I'm Emma Castine, and no, I don't hold with that nonsense. Neither does my husband." She made change for Belle Saugus, watching the other woman through narrowed eyes.

Mrs. Saugus snatched her parcels, the tea and something that sloshed. A flask, Diana decided, which might account for the empty whiskey barrel. "Some people wouldn't know an opportunity to make a profit if it hit them in the fanny."

"Oh-ho! Fine talk! My Elmer's got a head on his shoulders, he has."

"Is that why he leaves you to do all the work while he spends his time gossiping at the livery stable?"

"That's his brother's place," Emma Castine shot back. "They get together to discuss town business, not that it's any of *your* concern."

Ordinarily, Diana would have left. Or attempted to make peace between the two women. In this instance, she thought it might be more useful to let them argue. That Horatio Foxe would approve of this method of getting information gave her pause, but she still refrained from interrupting.

"Come here all hoity-toity, thinking you're better than the rest of us," Mrs. Castine complained. "Well you're no better than you should be, I say."

"You miserable old hag. What do you know about anything! I don't have to listen to your insults."

"Leave then. We got along very nicely, thank you, before you and that husband of yours came here."

"Did you? This place hasn't changed a bit in ten years. It's still a cesspit in the back of beyond."

"Why are you here then? That's what I'd like to know." Hands on hips, she glared at her opponent from behind the counter. "Why don't you just go back where you came from?"

Instead of answering that question, Belle Saugus tossed her head and declaimed: "'I hate ingratitude more in a man than lying, vainness, babbling drunkenness, or any taint of vice whose strong corruption inhabits our frail blood.'" Then she whirled and strode out of the shop.

Diana had to hurry to catch up. "That was a supurb exit line," she gasped, breathless from chasing after the other woman. She wasn't sure it had suited the situation, but it had certainly been delivered with flair. And it had left "the enemy"—Mrs. Castine—in a state of confusion.

"She irritates me," Mrs. Saugus said. "Her husband hasn't the sense to come in out of the rain, and yet she dares criticize my Norman."

Diana gave the lowering sky a wry and wary glance and

quickened her pace even more. Belatedly, she realized they might have done better to remain in the store.

"My Norman is ten times more clever than anyone else in this god-forsaken town," Belle Saugus continued, apparently oblivious to the scattered drops of moisture already beginning to fall. "He's proven that before and he'll do it again."

Proven how? Diana wondered.

Abruptly, Mrs. Saugus came to a halt in the middle of the road, hands fisted at her sides. "Give me a moment. I must regain control of myself."

She'd seemed in excellent control to Diana, who knew very well how easily temper could overcome common sense. Hard upon that thought came another. This woman's self-possession, her customarily blank expression, her dramatic departure from the general store—all these things suggested theatrical experience. So did the word "stage," overheard during the previous night's argument.

It might be that Belle Saugus was simply a natural actress, that she'd grown accustomed to "performing" in certain ways. Most women did, to some degree. But there had been a level of skill, a certain projection of the voice and an attitude evidenced in the lines she'd delivered from Shakespeare's *Twelfth Night* that made Diana, who knew something of actors, think this particular woman must once have trod the boards.

She contemplated coming right out and asking, but there were pitfalls in such directness. In some circles, actresses were considered only a step above whores. She'd get nothing out of Belle Saugus if she insulted her.

"Shall we walk on?" Mrs. Saugus asked. "I am quite recovered now."

"I think we should, and quickly." What had been only an occasional drop of rain had suddenly become a steady drizzle.

Moving as fast as corsets and bustles would allow, the two women scurried towards the hotel. "Wait," Mrs. Saugus begged as they reached the turning into the long driveway. "I need to catch my breath." She ducked under a convenient maple tree and Diana followed.

The leafy branches overhead did not offer much protection, especially when the drizzle turned into a downpour, but there was no going on then. They'd have to wait out the rain.

A cold rivulet of water slid inside Diana's collar and down her back, making her shiver. "Useless bit of fluff," she complained, pulling off her hat and shaking moisture from the brim.

"Perhaps you could borrow that one," her companion suggested, pointing to the enormous straw chapeau sported by a scarecrow in a nearby field. Its stuffed appendages flapped with every gust of wind, calling attention to the rest of its natty attire—a ragged plaid shirt and overalls.

Diana laughed. "Perfect for providing protection from the rain, but *so* unstylish!"

They stayed where they were until the storm abated, but Diana learned nothing of use about her companion. Mrs. Saugus kept the conversation on fashion, about which she seemed to know a great deal . . . most of it dead boring.

At length, they continued on towards the hotel through heavy mist. By the time they reached the veranda, they were both thoroughly damp. With no more than a perfunctory farewell, Diana went to her room to change into dry clothing.

Twenty minutes later, wearing a silk wrapper, she sat with lower limbs curled beneath her on the window seat, a pencil in one hand and one of the notebooks she always carried with her resting in her lap. As she recorded her impressions of the morning, she couldn't help wishing she'd followed Mrs. Saugus's example and purchased China tea at the general store. She'd used the annunciator to have one of Mrs. Ellington's hot brews sent up but she did not recognize the taste and could not say she cared for it. She set the cup aside and consoled herself with gumdrops.

There was much to consider, Diana thought, as she nibbled

one of the sweet candies, but if Belle Saugus *had* been an actress, Diana knew exactly who to consult to find out more about her. Her landlady in Manhattan, Mrs. Curran, knew everyone who'd been involved in theater for the last forty years.

She would write to Mrs. Curran, Diana decided, describing Belle and asking the older woman to find out what she could. She paused, pencil over paper, as a thought struck her. She could do better than that. If Mercy's discarded drawings were still in the kitchen kindling box, she could include one of them with her letter.

Pleased with this plan, Diana pondered what else to write. Should she make some mention of the Saratoga trunk and the boxes she'd left stored in the house on Tenth Street? She *could* ask Mrs. Curran to send them directly to Maine. That way, there'd be no need for her to return to New York . . . if she resigned her position at the *Independent Intelligencer* by telegram.

But was that what she really wanted to do? Her recent conflict with Ben still fresh in her mind, Diana sighed. She hoped the tension between them was just pre-wedding jitters, but what if it was more than that? So far, Ben had yielded every time she had insisted upon having her own way, but what if there was a limit to his tolerance?

With another, deeper sigh, Diana rose to dress. She would go down to the kitchen, filch a sketch of Belle Saugus, then retire to the writing room to compose her letter to Mrs. Curran. She would not ask that her trunk be sent on. Not yet.

Diana had not set out to test Ben's limits, but she had to be practical. She would be far better off in the long run if she found out what they were *before* she married him.

CHAPTER SIX

༄ ☙ ☜ ༄

By the time he returned to the livery stable that afternoon, Ben had wasted a great deal of time trying to speak to Myron Grant. If he was in the hotel, he was avoiding Ben. Ben hadn't caught so much as a glimpse of Norman Saugus or Floyd Lyseth either.

A rain shower had delayed him further. He'd waited it out in the company of Sebastian Ellington, playing a game of billiards to pass the time. The young man was pleasant enough to talk to but had carefully steered the conversation away from anything to do with his family. About Elly Lyseth he knew nothing. "I've lived here less than two years," he told Ben. "I'd never even heard of the woman until they dug up her bones."

When the precipitation at last let up, Ben set off for town. He half expected to encounter Diana on her way back from the Lyseth house. He did not. He assumed she'd returned earlier. Either that, or she had taken shelter in one of the stores in the village.

The livery stable smelled of leather and horses. Three men were already present when Ben entered. Luke, Mercy Grant's swain, was hard at work cleaning harness. The other two, Castine the blacksmith and another man of about the same size and proportions, had abandoned labor to tip back in two identical wooden chairs and drink coffee.

"He was a fool not to have more insurance," Castine was saying as Ben came in.

"Any man who can't rebuild a barn for three hundred dollars shouldn't be farming," his companion argued.

"Got to insure more than the building," Castine countered. "What if he'd lost livestock in the fire?"

"But he didn't. That's the point."

"How much insurance you got on that store of yours, Elmer?"

"Ten thousand dollars," Elmer grudgingly admitted. In a defensive tone, he added, "That's how much I've got in stock. Got to protect my investment, don't I?"

Castine was chuckling when he looked up and saw Ben. "Dr. Northcote. Come for that surrey?"

"Looks like I won't be needing it today, after all." With a silent apology to Diana, he put into effect an idea he'd had while walking from the hotel to the livery stable. "I wanted to get the wife away from here, what with finding bones under the building and all, but she won't budge. You know women. Stubborn as all get-out."

They agreed that women were the very devil to live with.

"That Norman Saugus has got the worst one, though," Elmer said. "Never marry a red-headed woman."

"Have you seen Saugus today?" Ben asked. "The hotel is all but deserted. I haven't caught a glimpse of him, or either of the Grants, or even Floyd Lyseth."

"Floyd drove Howd and Myron past here early this morning," Castine said. "Came back during the rain storm, but Myron was the only passenger." He shrugged at Ben's raised eyebrow. "Can't get much of anywhere without going past my place."

"Funny about them bones," Elmer said, breaking into Ben's speculations.

"This here's my brother Elmer," Castine said. "He owns the general store."

"You got a real close look, Doc," Elmer said. "Was she

murdered?"

"I got a close look, too," Castine objected, "seeing as how I was a juror and all."

"It's hard to say after all this time," Ben answered. "It was sheer luck we were able to identify her. If she hadn't been wearing that locket Howd Grant gave her—"

Too late, Ben realized that the locket had not been mentioned at the inquest. Coroner Buckley had simply stated that the bones had been identified as those of Elly Lyseth.

Elmer shot out of his chair, sending it tumbling over backwards. "By God, Erastus! What were you thinking? How could you let him off?"

"What's this about a locket?" Castine asked Ben.

"Howd Grant identified the necklace Miss Lyseth was wearing as one he'd given her shortly before she disappeared."

"He was *courting* her?"

"It appears that way."

"Should have locked him up and thrown away the key," Elmer muttered.

"That's quite a leap," Ben said, righting Elmer's chair, "from giving a woman a gift to taking her life."

"Just once, Howd Grant ought to get what he deserves." Elmer's eyes gleamed with suppressed fury. "Thinks he's God's gift to women. Well, he ain't."

Ben tried in vain to make sense of the colorful spate of words with which Elmer Castine proceeded to cuss out Howard Grant. He wound down after a while and, having vented his spleen, abruptly declared it was high time he got back to the store.

His brother watched him leave the livery stable, shaking his head. After a moment, he turned to Ben. "Some people just never let go. Elmer and Howd were rivals once upon a time for the hand of Mercy's mother."

"He's not the only one who never lets go," Luke grumbled from his perch in the adjacent tack room.

The blacksmith's countenance darkened. "I told you why you're to stay away from that girl." Lowering his voice, he said, for Ben's benefit, "I ain't entirely sure she's not his cousin."

"But if she married Grant—"

"It was *after* that Howd and Elmer fought over her. Elmer said he wasn't treating her right. Howd denied it. Then he near killed Elmer with his bare fists. Some say Howd's got a temper worse than Myron's."

"Has he ever been violent towards women?" It was one thing for men to get into fights, quite another for a man to abuse a member of the weaker sex.

"As to that, who's to say? What goes on in a man's home is between him and his wife. But I will tell you this. Howd Grant is a real strange duck. Goes off by himself a lot. No real friends. He thinks more of animals and birds than he does of his fellow man."

"I take it folks in town had no idea he was courting Elly Lyseth?"

Castine shook his head. "Hard to picture what she'd see in him. She was a pretty little thing. Full of life." He thought for a moment. "Kinda reminded me of the youngest Grant girl. Elmira. Maybe that's why it was so easy to believe Elly ran away. Folks in my generation, we remembered when Elmira went. Kids Elly's age would have heard the story from their parents. Some folks mighta made it into a real romantic tale. Anyway, when Elly disappeared, everybody in town just figured she'd up and followed Elmira's example."

Ben would have liked to ask more questions, but Castine had one of his own. He wanted to know why Ben had come to Lenape Springs in the first place.

"I heard the fishing was excellent," Ben replied.

He wished he'd thought of another excuse when Castine launched into a discussion of angling that quickly left Ben in the dust. Ben had fished in the past, but was not an enthusiast. He counted himself lucky when he managed to extricate himself from the livery stable without agreeing to let Castine guide him to a favorite local trout stream.

All in all, Ben thought he'd rather spend a day bird-watching with Howd Grant than stand in icy running water, making endless casts with a fishing line.

❧

An hour after Diana's return to the hotel, she had composed her letter to Mrs. Curran and was ready to put it in the mail. She exited the writing room and crossed the lobby to the check-in desk, behind which Mercy stood talking to Tressa Ellington and Myron Grant.

"Here she is now," Mercy said, catching sight of Diana. She did not sound friendly.

Diana stopped in her tracks. "Is something wrong?" Her voice, annoyingly, broke on the question. Had Mercy seen her take the discarded sketch from the kitchen?

"We know about you." Uncle Myron's belligerent tone added force to his statement.

Diana felt the color drain from her face and she had to grip the front of the check-in desk for support. Somehow, they'd found out that she was Elmira's daughter. A bit frantic, Diana looked around for Ben, but there was no sign of him. She glanced a second time towards the door to the veranda, wondering if she should make a run for it. She managed to quell the impulse, but her heart was racing as she forced herself to face the angry triumvirate.

"I did not set out to deceive anyone," she said in a small voice.

"Liar!" Myron Grant was livid. His eyes, hard and unforgiving, bored into her.

Swamped by guilt—for she *had* lied to them—she suddenly wanted to confess everything. It would scarcely make them feel any more kindly towards her, but she hated the deceit, hated "acting." Besides, she was no good at it. She never had been. She'd been laughed off the stage the two times she'd been persuaded to fill in for one of Evan's ailing colleagues.

Before she could find a way to begin, Mrs. Ellington spoke. "You're probably wondering how we knew," she said. Although her arms were folded across her bosom and her face wore an implacable expression, Diana thought for just a moment that she detected a hint of amusement in the housekeeper's eyes. "Scorcher reads telegrams before he delivers them."

Diana blinked. What did Scorcher have to do with anything? Surely her mother hadn't sent a telegram to the Hotel Grant.

"Not surprising, really," Mrs. Ellington continued. "They all listen when the messages come in. Anybody who understands Morse Code can figure out what they say. And I'm quite sure Mr. Nicholls at the post office reads our mail if the letters aren't sealed."

Understanding swept through Diana, leaving her dizzy with relief. Scorcher had told them the contents of her telegram from Horatio Foxe. They didn't know *who* she was. They only knew *what* she was.

Her sense of having been reprieved was short-lived. These good people still had plenty of reasons to be upset with her. Thanks to Scorcher, they must believe she intended to write an exposé about the hotel—a scandal-filled story built around the grisly death of a young female employee and culminating with the discovery of her remains and, if Foxe had his way, the arrest of her murderer.

"Are you a reporter?" Mercy asked. "Like that Nellie Bly who writes stories for the *World?*"

"Not quite like Nellie Bly."

"I should say not," Mrs. Ellington cut in. "She risks her life to expose the terrible conditions people have to endure. First it was the insane asylum, and since then she's been locked up in jail, and worked in a factory, and exposed an employment agency that was—"

"I am a journalist, not a stunt girl," Diana interrupted.

"What do *you* write about, then?" Mercy wanted to know.

Another perilous subject!

"I review books." Diana saw no need to mention that she also reviewed plays and reported theatrical gossip. That might give the wrong impression.

She was pleased to find that her voice was steady again.

"That Mr. Foxe who sent the telegram," Uncle Myron said. "Scorcher says he's from the *Independent Intelligencer.* That newspaper's got almost as bad a reputation as the *National Police Gazette.* Nothing but sensational stories and half-truths. Fit for the barber shop or the barroom, but not for decent people to read."

"It's not *that* bad," Diana protested, offended in spite of the kernel of truth in her uncle's assessment. "And how does a boy Scorcher's age know so much about it anyway?"

"He's a reader, "Mrs. Ellington said. "Reads every newspaper he can get his hands on. Books, too."

"Never mind Scorcher," Myron Grant cut in. "I want to know why you came here. Danged strange it wasn't until after you arrived that they dug up those bones."

All three women gasped at this suggestion, but Diana was the first to recover. "That's nonsense and you know it. I had nothing to do with the discovery. And I did not come here looking for scandal." It had found her, Diana thought, and it had been sheer bad luck for them all that Horatio Foxe had also been able to locate her.

"Your husband said you came because you know my sister Elmira." Myron's glower intensified. "Just how do you know her? That's what I want to know. What scandal was *she* involved in?"

Once again, Diana considered confessing the truth. Then she realized how much explaining she'd have to do. Her mother had been, and continued to be, involved in more than one questionable situation. What if Uncle Myron asked for details? She shuddered to think what he'd make of Elmira Grant Torrence's current profession.

She cleared her throat. "Mrs. Torrence lives in Denver, Colorado," she said. "I was there recently, on a matter that had nothing to do with my employment by the *Independent*

Intelligencer. Once that was dealt with, however, I did write several travel articles for the newspaper."

Everything she'd just said was true, but her statements left out a host of details. Certain Uncle Myron, and probably Mercy and Mrs. Ellington, as well, could tell she was hiding something, Diana waited for the ax to fall.

"Why did the telegram come addressed to Mrs. Spaulding?" Mrs. Ellington asked. It was the second time she'd provided a welcome distraction.

"That is the name which appears as my byline." A note of pride came into her voice. Until quite recently, all her pieces, even her column, had been published anonymously. It was a mark of success to be acknowledged as the author of an article.

"Is that what they call a pseudonym?"

"Pseudonyms are assumed names. Diana Spaulding was my legal name at the time I started writing for the *Independent Intelligencer.*"

"That's right," Mercy murmured. She spoke to her uncle. "The telegram came addressed to Mrs. Spaulding. She's a newlywed. She said she was a widow when she met Dr. Northcote."

Myron seemed calmer now. He scratched his chin. "Is Northcote really a doctor?"

"Oh, yes," Diana assured him. "He's a very fine physician."

"He doesn't seem to think much of my spring."

"He didn't come to take the waters," Diana said honestly.

"He didn't come to fish, either. Don't bother to deny it." Myron was back on the attack. "There were no fishing poles in your gear. I want you and your husband out of my hotel, Mrs. Northcote. And you'd better not be writing about us for that newspaper of yours, either."

Diana at last let go of the check-in desk and stood on her own two feet, back straight, chin thrust forward. "I never intended to write anything negative about the Hotel Grant. My editor, I admit, likes sensational stories. And I have written about crime in the past, from a female point of view. But—"

"You'll not be writing about crime here," Myron declared. "We don't need that sort of notoriety."

"Besides," Mercy put in, "there *was* no crime."

"She told you she'd been writing travel articles," Mrs. Ellington interrupted. "I should think it would be obvious that's why she came here. She was going to do a piece on the Hotel Grant. Free publicity, Myron. Do you want to throw that away?"

Diana seized the life line she'd been thrown. It meant lying to them again, but at this point, she couldn't quibble. She didn't want to leave here. Not now. Her family needed her help, whether they realized it or not.

"The story of the discovery of Elly Lyseth's bones has already spread beyond Sullivan County," she said. "You won't be able to avoid the notoriety entirely. Murdered or not, there's a mystery surrounding that young woman's death."

"She wasn't murdered," Myron insisted. "It must have been an accident." He could not quite hide the flash of doubt in his eyes.

He was worried that his brother might be blamed for the girl's death. Diana sympathized. She wished she could tell him the real reason she had no intention of digging up scandal on the Grants, but she'd have to work with what she had.

"I envision an article on this hotel that praises all its amenities, and the healthful qualities of the spring water, *and* shows its owners to be the sort of people who care about justice. The only way to clear your name is to discover what really did happen ten years ago, and I can help you do that."

"How?" He didn't sound convinced, but at least he wasn't hustling her out the door.

"By talking to people. By asking questions."

"That'll only stir up trouble." Myron objected.

"We've already got trouble," Mrs. Ellington said. "That blasted preacher is pushing Celia to denounce the hotel and say Elly died because she worked here for us."

"Mrs. Northcote meant to visit her earlier today," Mercy whispered. That Celia Lyseth might already have talked to a reporter clearly alarmed them all.

Diana met their accusing stares with an equanimity she was far from feeling. "Mrs. Lyseth did not denounce anyone to me. She wouldn't even talk to me." Of course, she hadn't known Diana was a journalist then, either.

Myron started to speak, then closed his mouth with an audible snap. He stood in silence for a long moment, mulling over what she'd said. "You came here to write a travel piece?" he asked at last.

Diana couldn't bring herself to lie outright, but she managed a nod.

"Good publicity, you think?" He looked at Mercy.

"Excellent publicity."

"There's a saying," Diana reminded them, "that any publicity is good publicity." She'd never been sure she believed it, but the argument seemed to convince her uncle.

"Guess if we had a reporter on our side, that might be an advantage. You can stay."

"And you'll cooperate with me?" Diana persisted. "Talk to me. Answer my questions, even if you think they're intrusive?"

He agreed with a reluctant nod.

"Excellent. I'm sure your example will persuade the rest of your family to follow suit. Do you have any influence over Mr. Saugus?"

Myron Grant's expression cleared for a moment and he almost smiled. "I don't suppose you could prove he killed Elly? That would solve a host of problems."

"I'll see what I can do," she promised, hoping he caught the sarcasm in her tone. "In the meantime, let's get started on that interview."

Myron looked puzzled.

"I thought I made myself clear. I'll need to talk to each of you, to ask questions about what happened ten years ago. You're here. I'm here. I might as well start with you."

"Now?"

"Now."

Myron grumbled a bit, but finally gave in. "Come into the kitchen. I've got a hankering for a cup of coffee to whet my whistle before we begin."

A short time later, seated at a freshly scrubbed pine table with steaming mugs in their hands, Diana began her inquisition. She had her notebook and pencil at the ready, but first she simply studied her uncle's face, looking for Elmira in the planes and angles.

There was no physical resemblance that she could see, but there was a similarity in attitude. Like his sister, Myron was impatient, brusque, and did not suffer fools gladly. "Get on with it," he ordered.

"How did you first meet Norman Saugus?" She set aside family feeling and became all business. This was a murder investigation. It must be undertaken with utmost efficiency.

Her uncle grimaced at the question. "About eleven years ago. Went into the City to meet with some buyers—had a herd of dairy cows then and was selling the milk."

"The city?" Diana interrupted. "That would be Middletown? Or was it Newburgh?"

He snorted. "Don't you know there's only one City when you're from these parts? New York City, Mrs. Northcote. Manhattan."

"Very well. And you met Mr. Saugus there?"

Myron sipped coffee, a reminiscent gleam in his small eyes. "We were staying in the same boarding house. Seemed a nice enough fella. And when he heard I owned a hotel in the mountains, he said as how he'd been meaning to get out of the City for a spell. Next thing I knew, he and Belle decided to come back with me. Paying guests, they were . . . at first."

"And later?"

"Well, once we got to talking, and I told him some of the things I'd thought about doing with the hotel, he told me he was in the business of finding money to invest in profitable enterprises. That's what he called them—profitable enterprises.”

“Did you ask for references? Check his credentials?”

“Never thought to. Well, I knew him, you see. He’d been staying here a couple of weeks by then, paying his bills as regular as can be.”

Diana kept her thoughts to herself, but Myron’s words put her in mind of two types of criminal she had learned about when she was writing crime stories for the *Independent Intelligencer.* One was the boarding-house thief, a breed with which she’d had personal experience. The other was the hotel thief. Both tended to operate in cities, where it was easier to dispose of the plunder and disappear in a crowd, but what Saugus had told Myron about wanting to get out of New York for a while rang true. If he’d tried his game too often, the police probably knew what he looked like.

There were a great many confidence *women*, too, she recalled. “You said Mrs. Saugus was with him when you met?”

Myron nodded.

Diana frowned. The type of criminal she’d been thinking of didn’t usually work in pairs. Or rather, when they had confederates, they didn’t allow anyone to see them together. “Tell me,” she urged, “why does the idea of Norman Saugus as Elly’s murderer appeal to you?”

“I don’t like the man.”

“Why do business with him, then? The second time, I mean.”

“He’s the only backer I could find,” Myron admitted, “and he had ready money.”

“How long did you search?”

He shifted uncomfortably in his chair. “I didn’t want to waste a lot of time. I saw what my sister did with her place, and Sebastian came back with me after that visit, expecting I’d do even better. Got to give the boy credit—he’s born to the business on both sides of the family.”

“Your sister and her husband have a hotel?”

Myron nodded. “In the Adirondacks.” He started to say more

but she cut him off.

"You can tell me about it later. Right now we need to stick to Norman Saugus. How did you find him again?"

"He found me."

"How convenient."

Myron missed her sarcasm. "Must have heard I was planning to expand. He wrote and offered to invest. Said he was sorry it hadn't worked out before."

"What stopped you the first time?"

"Thought you knew that. Spring dried up. Then there was the fire. Thank the Lord it was after the season. No one was killed or injured. But if the wind had been from the other direction that day, it would have taken the entire hotel."

"So he knew you'd rediscovered the source of the spring?" Diana asked.

Myron started to say yes, then hesitated. "You know, he never mentioned the spring. Must have heard, though. Why else would he be willing to put his own money into the resort?"

Why, indeed? Diana made a few more notes and considered what to ask next.

Her uncle's fingers drummed on the tabletop, signaling that he grew impatient with her questions. She was not surprised when he challenged her. "Where does all this get you?"

"Nowhere . . . yet. But let's go back ten years. Saugus and his wife were here. Did they know the Lyseths?"

"Had to. All three of them worked at the hotel."

"Any closer contact?"

"Not that I saw."

"What do you remember about Elly?"

"Flighty little thing. Always complaining. Always finding ways to get out of work, too. And she sassed the customers. I had to complain to her father about that once. He took a switch to her, but it didn't help much. Just made her sulky."

Diana winced, but didn't comment on the punishment. "Sassed

how?"

"Disrespectful. You know. Someone would need towels and she'd say, 'Hold your horses, mister. Do I look like some darky slave?' Puzzles me what Howd saw in her."

"He never talked to you about her?"

Myron shook his head.

"Where is Howd now?" Diana asked.

"Danged if I know. Said he had something to take care of in town."

"In Liberty?"

Myron nodded. "First thing this morning, Floyd and me went in to pick up supplies. Howd wanted to go along, so he did."

"How is Floyd Lyseth taking all this? Does he think his daughter's death was an accident?"

"Hard to tell what Floyd thinks. He didn't say a word the whole trip, going or coming back. But to tell you the truth, Howd seems more upset than Floyd is. I figure that's why he wanted to go into town—to get away from here for a while. Sometimes he walks when he's upset. He can walk the five miles from Liberty to here easy enough when he's ready to come home. Then again, could be he headed for the hills."

"Let's hope not. I need to talk to him. He's the one who seems to have known Elly best."

"In the Biblical sense, maybe," Myron muttered. "Doubt he had any idea what else she was up to."

Diana let that pass.

"You got any more questions?" Myron demanded. "I've got work to do."

"That's all I can think of for now," Diana admitted. "I want to interview Mrs. Ellington and Mercy, and Howd when he returns."

"What about Saugus and his wife?"

"I'll talk to them, too, but not, I think, as a journalist. Would Scorcher have told anyone else what was in that telegram?"

"Hard to say, but I doubt the Sauguses will have heard. Neither one of them is friendly with anyone from the village."

"Good. I'd just as soon they not find out I work for a news-paper."

"I'll send Tressa in." Myron was on his feet, already heading for the door.

"Ask her to meet me in the writing room," Diana called after him.

She arrived first and used the few minutes of privacy to scrawl a hasty note to Horatio Foxe. She had changed her mind about contacting him by telegram. She did not want to take the chance that its contents would get out. With luck, her letter would be sent to Manhattan by train and reach him tomorrow.

She'd just finished addressing the envelope when Tressa Ellington joined her.

"Are you sure you need to dig up old scandal?" she asked. "Perhaps your editor would be satisfied with a travel piece."

"If I don't write about Elly, some other reporter will. And as long as there are no answers, suspicion will continue to hang over Howd Grant."

"Mr. Buckley's letting the matter drop."

"Just because the authorities aren't investigating doesn't mean the discovery of those bones will be forgotten."

"No, I suppose you're right. The newspapers will keep the story alive." She sounded bitter, and Diana couldn't blame her.

"You knew Elly Lyseth when she worked here," Diana said when the other woman finally selected a straight-back chair and sat. "What can you tell me about her?"

Mrs. Ellington held herself stiffly, hands clasped in her lap. "I was not well acquainted with the girl."

"I know that it is repugnant to speak ill of the dead, but sometimes it is necessary. Was there anything about her character that might have caused someone to murder her?"

"Well, she was no better than she should be. That's certain."

"Did you know Howd Grant was . . . courting her?"

A flicker of some deep emotion shone in the older woman's eyes. "There were hints of it. The way he looked at her sometimes when he didn't think anyone would notice. Damned old fool!"

"He was an older man. He is pleasant-natured, attractive—"

"He did not seduce that flighty young chit, if that's what you're hinting at. If anyone took advantage, it was her."

"You didn't like Elly much, did you?"

"I didn't know her, except as a lazy, slovenly chambermaid. I told Myron not to hire her, but with Celia and Floyd already working here, he didn't see as he had much choice."

"It wasn't unexpected when she disappeared, then? You accepted the story that she'd eloped with a peddler?"

"Oh, yes. It only surprised me that she didn't manage to catch one of the guests. She was always flirting with them. And more than that, I suspect."

"But you have no proof? She was never caught with a man in a compromising position?"

Mrs. Ellington shook her head. "More's the pity. That would have gotten rid of her, maybe before she got her claws into Howd."

"What about Norman Saugus? Did you ever suspect he was one of her, er, conquests?"

Tressa Ellington blinked at her, clearly taken aback by the suggestion. "I don't believe I ever saw them together."

"All right. What about Mr. and Mrs. Saugus? What are your impressions of them, then and now?"

"Charming when they want to be. Snippy when they don't."

"Do you trust them?"

For once an answer came without hesitation: "No."

"Why not?"

"Underneath all the well-tailored clothes, he still talks like a snake-oil salesman, and no fashionable gown can hide what she is, either. With all that red hair and the overblown figure, she still looks more like a girl in a chorus line than a proper lady."

"That doesn't make them murderers," Diana said, fighting a

smile. "Or even small-time criminals." She thought for a moment, then asked, "What if Howd found out about other men? Do you think he'd—"

"Certainly not!" Mrs. Ellington went rigid with indignation. "He's not that sort of man."

Gracious, Diana thought. *How swift she is to rise to his defense.* She wondered if Howd knew the housekeeper had been jealous of the maid.

"May I go now?" She stood. "I have work to do."

"So do we all. Can you see that these are mailed today?" she asked, handing over both the letter to Foxe and the one to Mrs. Curran.

Mrs. Ellington accepted the missives, promising to see that they were sent, and headed for the door. She stopped just short of her goal and glanced back at Diana. "I didn't mean to snap your head off. I'm worried about Howd, that's all."

"I understand," Diana assured her. Perhaps more than Mrs. Ellington realized.

Mrs. Ellington managed a cautious smile. "I believe I'll take your letters to the post office now. Nothing like a brisk walk to restore both mind and body."

"Send Mercy in, will you?" Diana called after her.

She didn't have much expectation that her young cousin would add anything new to the information she'd already gathered. Mercy had already denied remembering much about Elly Lyseth. But it wouldn't hurt to talk to her again. At least this time Diana could be open about what she wanted to know.

But Mercy did not appear, and when Diana went out into the lobby to look for her, the young woman was nowhere to be found.

CHAPTER SEVEN

Խℭ

Ma'am? Mrs. Spaulding?"

The voice was young, male, and had a hitch in it, as if the speaker were nervous. Diana turned to find Simon "Scorcher" Tanner standing just inside the lobby entrance of the hotel.

"Do you know where Miss Grant is?" she asked him.

"No, ma'am. But I have another telegram for you. From your editor."

She sighed and extended her hand for it. "I suppose everyone in the telegraph office knows the contents of this one, too."

"Just me and the operator, ma'am."

"Let's keep it between the three of us, shall we?"

"Yes, ma'am. I'm sorry, ma'am. Didn't mean to cause trouble, ma'am. It's just that it's so exciting to have a real reporter here. I read every newspaper I can get my hands on. Hotel copies, mostly. The *Independent Intelligencer* is the stuff, begosh, and you were the one who caught that killer who murdered those other reporters." There was such admiration in his voice that Diana immediately softened towards him. He hadn't meant to create new problems for her with the Grants.

The lad's earnest blue-eyed gaze and the eager expression on his freckled face left Diana feeling a bit bemused as she opened the telegram and read Horatio Foxe's latest missive. At once, annoyance furrowed her brow. Foxe's last request had been an imposition, too, but at least she had a personal interest in finding out what had happened to Elly Lyseth because of the hotel and her own family's involvement. This new assignment irritated her. Didn't Foxe realize carrying it out would be an interruption? A distraction? She had no time to pursue a second story.

She answered herself—obviously he was not at all concerned about disrupting her plan for a quiet reunion with long lost relatives, or interfering in her efforts to clear one of them of suspicion of murder. Now that it had occurred, Diana supposed she should have anticipated this development. She knew Horatio Foxe was not one to waste his resources. She was on the spot. Naturally he would want her to look into that other murder, the one that had taken place the previous fall.

Ben was not going to like this. He already thought Foxe took advantage of her.

Perhaps she'd put off telling him. There was no real question about accepting Foxe's new assignment. If she was to retain any measure of independence after her marriage, it behooved her to keep her job. That meant looking into the notorious "Sailor Jack" case whether she wanted to or not.

Resigned, Diana folded the telegram and put it in her pocket. Only then did she realize that Scorcher was still watching her intently.

"I could help you with this story, ma'am."

"*How* can you help?" she asked him.

"I know all about Sailor Jack. It's been in the local papers for months. Everyone says there's going to be a hanging when the trial's over. I'll bet they let newspaper people witness it. You could take—"

"No!"

His face fell. "I wouldn't be any trouble. And I'd like to see a hanging. There won't be many more after this year. They got one of them electric chairs now, at the state prison."

Diana gave him a sharp look, thinking he seemed to have an unhealthy interest in the subject of murder. Then again, she supposed there were those who would say the same thing about her.

"Only certain people are allowed to witness hangings, Scorcher. In addition to the sheriff and his deputies, the district attorney and a judge, and two physicians, there can be no more than twelve citizens— 'reputable' citizens. That means no women and no minors."

"But—"

"No. On the other hand, Mr. Foxe, my editor, will pay you for any useful information you have."

Putting a hand on the lad's bony shoulder, Diana steered him to the pair of lounging chairs arranged in one corner of the lobby. They were old, of the tubby and rounded style popular before the Civil War, but comfortable, and it was warmer there by the windows than it was next to the unlit fieldstone fireplace at the other side of the large, open room.

"Sit. Tell me what you know."

With renewed enthusiasm, Scorcher spouted facts while Diana scribbled rapidly in her notebook, hoping she could read her own handwriting later. Scorcher knew what he'd read in the newspapers and what he'd heard people say. Diana couldn't rely exclusively on either source, but the boy's fascination with the murder would save her a great deal of time and effort.

In short, John Allen, known as "Sailor Jack," had killed one Drucilla Ulrich of Swiss Hill, near Jeffersonville, while he was intoxicated, and had robbed her afterward. He'd been caught because she'd been killed with a heavy charge of bird shot and Allen had been the only one out hunting with a shotgun in that neighborhood.

"He claimed he was innocent, but when they searched him

they found a large jackknife and a dollar and nine cents in money, and a newspaper." Scorcher leaned closer, lowering his voice conspiratorially. "The newspaper was torn because several pieces had been used for gun wadding, and they matched paper found on the kitchen floor where the crime was committed."

"Was the knife significant?" Diana asked.

His nod was so vigorous it made his scraggly blond hair bounce up and down. "A bureau in Mrs. Ulrich's house had been hacked at with a knife to get the drawers open and Sailor Jack's blade exactly matched the cuts. Then, when they searched the road between Mrs. Ulrich's house and town, they found a five dollar bank note, and someone remembered seeing Jack with one in the village the evening before. They figured he must have thrown it away while he was being dragged back to the scene of the crime. Anyway, Mrs. Ulrich's son Joe identified the bank note as one his mother had owned. Don't know how. Must have had a mark on it or something. Anyway, he said she'd had it at least fifteen years."

As evidence went, even second hand from the mouth of an overeager young man, Diana found this convincing. She wished all murder cases were as straightforward. On the other hand, there didn't seem to be much of a story in what Scorcher had told her. The hunt for the killer was over. The trial would not be held until June. She wrote: "Interview Sailor Jack?" in her notebook. That would mean a trip to the county seat in Monticello, taking her away from where she wanted to be, but she couldn't think of anything else that would provide a newsworthy angle.

She smiled at Scorcher. "You've been a wonderful help. Thank you."

"How much do you think he'll pay me, your editor?"

"How does five dollars sound?"

His eyes went wide with pleasure. "You're the stuff, begosh!" At once the pale skin behind the freckles pinkened. "I mean to say . . . well . . . thank you, ma'am. That's more than I'd likely make in a month of delivering telegrams."

"Just one thing, Scorcher."

"Yes, ma'am?"

"Not another word to anyone else from now on about any of this. Not about my interest in Sailor Jack or about the remains that were found here at the Hotel Grant. And the content of any telegrams I receive from now on is to be treated as privileged information."

"Yes, ma'am. Word of honor. And you be sure to let me know if there's anything else I can help you with." He was whistling cheerfully as he left the lobby.

"You've won his heart," Mercy said from behind Diana.

"It's not difficult to do with a boy that age."

Diana rubbed her fingers together, hoping to warm them. She'd have written with gloves on if it had been practical, it was that nippy in the lobby. She wondered why Mercy didn't spend half her time blue with cold. She supposed her cousin kept warm enough when she was polishing furniture or dusting or sweeping, but she must become thoroughly chilled when she worked at less active tasks behind the check-in desk.

"Aunt Tressa said you wanted to talk to me."

"I have a few questions."

"It's almost time for dinner. Will they wait?"

Since Ben had just come in from the veranda, Diana agreed that it could. She'd far rather return to their warm, cozy suite to compare notes with him than badger Mercy for answers.

The first Grant to arrive in New Netherlands was looking for a lead mine," Mercy Grant said over dinner in one of the small, private dining rooms. "He and his brother had a map they'd gotten from some Indians."

"Lead?" Diana's brow furrowed in puzzlement. "Is lead valuable?"

"It was back then," Ben told her. "They made bullets from it."

They still did, he supposed.

"And arrowheads," Myron put in. "The story of the lost Indian mine is nonsense, but back in my great-great-great-great-great—" he counted them off on his fingers—" grandfather's day, the Grants had a store where the Indians came to melt lead for arrows."

"Wouldn't that be a smelter?" Diana asked. She'd grown up in the mining country of Colorado.

"The story I heard said it was a silver mine," Sebastian interjected.

"Lead," Mercy insisted, "and I'm telling the story."

Sebastian subsided, but he mouthed the word "silver" just to annoy his cousin.

Ben and Diana and Mr. and Mrs. Saugus had been invited to share the evening meal with the Grants and Ellingtons, since there were no other guests in the hotel. Belle Saugus was present, but she'd informed them, rather curtly, that her husband was "indisposed."

Howd had not yet returned to Lenape Springs.

Ben watched Diana as Mercy resumed her story. He didn't pay much attention to the words. She chattered like one of her father's birds—a junco, perhaps, or a jay.

Since Ben's return to the hotel, Diana had brought him up to date on developments, including Mercy's clear desire to avoid an interview. The girl evaded Diana's eyes even now, babbling on about ancestors she had no idea she and Diana shared.

"William Grant had two children, twins, a girl named Mercy and a boy named Justice. It's said they could communicate with each other without words."

"A dangerous thing, I should think, in those unenlightened times. If the wrong person knew of it, either or both of them would have been accused of witchcraft."

"But so convenient, don't you think, Diana? Especially in light of what happened to them. You see, bandits who wanted the map to the lead mine attacked the Grant home in what was then the

Connecticut colony. They'd built their farmstead in a very remote spot, so no one was nearby to help. The villains burned it to the ground, killed two servants, and kidnapped Justice. Mercy only escaped because she'd been off in the woods gathering berries when they struck."

"Their father wasn't at home?" Diana asked.

Ben could sense her fascination with Mercy's account. He supposed he shouldn't be surprised. These were, after all, her family's stories.

"William had already left with his younger brother. The map wasn't there, either. The robbers found nothing. There was a copy, but William had given it to his daughter and Mercy had taken the precaution of sewing it into the lining of her skirt."

Diana's cousin went on to tell them how the first Mercy Grant had tracked her twin, with the aid of their otherworldly connection and the assistance of a handsome stranger named Sebastian Tanfield.

"Did they ever find the mine?" Diana asked.

Myron snorted. "Lot of nonsense. All of it."

"A gold mine might be, but there could be silver," Sebastian said.

"*Lead.*" Mercy sounded exasperated. "And there *is* lead in the mountains. There's a mine over near Wurtsburo."

"Which mountains?" Ben asked. "The Catskills or the Shawangunks?"

Mercy giggled. "It's pronounced Shon-gum," she corrected him.

Ben bore the amused smiles with good grace. There were a few place names in Maine, too, that tricked the unwary visitor from away.

"Our mine was probably up around Sundown. That's where the Grants lived before they came here. We still own the old homestead. My father uses it when he wants to spend time by himself."

"Is that where he is now?" Ben inquired.

"I don't know where Howd's got to," Myron complained.

"I'd like to talk with him when he returns," Diana put in.

"I'll see to it," Myron promised. He glanced at Mrs. Saugus, who had not been informed of Diana's status as a journalist, and said no more.

"So," Diana said, "it sounds as if William Grant *did* find a mine."

Mercy sighed. "Truth is, there wasn't much to find. Turns out the Indians just dug lead out of a stream of water and took it to smelters to make into arrowheads. Or bullets. There was some lead to be had, but not enough to make their fortune."

"Unless that's just what they wanted people to think," Sebastian interjected. "I'm pretty sure it was illegal to mine without the Dutch government's permission in those days."

"What happened to the map?" Diana asked, taking a sip of the fine wine Mrs. Ellington had served with the meal.

"It used to be kept in an old blue chest in my grandfather's room, but one time he and Uncle Myron and my father took it and went looking." She cast a sly grin her uncle's way. He glowered back. "Apparently, by then, the stream had changed course or dried up because there wasn't a trace of it left."

"You should frame that map and display it," Diana said. "Tourists love that sort of thing."

"I would, except that now the map's missing, too. I went to look for it a few months ago and it wasn't in the blue chest." She cast a suspicious glance in Sebastian's direction. "No one admits to knowing what happened to it."

Ignoring her, Sebastian calmly went on eating.

This family had spotty luck with streams, Ben thought, but it did ease his mind when Myron continued to debunk the myth of the mine. If he'd really salted the brook, he'd jump at a chance to exploit a lost Indian mine.

"Seems I've heard similar stories," Ben ventured when there was a break in the soliloquy. "Wasn't there something about an

Indian who painted his face with gold?"

"Agheroense." Myron supplied the name with an ease that belied his lack of interest in the subject. "An Indian interpreter. Showed up at Fort Orange—that's Albany now—with shining face paint. Everybody said it was gold. The Injun took the authorities to the place he found it, but they kept the location secret and tried to send some of the stuff to Holland to be tested. Know what happened to it? Disappeared off the face of the earth. Oh, the ship it was on was seen once more, out in the harbor at New Haven, but only long enough to vanish in a puff of smoke." The sarcasm in his tone intensified. "A ghost ship."

"I was thinking of something a bit more recent," Ben said. "Perhaps fourteen or fifteen years back. The father of a friend of mine was one of a party that went to the Mountain House in Woodstock because they'd heard an Indian legend about a gold mine in the Catskills. They took a boy medium with them. He was supposed to be able to look through an enchanted stone and discover hidden treasure. It didn't work, but the treasure hunters apparently enjoyed the experience. As I recall, there was talk of organizing a stock company to work the mine. They were certain they'd find it on their *next* expedition."

"There's a sucker born every minute," Mrs. Saugus said, *sotto voce*. Everyone laughed, but Ben doubted they were all amused for the same reason.

Howd Grant put in an appearance shortly after Diana and Ben retired to their suite for the night. There had been time to turn up the gaslights, stir the embers and add kindling to the fireplace, and exchange their first conflicting opinions about where Ben was going to sleep that night.

"Myron told me to talk to you." Howd's curious glance went from Diana to Ben and back again.

"Come in, Mr. Grant," Diana said, stepping back out of the

way. "I have a few questions for you."

"Howd. Remember? Or Uncle Howd, if you feel better being a bit more formal."

Diana stared at him, but his expression was benign. She assured herself that he'd meant nothing more than to offer to be an honorary uncle. If he had any idea she was really his niece, surely he'd say so.

"Myron explained you want to help," Howd continued. "I'll cooperate all I can." He hesitated. "I didn't have anything to do with Elly's death, you know. I loved her."

"I want to believe you," Diana said, "but your word alone isn't good enough. You must see that your secret courtship of Miss Lyseth makes you *look* suspicious. Even your brother was beginning to have doubts when you didn't return to Lenape Springs by this evening."

If she'd hoped he'd tell her where he'd been and what he'd been up to, she was disappointed. He simply made himself comfortable in the armchair, leaving the sofa for her, and waited for the inquisition to begin.

"Tell me about Elly Lyseth." Diana sat gingerly on one end of the sofa, glad she hadn't yet put out the blanket and pillow for Ben.

"I don't know where to start."

"Start with the way things were ten years ago. Why not court her openly?"

"She was a lot younger than me. I figured we didn't need to hear what folks thought of me robbing the cradle."

"Your idea, then?" She looked up from her notes.

He frowned. "No. I was pleased as punch she seemed to like me. I wanted to show her off. Take her to dances. She wouldn't go."

"A religious issue?" Ben had been standing with one shoulder propped against the elaborately finished terra cotta and pressed brick fireplace. Now he gave the fire a last stir and, satisfied that it was burning well, returned the poker to its rack, put the fire screen in place, and crossed to the sofa. He sank down next to Diana, sprawling elegantly and taking up far too much room.

"You mean her mother?" Howd asked. "No. Celia wasn't such a stickler back then. She wouldn't have begrudged Elly a little fun. It was Floyd Elly was leery of. When she was younger and misbehaved, Celia'd take a switch to her, but Floyd, he'd use his fists."

"Was she afraid of her father?"

"Just careful around him."

Diana knew corporal punishment was the way most parents dealt with their children. Only the degree varied. Still, it bothered her to learn that Elly Lyseth had been beaten. "Did she think that if she ran off and got married she'd escape him?"

"Once the deed was done, he couldn't touch her. Not legally, anyway."

Diana did not respond aloud to that comment, but her hands involuntarily clenched into fists. Carefully, she straightened her fingers. She knew far too many women who had tried to escape a tyrant of a father only to end up in a far worse situation. A woman might escape parental discipline when she married, but once she was wed, then her husband could beat her with impunity.

As if sensing her thoughts, Ben shifted his position until his thigh brushed her skirt. She took comfort in the contact, as he'd no doubt intended. She kept her eyes on Howd, however, and most of her attention on the interview she was conducting.

"Did Elly ever talk about running away? No one seems to have been surprised when she simply disappeared. Even you didn't suspect foul play at the time."

"Elly was a spirited girl. And outspoken." A faint smile curved his lips. "They had some fierce, loud quarrels, her and her parents. Elly'd be yelling, and Celia'd shout: 'Do you want the neighbors to hear?' And Elly, she'd raise her voice even louder and bellow: 'Yes! Let's give them something to listen to! What do I care?'"

"Someone told me she'd run off with a peddler."

"That's the story that was going around," Howd agreed. "I believed it myself."

"Why?"

"Well, given a choice, who'd pick me over a good-looking young man? There was a drummer come through here just about that time. Not the old fashioned kind, selling pots and pans and mending them. This fella was a jobber for a men's clothing company. Called himself a commercial traveler. Dressed real fine and drove a wagon and team owned by his firm because he had to handle two big trunks, one for patterns and another for goods. He called with the summer line in early spring and the winter line in early autumn. Everybody saw how Elly noticed him the first time he visited Castine's store. He came through again just before she disappeared."

"Was she seen with him?"

"I saw her watching him. Can't say for sure, now, if they even spoke, but she was interested all right. I was jealous at the time. That's why I decided to give her the locket."

"Speaking of that locket, was there a picture inside it?"

"See for yourself." He reached into a pocket and produced it.

Diana opened the delicate gold heart and looked down at the smiling face of a younger, thinner, happier Howard Grant.

"Got it back from the coroner," Howd said when she returned it to him. "He didn't need to keep it for anything."

"Did you ask her to marry you?" Diana asked.

"I was going to, but she . . . well, she wasn't herself that day."

"How do you mean?"

Howd sighed. "She was always so vivacious. Reminded me of an overeager puppy sometimes. She'd never remember until it was too late that puppies who make a nuisance of themselves are more likely to be kicked than petted."

What a strange thing for a lover to say, Diana thought. Unbidden, her gaze slid to Ben, then quickly away when she found him watching her instead of Howd.

"Anyways, that day she was real quiet. I thought she'd be excited when I gave her the locket. She knew how much it meant to me, having been my wife's and all. But she just took it and slipped it around her neck and thanked me. Said I was very sweet."

"So later, when she disappeared, you thought she'd been planning to go all along?"

"I'm ashamed to say that's exactly what I thought—that she was a rounder who'd been two-timing me. I thought about going after them. I was angry about the loss of the locket too. And I confess I would have liked to kill that drummer. But I'd never have hurt Elly and I *didn't* go after them. I went up to my place in the woods for a spell, till I calmed down, and then I tried my best to forget all about Elly Lyseth."

Diana put a sympathetic hand on his arm. "I'm sorry," she said.

"We'd best add the clothes jobber to our list of suspects," Ben said, "although it may turn out he never even met Elly Lyseth. Do you know his name?"

"Never heard one. And I'm told he hasn't been seen in these parts since then." A faint smile played around the corners of his mouth. "Folks figure he heard Floyd Lyseth was wanting to tar and feather him."

"Mrs. Castine might be able to identify him for us," Diana said, "and the company that employed him." She scribbled a note to herself, then looked up expectantly at Howd. "Were you working at the hotel then?"

"I never had much to do with the business of running the hotel. After our father died, Myron took over. I stayed around, helped out in the season, but my paintings and my nature studies take up most of my time."

"You'd been married. Had Mercy. Lost your wife."

He nodded. "She died two days after Mercy was born."

"Did you live here?"

"Yes, although I was gone a lot. Mercy stayed put. She needed people to look after her. Tressa Ellington's been a marvel. She's no blood kin, but she loves Mercy like she was her own and Mercy calls her Aunt Tressa."

"How long has Mrs. Ellington been here?"

"Ever since our youngest sister, Elmira, got married. Myron hired Tressa as housekeeper right after. Our oldest sister, Sally Ann, is married to Tressa's brother."

Diana wanted to ask about Elmira, but she didn't dare. She had no reason to be interested in the sibling who'd left thirty-three years earlier. After exchanging a look with Ben, she changed the subject.

"What did you know about the plans your brother had with Norman Saugus?"

"Ten years ago? They meant to enlarge the place." Howd frowned. "It wasn't nearly so grand a scheme as the one they've come up with this time. They talked about making the Hotel Grant into one of those resorts that has everything guests could want, all in one place, so they don't mind traveling out of the way to get here. They've got that sort of thing up to Blue Mountain Lake in the Adirondacks, near where Sally Ann's place is."

Diana knew such resorts existed, although she'd never stayed at one. Visitors came great distances to live in luxury. It took a considerable investment to build a hotel with all the amenities and an enormous amount of publicity to spread the word of its existence to patrons wealthy enough to afford the rates.

"So Norman Saugus had money to invest?"

"That's what he claimed. But he was greedy for profits. Why Myron let him pressure him into trying to enlarge the fountain, I'll never know."

"The spring was lost. Then there was a fire. After all that, I'm surprised Saugus is willing to risk capital a second time."

Howd gave a derisive snort. "Still greedy, I guess."

"What if he didn't lose by it?" Ben asked, causing Diana's

eyebrows to shoot up. "What if he had insurance?"

"I didn't hear about it if he did." Howd sat up straighter in his chair, his hands gripping the arms. "He sure carried on something awful at the time."

"Did Myron have insurance?"

"Not enough."

"That could be why Saugus didn't mention any recompense he received."

"What are you thinking, Ben?" Diana turned towards him fully, tucking her limbs beneath her on the sofa as she did so.

"That you're right to think Saugus wouldn't come back again if he'd lost money the last time. I wonder—would he have done even better for himself if the entire hotel had burned to the ground ten years ago?"

"Arson?" It was Howd who gave voice to the word on all of their minds.

"It's worth investigating." Ben rose and went to check the fire in the fireplace, which was crackling merrily in the background. "I have a hard time believing in the grand plans he's been talking about. What if it was just talk the last time, too? What if he only appeared to invest in the hotel and meant all along to destroy it for the insurance?"

"But he has investors this time," Howd protested.

"Does he?"

"Surely he'd not take such a risk, Ben," Diana protested. "Once perhaps, but a second time? When there are people living here?" The idea that Saugus might try to burn the hotel down over their heads had the breath backing up in her throat. Bad enough that he cared so little for property, but to disregard human life was intolerable.

Plainly agitated, Howd also rose. "Saugus doesn't know about all the renovations. Maybe I should tell him." He gestured toward the fireplace. "Last year, before Saugus reappeared, Myron wanted to put in a new steam heating apparatus to heat the rooms, but it was too expensive. It was a choice between that and doing something about the water supply. We ended up digging an artesian well and putting in pipes to bring hot and cold running water to the rooms . . . and to two hydrants on either side of the hotel. They're mostly used to sprinkle the lawn, but they're there in case of fire, too."

Diana found she could breathe again, but the possibility Ben had raised was still a terrifying one. Someone who had no regard for casualties of arson was not likely to balk at outright murder.

"This doesn't make sense," Howd muttered. "Saugus must have gotten money somewhere. He financed most of the renovations we completed this year."

"Credit?" Ben suggested.

"I'm sure I'd have heard complaints by now it if the local builders hadn't been paid."

"Then perhaps he does have investors. Perhaps he means to defraud them, too."

"You're very cynical," Diana said, but there was no heat behind the accusation.

"In this case I think it's warranted. Who was it said that Saugus reminded them of a snake-oil salesman?"

"Mrs. Ellington," Diana supplied.

"Yes. And you said you suspect that his wife has theatrical experience. I wonder if this is nothing more than an elaborate confidence game."

"All for insurance?" She didn't want to believe it, but the idea was beginning to sound plausible.

"If it is, then the real question is not whether Saugus was guilty of arson ten years ago, but whether he also committed a murder to cover his tracks." Ben looked at Howd, who now stood beside him at the hearth. "Could Elly have found out what he was up to? Might he have killed her to keep her quiet?"

He looked appalled at the idea. "She'd have told me!"

Diana wasn't so sure about that.

Ben clapped a hand on Howd's shoulder. "We'll pursue the matter. In the meantime, say nothing to anyone of what we've discussed here tonight. After all, it's just a theory. We may be wrong."

"We'll find out the truth," Diana promised as she showed her uncle to the door. "You can count on us."

"I'll hold you to that," he said in a choked voice. And then, looking as if he might burst into tears any moment, he made a hasty exit.

Ben glanced up from the fire as she closed the door and leaned against it with a deep sigh. "You'll have more perspective on the matter after a good night's rest."

"I am too agitated to sleep."

He reached her in two long strides and pulled her into a comforting embrace. "I know how to relax you."

"Still trying to get me to go to bed?" She managed to inject a note of teasing into her voice but the mood was not reflected in her eyes.

With another sigh, Diana eased far enough away from Ben to retrieve the list of suspects she'd tucked into his jacket pocket for safekeeping while they were dressing for supper. She carried it back to the sofa and, using her notebook as a lap desk, she added "unknown drummer" to the bottom. Earlier she'd written in Mrs. Ellington's name. If she'd been jealous of Elly, she might have killed her, hoping to win Howd's affections for herself once her rival was gone.

Turning the paper over, Diana continued to write.

"Another list?"

"A timetable. I need to organize what we've learned."

She wrote quickly, with Ben standing behind her to point out anything she forgot. "We need specific dates," she murmured. "We can't just say 1878."

"Put down what you have. What happened first?"

"Saugus came to Lenape Springs as Myron's financial backer."

"His wife came too."

"Yes. The hotel was to be enlarged into a self-contained destination resort."

"It could have succeeded. I know plenty that have. The Poland Spring House in Maine. The Catskill Mountain House overlooking the Hudson River."

Diana glanced at him. "Both places are too expensive for a third-rate acting troupe on tour to afford. Have you stayed at either of them?"

"Both. And others, on the trip I took with friends from college."

"The same journey that brought you to Denver and up Pike's Peak?"

"That's the one. That was back in 1877, so what I saw would have been similar to what inspired Myron to think he could succeed."

She nodded and continued to list items under the year 1878:

Howd and Elly secretly courting
Myron tries to enlarge fountain and loses source of spring
Handsome drummer visits Lenape Springs
Howd gives Elly a locket
The next day Elly is gone—said to have "run off with a peddler"
A few days later—fire destroys west wing of hotel
Saugus leaves—collects insurance?
Howd leaves

"It was in the autumn of the year," Ben said. "Myron said the season was over when the fire broke out."

"I forgot to ask Howd where it was that he last saw Elly," Diana said.

"It may not matter what questions you ask. At this point we don't know what's important and what's not. For that matter, we have no way to separate truth from deception. For all we know, they may all be lying through their teeth."

Diana knew he was right, but made no response to the implied warning in his words. "I can't think of anything else we know about 1878."

"Then skip ahead to 1886."

"What happened in 1886?"

"Myron visited his oldeset sister and brought Sebastian Ellington back with him to help out at the hotel."

She didn't see what connection that could have to the murder, but she wrote it down anyway. Then she added several more items without comment:

> *Spring 1887*
> *Camp meeting near Liberty Falls; Riker one of the preachers*
> *Summer 1887*
> *Jonas Riker marries Lida Rose Leeves*
> *Lenape Springs Villa turned into a temperance house*
> *Myron rediscovers source of spring*

"Or salted it," Ben said dryly.

"You don't believe that."

"I wouldn't put it past him, but I also know it wouldn't have worked."

She wrote down: *rumors of salted spring.* "Whose idea was it to expand the Hotel Grant on an even grander scale?" she wondered aloud. "Myron's? Or Saugus's?"

"Another question we'll have to ask."

Diana went back to her notes.

> *Fall 1887*
> *Renovations start*
> *Spring 1888*
> *Saugus returns talking of telegraph line*

"Can we find out more about that? Wouldn't he have had to file papers?"

"Yes, and obtain the right-of-way from landowners. If the proposal was a scam from the beginning, there won't be any. I can also find out more about this joint stock company he says he's formed. He could be bilking the investors, even though there is building going on."

"Something Mrs. Saugus said . . . ." Diana struggled to recall what it was, but the long day had caught up with her. She was too tired to think straight. Hastily, she scribbled the last few lines of her timetable.

> *Saugus keeps workers away from the burned out wing*
> *Elly's body found*
> *Saugus spent the next day in his room drinking.*

"How do you know that?" Ben asked.

"His wife bought whiskey at the general store. Then he wasn't seen all day, including at supper."

"She said he was indisposed."

"Did she ask you to examine him? If he was ill, he'd have wanted a doctor."

"Perhaps, but at the moment this is all speculation, and there's no way to find out more about Mr. Norman T. Saugus tonight." He gently pried Diana's notes and pencil away from her and tossed them on the nearest table. Then he tugged her into his arms and lowered his head until his lips were almost touching hers. "Perhaps you'd care to concentrate on Dr. Benjamin Northcote instead?"

"Perhaps," she replied, and closed the distance.

CHAPTER EIGHT

❧❦❧

Whatsoever a man soweth, that shall he also reap," Pastor Riker intoned.

"Amen!" chorused his congregation.

The interior of the church would have been stuffy with the windows closed, but opening them allowed insects to swarm in. Sticky curls of arsenic paper suspended above Diana's head did little to reduce the annoyance. She noticed an audible hum as flies settled on a sticky spot on the back of a pew two rows in front of her.

A pity no one had installed screens, she thought. Castine's store had them in stock. They also sold palm leaf fans, but she'd not had the foresight to buy one. Not only would it have helped keep the bugs away, it might have dispelled some of the unpleasant odors rising around her.

She recognized one smell as shoe blacking, far too liberally applied. Another, she suspected, was a mixture of ingredients designed to repel mosquitoes and other flying nuisances. Rubbed into the face and neck and hands, it did a good job of preventing bites and stings but the stink of oil and tar also forced the wearer's friends to keep their distance.

"Set your affections on things above, not on things of the earth," the preacher exhorted his listeners. "Eschew whited sepulchers, which indeed appear beautiful outward, but are within full of dead men's bones. The love of money is the root of all evil. The wages of sin is death."

Riker, Diana realized, was not so much delivering a sermon as stringing Bible quotations together. She closed the little notebook in her lap. With its green leather cover it looked enough like a book of psalms to escape notice. Still, she doubted she'd be writing anything down. Funerals might make good copy, but this interminable worship service would not.

Pastor Riker continued elaborating on a fire and brimstone theme for fully half an hour while Diana, Ben, and the good people of Lenape Springs sat in uncomfortable silence on hard pews. The preacher did not mention Elly Lyseth's murder or the Hotel Grant, but there was no doubt in Diana's mind that he'd deliberately chosen texts likely to escalate the level of disharmony in the village.

Everyone in the community seemed to be in attendance, with three notable exceptions—Myron Grant, and Norman and Belle Saugus.

Having worked the crowd into a fine fervor, Riker called upon members of his flock for their testimony. Celia Lyseth was the first to stand up and tell the others how she'd found salvation. It was a story they must have heard dozens of times before, but they listened with rapt attention.

The rambling account was delivered with a fervor Diana had not expected, though she should have. Mrs. Lyseth's eyes gleamed. She threw her whole body into the narration. Boiled down, it amounted to very little. She had gone into "a decline" shortly after giving birth to her only child. Then she'd seen the light . . . literally.

It sounded to Diana as if she'd fallen asleep and been awakened by the sun shining into her face through a window. In Celia Lyseth's interpretation, however, she'd seen the face of the Lord Jesus Christ in among the dust motes, and He'd spoken to her, telling her to rise up and accept salvation.

No more vapors after that! She'd become an earnest churchgoer, and started attending camp meetings, and been partly responsible for bringing Pastor Riker and his church to Lenape Springs.

And where, Diana wondered, had Elly fit into all that? It was no wonder she'd rebelled. Diana even began to feel a certain sympathy for Floyd Lyseth. It could not have been easy living with a wife who'd rail against sin at the drop of a hat.

Hearty cries of "Amen, sister!" followed the recitation. Mrs. Lyseth was flushed and smiling when she resumed her seat in the pew beside her taciturn spouse.

Riker knew better than to ask Floyd Lyseth to testify and passed on to another local man who told how he'd been freed from his addiction to demon rum by the Lord's intervention. Riker skipped over the Grants and Ellingtons too, and none of the villagers he did call upon revealed anything scandalous. No lovers. No thefts. No murders.

"You, sir," Riker said, looking right at Ben. "Have you been saved?"

Diana's heart began to race. She knew better than to think Ben would betray her by admitting that they were only pretending to be married, but she feared his reaction to Riker's demanding tone. She had felt Ben grow more and more tense throughout the recitations and she feared he might respond now, as his mother assuredly would have, by saying something outrageous.

"What have you to confess?" Riker's gaze held Ben's and the tension between them was palpable in the silence that followed.

Ben forced a smile. "I am a man of science," he said slowly.

He clearly intended to expand upon this announcement, but Riker was no fool. "Better than nothing," he snapped. With a peremptory "Next!" he moved on to a new target.

"Did you mean to deliver a lecture on Darwinism?" Diana whispered.

"I was considering telling him I was an atheist." He waited a beat. "Or perhaps an Episcopalian."

Diana stifled a laugh.

The church services wound down at last with the singing of "Nearer My God to Thee." The funeral followed immediately. Rather than have the body laid out in the Lyseth home for viewing, as was the custom in most instances, the remains had been turned over to Pastor Riker. The coffin was carried in by four pallbearers and set down in front of the altar. Once again, the preacher spoke of sin rather than redemption, as if the young woman's death had been her own fault. Diana's hands had clenched into fists by the time he wound down.

"Horrible man," she muttered as they trooped out of the church and walked the short distance to the cemetery.

The words said over the grave were the familiar ones— "Ashes to ashes, dust to dust" —but Diana thought Riker's tone seemed grudging.

Some of those who filed past the grave site when the service was over dropped flowers onto the casket. Diana stopped for a moment to stare at the brass plate that read: *At Rest.* Elly Lyseth would not be, she thought, until they had brought her murderer to justice.

A woman Diana had not noticed earlier spoke up as the crowd began to disperse. "You must all come back to the villa for refreshments. Mr. and Mrs. Lyseth haven't room enough to accommodate such a crowd."

Diana looked at the speaker more closely. If this was Lida Rose Leeves Riker, she possessed only the most superficial resemblance to her brother. Ed Leeves looked like what he was—a professional gambler. His sister was the epitome of the domesticated female— plump, red-cheeked, and anxious to please.

"Can you tolerate any more?" Diana asked Ben.

"If you can."

"Then I think we should go. It will be an opportunity to learn more about the town."

Tressa and Sebastian Ellington came up beside them as they walked through the village. "None of the Grants are coming," Mrs. Ellington said. "Feelings run too high against Myron's plans."

"What has that to do with Elly Lyseth?"

"What did anything Pastor Riker said in there?" Mrs. Ellington asked as they left the little white clapboard church behind. "Well, you'll enjoy seeing the villa. Old Cyrus Leeves, Lida Rose's father, had his own style."

"In what way?"

"Take a look at the ladies' outhouse," Mrs. Ellington suggested.

Diana made a point of it. It was a small replica of the main house, complete with mansard roof and window boxes full of flowers. The inside was paneled with black walnut and the seat had been made from a two-inch thick mahogany plank.

The interior of the hotel was also interesting, but it had suffered from Jonas Riker's occupancy. Although the paneling was exquisite and the furniture of good quality, it appeared that all frivolities, such as mirrors, had been removed. Likewise, Pastor and Mrs. Riker dressed very plainly, although their clothing was of excellent quality.

As an ornament at Ben's side, Diana was relieved of the necessity of making small talk. Instead she could simply listen and absorb. It was one of the things she did best. She made no attempt to sort through what she heard. That would come later.

"Had to melt snow to water the cows after the blizzard," a farmer complained. "Couldn't get through to the spring on the back lot."

"Heard Gil Tanner, over to Liberty Falls, put a windmill over his spring as soon as the snow melted. It pumps water into a cistern above the orchard and he gets a good force of water in the barn and in the house. Lucy's already put in a bathtub."

"I've got twenty-five cows now. Ship four forty-quart cans of milk a day to the City on the O&W."

"What are they charging for freight?"

"Ten cents a can. Too bad half the milk bill goes for feed during the year."

Before Ben moved on, Diana had also learned that a good milk cow sold for thirty-five dollars and a newly born calf for a dollar.

"Nothing but gambling and racing and loose morals in Saratoga Springs," Pastor Riker told a parishioner.

Diana wondered how he knew.

"Norman Saugus goes through with his plans and that's what we'll have here. The man's got to be stopped. It'll be the ruination of Lenape Springs if he's not."

A child tugged at Diana's sleeve. She looked down into wide hazel eyes and saw, with some surprise, that the girl was holding out an autograph book and a pen. "My mama says you're just like Nellie Bly. Will you write something in my book?"

Unsure whether to be flattered or alarmed, Diana took the leather-covered volume and searched for a blank page. The first entry was a sentiment from mother to daughter:

> Let the road be rough and dreary
> And the end far out of sight
> Foot it bravely, strong or weary
> Trust in God and do the right

"Who is your mama, child?" Diana asked. "And what is your name?"

"I'm Rose Castine," the girl said. "My mama and papa own the general store."

And that meant, Diana realized, that the entire town must know she worked for a newspaper. She was surprised no one had made any mention of that fact, but supposed respect for the dead might account for their reticence.

Several of the autographs in the little book made mention of roses, while one concluded "in this quiet little spot, I'll plant a sweet forget-me-not." Diana pondered. She did not want to wax sentimental. After all, she was a stranger to this child. Nor did she wish to spout off about God, as others had. Finally, calling to mind a rhyme her school friend Rowena had liked to write in autograph books, she scribbled:

> *When you are tired of life*
> *And all its changing scenes*
> *Go out into the garden*
> *And hide behind the beans.*

Rose giggled happily when she read the words and scurried away to show them to her mother. Diana went back to eavesdropping on conversations, a little less certain than before that she would overhear anything worthwhile.

Most of the talk was about the weather—how cold this year had been; that the speaker had never seen so many empty barns as now; that the outlook for the corn crop was discouraging.

"It's been a backwards spring," one man said.

"I heard," his companion remarked, "that they had frost three days last week over to Shinhopple."

"Mrs. Northcote?" a soft, female voice inquired.

Diana turned to find Mrs. Riker standing behind her. She seemed nervous, and glanced over her shoulder to locate her formidable husband before she spoke again.

"Someone said you were in Colorado recently. I wonder . . . well, that is, I think that's where my brother is, but I haven't heard from him in many years. I suppose it would be a very great coincidence if your path crossed his, but—"

"In fact, I did meet your brother," Diana interrupted. And she'd been under the impression that Ed Leeves had been in touch with his sister, since he'd known more about what was going on in Lenape Springs these days than Diana's mother had. Now that she thought about it, she supposed it was far more likely that an "entrepreneur" like Leeves would hire someone to send him a report on his relatives.

"Is he well?" Mrs. Riker asked.

"He's successful."

Her faint smile told Diana she suspected what that meant but she did not ask further questions. Instead, taking note of her husband's approach, Lida Rose Leeves Riker simply thanked Diana for the information and drifted away.

Diana moved on, too, past Celia and Floyd Lyseth. They stood close together but there was no sense of intimacy between them. They weren't speaking, either. Now that she thought about it, Diana didn't believe Mr. Lyseth had said a single word all day, not even when he stood in the receiving line that greeted mourners as they entered the Lenape Springs Villa. And Mrs. Lyseth, after her testimony in church, seemed to have been drained of both speech and emotion. After ten years, a display of grief would not have rung true, Diana supposed, but she found her impression of Elly's parents as cold, heartless people profoundly disturbing.

A loud voice distracted Diana from her musings. "He's always trying to change things," a man complained. Diana recognized him as the blacksmith. "What's wrong with the way things are? That's what I want to know."

"The whole hamlet will change if he gets his way," his companion said. "Heard he wants to create places for folks to promenade. Going to hang Chinese lanterns all over creation, or maybe put in gaslights."

"I heard electric lights on strings," a third man contributed

"Bad for the farms if a lot of strangers come in," said the blacksmith. "They'll trample the fields. Scare the cattle."

"What about the extra income from selling produce and milk to the hotel?" someone else asked, plainly trying to strike a positive note.

"He puts in a race track, they won't be coming to eat and drink. Not milk, anyways."

Rueful laughter greeted this comment.

Ben was more than ready to return to the Hotel Grant by the time Diana signaled him that she wanted to leave. More than two hours had passed since the end of the burial service. Tressa Ellington's departure with her nephew had preceded theirs by a good hour.

They found all the hotel's residents, except Norman Saugus, in the family parlor, where a heated argument was in progress between Sebastian and Mercy.

"You shouldn't be playing cards on a Sunday," Mercy scolded.

"Since when have you been a Free Methodist? Today's the first time I've seen you go to church since I got here."

"I hope I'm a good Christian," Mercy shot back, grabbing the deck of cards he'd just opened.

"There are board games in the sideboard," Mrs. Ellington interrupted, and crossed the room to open its lower doors. A moment later she'd extracted a stack of boxes. "Look here: *Parlor Base Ball Game, District Messenger Boy, Buffalo Hunt, The Great Wall Street Game,* and even *The Game of Playing Department Store.* Take your pick."

"I had my heart set on cards, Aunt Tressa."

"Old Maid?" Mercy suggested.

He made a sound of disgust. "That's for girls."

When the bickering continued, Mrs. Ellington made an arbitrary choice and put away all the boxes except *District Messenger Boy.* She unfolded the board and began setting out metal figure tokens.

"Better not be any dice," Sebastian teased. "That would make it gambling."

"Be easy in your mind. There's a spinner. Now, then, players start as messenger boys. The winner becomes president of the telegraph service, having passed all the subordinate positions."

"Boring," Sebastian declared, but he sat down at the square table his aunt cleared of framed family photographs and a vase of flowers, and took a metal figure to represent his messenger boy. When Mercy and Mrs. Ellington and Belle Saugus joined him, the room quieted.

Howd, ensconced in a comfortably padded armchair, his feet propped up on an ottoman, watched his daughter with pride and affection. "Just like her mother, God rest her soul."

"How so?" Ben asked.

"Grace didn't hold with me playing cards on Sundays either. Or dice. Unless I was sure of winning, that is." He chuckled. "One time I took a chance on one of ten turkeys at a turkey raffle at the blacksmith shop, but the raffle was on a Sunday and was to be decided by a throw of dice, so I sold my chance to Bill Manion. I made a profit of forty cents for a ten cent investment. Only thing was, Manion threw the dice and won the turkey, and it was worth about a dollar. Grace said I should have kept the chance."

"Sounds like she knew you pretty well." Ben took a seat on the faded yellow velvet sofa opposite. Unlike the simpler, square-backed Eastlake style furniture in their suite, this one was heavily padded— the only bit of wood showing was in the form of tiny legs—and the back was humped in the middle and at both sides.

He looked around for Diana and found her examining the photographs Mrs. Ellington had set aside.

"Grace knew me inside out," Howd admitted. "A pity we didn't have much time together. I waited a good long while for the right girl to come along."

"How did you meet?"

"She came to work at the hotel one summer." He chuckled again. "She was the age of marriage and she was after a husband. She expected she'd get one of the two eligible men who worked in the hotel."

"You and Myron?"

"Myron was a confirmed bachelor even then. No, the choice

was between me and Elmer Castine."

Ben toyed with mentioning the fight he'd heard about, but Howd was talking again.

"One time I took Grace to a dance in Liberty. People came from all over. There were two-seated buckboards and four-horse carriages and two-horse turnouts and surreys. There was even a tally-ho and six. Called it a 'grand hop.' Quite an event it was, too. Virginia reels, a 'grand march,' a 'choice collation' at intermission, and after that a social 'sing' accompanied by piano. It was after midnight before we got back here. Almost lost Grace that night."

Ben's attention sharpened. "How so?"

"Oh, no harm came to her. It was me. Up till then, I used to carry a bottle of apple wine about with me. Early that evening, I offered Grace some. That made her think I was a toper and she said she wouldn't dance with me—or anything else—so long as I had that devil's brew on my person. Well, I saw my mistake real fast, and I threw the nearly full bottle away on the spot. Never indulged in spirits again." He winked. "Well, not when Grace could see me, at any rate."

Keeping his voice too low for anyone else to hear, Ben asked, "Speaking of drink, is Saugus still 'indisposed?'"

"So Mrs. Saugus says." Anger replaced the reminiscent gleam in Howd's eyes. "Do you know how hard it is for me to be civil to her after what we talked about last night?"

"We'll find out the truth," Ben said. "Tomorrow we'll be able to ask officials in Liberty about right of ways and the like." This being the Sabbath, he had been unable to pursue the investigation of Saugus's business dealings. Nor had it been suitable to ask questions at Elly Lyseth's funeral about the drummer she had been flirting with ten years back.

"I'm of a mind to warn Myron."

Howd's brother had set himself apart from the rest of the family, pulling one of the balloon-back chairs close to a second table, the twin of the one being used for the board game. It was covered with slips of paper and what appeared to be clippings from newspapers.

"The railroad puts out a guide to hotels and boarding houses every year," Howd said, seeing the direction of Ben's gaze. "Myron has only a few more days to put together our advertisement. It's not easy deciding what to include." A hint of sarcasm came into his voice when he added, "How does one decide between saying 'No Jews Taken' and 'Christian Only' and 'Guests taken to church free of charge' when they all mean the same thing?"

Diana, who had been wandering rather aimlessly about the parlor, chose this moment to fetch up at Myron's side. When he glanced up and saw her, he gave her a speculative look.

"Perhaps you can make yourself useful while you're here, Mrs. Northcote. Since your husband doesn't seem inclined to endorse my spring water, what do you think of using this description?" He cleared his throat and read from one of the clippings: "The water has millions of silver globules which sparkle as though rejoicing at their liberation from the dark caverns of the gnomes."

"That's a bit extreme, don't you think?" Diana didn't bother to hide her smile, but she pulled a second chair up to the table. "Let's see what else we can come up with."

"Your wife will be occupied for some time," Howd said to Ben. "Care to take a walk? I'll give you a quick introduction to the birds in the area."

"I'm thinking of setting up a gypsy camp," Myron was telling Diana as they left the room. "Though Injuns might be better. Most resorts have one or the other. The gypsies tell fortunes. Injuns sell baskets."

On their way outside, Howd stopped in the lobby. "You might want to know this is here," he said, and opened the large drawer under the hotel register. The drawer contained nuts, several varieties of them. Scooping out two huge handfuls, Howd filled his pockets. "For the squirrels," he explained.

They crossed the veranda and the lawn, where Howd paused briefly to speak to the goat. "She's our mascot," he explained when they continued on. "She has the run of the place and pays us back by eating litter and keeping the grass trimmed. Of course, she also helps herself to anything left on window sills. Tressa lost a whole pie once."

Howd led the way to the start of a narrow path Ben had not previously noticed. It wound through oaks, maples, poplars, beeches, and veteran pines. "Look there," Howd said, pointing to a waxy-white flower among the pine needles that carpeted their path. "Pyrola. And that's pipsissewa beside it. Can you smell it?"

Ben caught a trace of the fragrance and nodded.

"The open fields are better for bird watching at this time of year," Howd said as they came out in a grove of hemlocks. "So much variety. Bobolinks and meadow larks. Red-wings, sparrows, tanagers, kinglets."

"But you didn't bring me out here to talk about birds, did you?"

"Not really. No."

"Gypsy camps?"

Howd grinned. "Had my fortune told once. I was eighteen at the time. The gypsy said that two girls lived very near me. One, with big blue eyes, wouldn't have me. The other, if I married her, would drag me through the dirt. I stayed away from Lottie Hosier after that. She worked here, too, and one time when I walked her back to her door—her room was right next to my parents' room on the first floor—she kissed me on the lips." He shook his head. "Back then, I thought that was pretty scandalous behavior."

"And later?"

"I like the ladies, Northcote. And they don't usually run away from me."

"Did you suggest privacy to tell me something more about Elly Lyseth?"

"No. It's Elmira we need to discuss. Oh—don't look so shocked. Did you suppose no one would find out Diana's her daughter?

Tressa overheard the two of you talking that first night in the private dining room and told me, but I think I would have figured it out on my own. There's a resemblance, you know."

Privately, Ben thought Diana and her mother had little in common, either physically or in their outlook on life, but he didn't intend to discuss his opinion of Elmira Grant Torrence, especially not with her brother. "Does Myron know?"

"No, and I won't be telling him. You know how he feels."

"Yes, so does Diana. That's part of the reason she didn't say anything to the rest of you."

"How's that husband of Elmira's?" Howd asked. "I know he stuck around long enough to become Diana's pa. I can see something of him in her, too."

"He's dead."

"Figured he might be. You want me to tell his father or are you planning to visit Torrence yourself?"

So Diana's paternal grandfather *was* still alive. "Would that be I. Torrence?" he asked, recalling the name he'd seen on the map.

"That's right. Isaac. Lives in Liberty. I talked to him yesterday. Told him about Diana. He wants to meet her."

Ben's conscience pricked him. He should have mentioned what he'd suspected about the Torrences to Diana before this. And he hadn't even considered that Isaac Torrence wouldn't know his son was dead.

"Torrence was upset when my sister eloped with his son," Howd said, "but he always liked Elmira. He'd have been glad if they'd come back. But he's never heard a word from Will in all the years since they left, and that's eaten at him. I think maybe he convinced himself that Will died in the war."

It took Ben a moment to realize what he meant. The couple had eloped in 1855. Diana had been born in 1864. If the family had no idea where they'd gone, it was reasonable to assume that William Torrence had enlisted in the Union Army and died a hero. Wrong, but reasonable.

Again, Ben considered how much to say. Torrence had died, violently, only a short time ago. And he and Diana's mother had been divorced for several years at the time. Diana would have to decide how much she wanted her new found relatives to know about the scandal.

"Does old Mr. Torrence have other children?" Ben asked.

"A daughter, Janette. She moved in with him after her husband died. She never had any kids of her own."

So, Diana was the only grandchild on the Torrence side. That meant Ben didn't really have much choice. He was going to have to arrange a meeting before they left Sullivan County.

"I'll tell Diana," he promised Howd, "but in my own time. With Myron still as adamant, I don't want to take the chance he'll find out."

"Probably wise," Howd conceded. "He was all set to throw her out of the hotel when he found out she was a reporter. Lord only knows how he'd react to learning she's Elmira's daughter."

❧❦☙

Diana was about to change into her green silk gown for the evening meal when she heard a loud crash in the suite below. It was followed by a bellow in Myron Grant's voice.

"You son of a bitch!" he shouted. "You tried to burn me out!"

By the time Diana reached the parlor of her own suite, Ben was on his way downstairs. She followed as quickly as she could, urged on by high-pitched feminine shrieks. She found Belle Saugus in the hallway, darting ineffectually about, clearly torn between rushing back inside the room and staying out of the way of the combatants.

"Stop them!" Belle wailed. "Make them stop!"

The thumps, grunts, and scuffling sounds Diana heard within the suite warned her there were fisticuffs in progress, but the sight that met her eyes when she looked through the door held her momentarily speechless. Howd sat on the floor, rubbing his jaw. Myron Grant had his hands wrapped around Norman Saugus's throat and was squeezing so hard that the smaller man's eyes bulged.

"Let him go, damn it!" Ben caught hold of Myron's arm and tried to loosen his grip. "You're going to kill him."

"He deserves killing." Myron spat, but he flung Saugus away from him. Saugus bounced against the wall and slid to the floor, gagging and clutching protectively at his neck.

Mrs. Saugus pushed past Diana into the room. Instead of going to her husband's side she marched up to Myron and poked him in the chest with one extended finger. "You're a damned fool, Myron Grant!"

He growled at her, making her retreat a step. "Don't you think I know that? And he's the one who made a fool of me." Fists raised, he turned towards Saugus. "I know what you tried to do."

Diana entered the parlor of the suite and closed the door behind her. She saw the sudden loss of color in Belle Saugus's face and the wince that crossed her husband's countenance, but she couldn't tell for certain what either reaction signified. Even if Howd had told his brother everything they'd discussed the previous evening, Myron had no proof of wrongdoing that would hold up against Mr. and Mrs. Saugus in court.

A quick survey of the room showed her that the furnishings were almost identical with those in her own suite. A few pieces of bric-a-brac had been broken during the fight and a chair had been shoved out of place. Discarded clothing lay scattered about, but Diana suspected slovenly habits were to blame for that, not Myron's enraged attack on his so-called backer.

In one corner sat a carton, the lid askew, that appeared to contain papers.

Ben knelt at Saugus's side to examine his injuries. "You'll have a black eye but nothing's broken," he said as he stood and offered the other man a hand. "Mrs. Ellington can no doubt provide ice for the swelling. I'd suggest honey and lemon in tea for your throat."

"Whiskey," Saugus croaked, reminding Diana of her theory that he'd spent the previous two days drinking. It was hard to say, now that he'd been beaten up, but she didn't think there were any outward signs of a hangover. His eyes were not bloodshot. She smelled none of the unpleasant odors usually associated with alcoholic excess.

Had he been ill? Or just hiding? And why would he hide? Myron obviously hadn't known a thing about the arson until Howd told him. She joined the latter, who was still nursing his jaw, while Mrs. Saugus poured whiskeys all around.

"What on earth possessed you to tell him?" she hissed.

"Stupidity?" Howd shook his head. "Believe me when I say it just slipped out. I was avoiding another topic." He hesitated, as if trying to decide whether to explain himself or not. "That doesn't matter now. Point is, Myron started going on and on about being worried about me, because of Elly's murder, and I said he was the one I worried about, and one thing led to another and I told him he was a damned fool to trust a man who'd tried to burn him out once and would probably do it again. Then I had to explain what I meant. And the next thing I knew, he was roaring like a bull and charging up here to beat Saugus to a pulp."

"I'll be damned if I'll go out to the ice house for ice for his eye," Myron muttered. "We need that ice for the season. Cost a fortune to harvest it from local ponds last winter. I paid—"

"Myron!" Howd snapped. "Enough."

Saugus made his way to the sofa. "This is all a misunderstanding," he croaked. "I never set any fire."

"Let's be accurate." Ben stood near the fireplace. "You've figured out that we can't prove you did. But we *can* prove you collected insurance after the west wing of this hotel burned. And we can find out if you have an insurance policy on the hotel right now."

While everyone's attention was fixed on Ben, Diana sidled over to investigate the box she'd noticed. It was indeed filled with papers. They were blank forms of some sort, but they were witnessed and sealed. Aware that proper authorities did not notarize unsigned documents, she slipped one into the pocket of her skirt before she made her way to Ben's side.

"Let's stop this now," he was saying. "You were lucky last time, Saugus. No one died in the fire. This time you might miscalculate. Do you want murder on your conscience?"

Saugus glared at him. "I'm not admitting anything, but let's say you're right. What's so wrong about wanting to recoup my losses?" He smirked at Myron, who was standing with Howd near the door. "You'd have done it yourself if you'd been smart enough to think of it."

"Get out." Myron's voice was soft now, and all the more threatening for the lack of volume. "I want you out of my hotel."

"We have a contract."

"Not anymore."

"I'll sue."

"Go ahead. I'd like nothing better than to meet you in a court of law."

Belle Saugus slumped onto the sofa beside her husband and burst into tears. It was a masterful performance, designed to melt the coldest heart. Diana had to admire it, even though she was certain it was all an act. And it was successful. By the time Belle's tears were stemmed, Myron had agreed to let the couple stay until noon the next day.

"Woman needs time to pack," he mumbled. "Guess it don't make no difference so long as you're gone soon."

Ben took Diana's arm and they joined Myron and Howd at the door. Myron opened it, then turned to glare at Saugus once more. "Did you ever deal honestly with me?" he demanded. "Or was the plan all along to burn me out for the insurance?"

Saugus didn't answer verbally, but the cocky smile he sent in Myron's direction rekindled the other man's rage. It took both Ben and Howd to keep him from charging the sofa. They hauled him out into the hallway and held on until they heard the lock click behind them.

Released, Myron stormed off. Howd and Ben exchanged a glance.

"He'll cool down," Howd said.

"Keep an eye on him."

"I will." He started after his brother, then stopped. "I doubt anyone will feel like sitting down to a meal this evening. I'll have Sebastian bring something up to your suite."

"What about them?" Diana asked, inclining her head towards the Saugus's door.

"Let them starve," Howd said, and went after his brother.

When he had gone, Diana looked wistfully at the closed door. "I have a few more questions for Norman Saugus."

"He's not going to answer them." Ben steered her towards the stairwell.

"I think it's a mistake to send Saugus away," Diana said when they returned to their suite. "If Saugus killed Elly Lyseth—"

"They won't leave sooner than they have to," Ben cut in. "I was thinking of driving into Liberty tomorrow anyway. I need to send a telegram and I thought we could—"

"You were going to look at local records!" Remembering his plan, she brightened. "You thought you might find proof of fraud. Will this help?" She produced the notarized document she'd stolen from the box in Saugus's parlor.

As Ben studied it, his brows lifted. "This is worth following up, certainly. Another thing we can do in Liberty in the morning. If you come with me, we—"

"Oh, yes. I'll come. I've been hoping for a chance to talk to the coroner."

The odd look he gave her made Diana realize she had yet to tell him she was supposed to be writing an article about Sailor Jack. That news could wait awhile longer, she decided. Perhaps until after they'd had a good meal in the privacy of their suite.

Perhaps until morning.

CHAPTER NINE

Monday dawned without rain and the temperature began to climb as soon as the sun was up. Diana and Ben rose early and were just finishing breakfast when Mrs. Ellington rushed into the private dining room.

"Dr. Northcote," she exclaimed. "Thank goodness you're still here!"

"Is someone ill?"

"Not ill, no. It's the Castine boy, Freddy. The blacksmith's youngest. A horse kicked him. Looks like the blow broke his arm."

"Say no more." Ben hastily wiped his mouth and tossed the napkin onto the table. "I'll fetch my medical bag and go at once."

Diana started to rise but he waved her back into her chair.

"Finish your breakfast. This won't take long, but it's best to set a broken bone as soon as possible."

"I'll walk to the livery stable to meet you," Diana called after him. "If his boy's hurt, the blacksmith won't want to leave him to bring the surrey out here."

Mrs. Ellington nodded her approval. "He's a good man, your husband," the housekeeper said.

"Yes, he is."

Tressa Ellington seemed about to say more, but instead just nodded and turned away. Diana ate quickly, polishing off steak and potatoes, her customary breakfast fare, before setting off at a brisk pace for the village.

She found the walking far easier than it had been the other day in the rain. The morning air had a fresh, clean smell, augmented by the fragrance of wildflowers. Diana smiled as she passed the tree where she and Belle Saugus had sheltered and glanced towards the comical figure of the scarecrow in the cornfield just at the foot of the Hotel Grant's long drive.

She had gone a few steps beyond that point when it struck her that something had changed. Turning back, she looked at the scarecrow again. She had not been mistaken. During the rainstorm, the straw man's limbs had flapped. Now they were stiff as boards. They looked . . . heavier.

Enough of a breeze stirred the leaves that there should have been some movement, enough to frighten birds away from the corn. Instead the straw-stuffed figured appeared to be attracting them in record numbers. Diana counted a half dozen crows pecking at the effigy.

"That's not right," she murmured.

Before she thought through what she was doing, she'd walked into the field. Her movements were hampered by the outfit she wore. In anticipation of the trip into town, she'd assumed full female regalia, including a breath-restricting corset, full skirts with several petticoats beneath, and a good-sized bustle. In spite of these impediments to rapid locomotion, she quickly closed the distance to the scarecrow.

Diana was almost on top of it before she suddenly realized what it was that had drawn the scavengers. She jerked to a stop, staring in disbelief at the figure before her. The old overalls and plaid shirt and weather-beaten, broad-brimmed hat were no longer stuffed with straw. There was a man inside the clothing—a very dead man.

Diana swallowed hard. Her hearty breakfast threatened to rebel.

Although she knew it was far too late to do anything for him, she moved closer, reaching out one tentative hand to feel for a pulse at the man's wrist. Her fingers touched cold, dead flesh, sticky with blood.

Helpless to stop herself, she peered up under the brim of the hat. The wide open but sightless eyes—one of them blackened—of Norman T. Saugus stared back at her. A vile smell assailed her at the same time. The combination was too much for her. Diana fled towards the road, stopping only to be horribly sick in a ditch.

Her steps unsteady, a foul taste in her mouth, Diana stumbled into town. It would have been closer to go back to the hotel for help, but Ben was in Lenape Springs. She ran the last few yards to the livery stable, staggered past a surrey, and stopped with a little cry of alarm when someone stepped in front of her.

"Mrs. Northcote? Are you ill?"

Belatedly, Diana recognized Luke, the blacksmith's oldest son, who must have been hitching up the horse when she stumbled into view. The expression of concern on his youthful countenance snapped Diana out of her panic. She'd come this far. She could not fail now. She had to tell Ben what she'd found.

"I'm not about to faint." Her tremulous, breathless declaration did not sound convincing even to her own ears. "It's just . . . I found a body."

"Ma'am?"

"A body," she repeated. Her voice shook less the second time she said it. Steadying herself with one hand against the side of the surrey, Diana ordered herself to calm down. This was no time for hysterics. "As soon as Dr. Northcote is finished setting your brother's arm, I must speak with him."

"*Whose* body?" Luke's agitated voice went so loud of a sudden that it made Diana jump. "Not Mercy?"

"No! Oh, no, Luke. It's Norman Saugus who's dead. Not another young woman."

"Thank the Lord."

"Amen," Diana whispered, and meant it. Bad enough to have found Saugus.

She hadn't liked him in life, but she'd known him. And now he was dead. Someone had killed him.

Someone had *murdered* him and left him in that field to be found.

The reality of what she'd seen struck Diana with such force that she swayed. Luke caught her before she could fall and steered her inside the livery stable.

"A chair. I'll get you a chair." He sounded in worse shape than she was.

"No. No, I'll be fine." She gripped the half door of an empty horse stall so hard her knuckles went white but she remained standing. She was afraid that if she sat, she'd collapse completely. She had to keep her wits about her. She had to tell Ben what she'd found.

Oh, God! It had been horrible! She'd never had to face that kind of death before. Death had always been remote. Something to write about. Something to hear about. She'd been that close to a dead body only once before, and although Evan, too, had been violently dispatched, he'd been cleaned up before she'd seen him, resembling a wax figure rather than what remained of a man.

To her shame, Diana knew she'd not been deeply moved by the discovery of Elly Lyseth's bones. The girl had been dead for years, and Diana had never met her when she was alive. But Norman Saugus had been real. She'd seen him only last night when—

Stifling a moan, she gripped the rail of the horse stall more tightly and with both hands. She was suddenly afraid she *might* faint.

She stared at the small wooden plaque attached to the top of the half door. "Jessie" it said. The horse's name. Ben had told her the little Morgan was called Old Jessie. Diana wished Jessie were still in the stall instead of hitched to the surrey. She could have used a soft equine nose to pat and the calming whuffling sound a horse made when questing for a bit of apple for a treat.

She drew in a deep, steadying breath and got her body under control again. Her mind was another matter. Her thoughts were racing. If Norman Saugus had been murdered, that meant someone had killed him, and the first name that came to mind was her uncle Myron's.

No, she told herself. Uncle Myron could not have done this terrible thing. He might have beaten Saugus to death last night if they hadn't stopped him, or strangled him, perhaps, but he'd never have struck him down in cold blood. Nor would he have put the body on public display, leaving it to chance who stumbled upon it first. What if a child had found him? Or Mercy?

Mercy? She frowned and lifted her gaze from the plaque to look at Luke. He was staring at her with an expression that was half trepidation, half concern.

"Why would you think that Mercy—"

She broke off, alerted to the fact that someone was coming by the clomp of heavy boots. A moment later Ben entered the livery stable in company with the blacksmith and several other men.

"Diana! What's wrong? You're pale as a ghost."

She threw herself into his arms, making no attempt to speak until she was safely clasped to his broad, comforting chest.

"She found a body," Luke said.

Ben's exclamation of surprise was nearly drowned out by the shocked outcries of the men who'd come back to the livery stable with him.

"It's Norman Saugus," she whispered. "Someone killed him and put him in the scarecrow's clothes and hung him up in the field by the road."

This time the exclamations held a note of disbelief, but the men of Lenape Springs were quick to go along and see for themselves. Within moments, Diana was alone with Ben. She stopped trying to be brave and buried her face in his shirt front.

"Diana," he said gently. "I need to go with them. They mustn't disturb the scene until the coroner comes. Do you want to stay here? I can get Mrs. Castine to—"

"No. I'll come with you." Although she shuddered at the thought of being anywhere near the scarecrow again, she had to go that way to get back to the hotel.

They left the livery stable, ignoring the curious stares of several village women and the postmaster. As they retraced Diana's steps, she explained how she had come to notice the scarecrow, and how she'd verified the body's identity. She was shaking uncontrollably by the time she'd finished the tale.

"Damnation, Diana! You shouldn't have had to see that."

"Someone was going to find him. It would have been worse if it had been a child."

"I should have noticed the crows. I went past there less than half an hour before you did."

"You were thinking about your patient. Is he going to be all right?"

"It's a clean break. But that's no excuse for my failure to—"

"Whoever came to the hotel to fetch you also passed this way without noticing. You can't blame yourself because I happened to be the first one who did."

He stopped arguing when they reached the field, but she knew he wasn't convinced. He was protective where she was concerned. Sometimes that was a good thing.

A cluster of men surrounded the scarecrow, hiding it from Diana's view. "Go," she said, giving Ben a little push. "Examine the remains. Send for the coroner. I can walk the rest of the way on my own."

Plainly torn, he hesitated, giving her a hard look.

"Go."

Ben did not appear entirely convinced of her recovery, but he obeyed. She watched until he reached the others, then went on. She still felt shaky, but her mind was functioning again. There were things to do at the hotel, things she could do better than the coroner or the police.

She told Myron first: "Norman Saugus is dead. Murdered."

He blinked at her in disbelief. Then slowly dawning horror suffused his features. "I didn't touch him! I swear to God I never saw him again after I left his room last evening. You were still there when I left. You saw me go. I didn't go back. I swear it."

Diana believed him. Besides, she would have heard the ruckus if he'd returned to kill Saugus. "Where *did* you go?"

"Here." They were in the family parlor. "I came here. Howd was with me for a while. We had some of Tressa's dandelion wine. Then I went to bed."

"And Howd?"

Myron's glare was ferocious. "If I didn't kill Saugus, Howd sure as Hell didn't."

"Did he retire when you did?"

"No. Said he was going for a walk."

"At night?"

"He likes to walk at night. Besides, the moon is nearly at the full. There was plenty of light."

"Don't be so defensive. I'm trying to help." Then she told him where and in what condition Norman Saugus's body had been found.

Her uncle grudgingly relented. "Howd's gone. I'm not sure when he left. Mercy might know."

"Gone? Gone where?"

"Probably up to Sundown. Damned inconvenient, if you'll pardon my French. Last time he took off I had to pay a boy to work at the hotel, and it cost me three dollars for ten days plus a fifty cent tip."

Diana left him to his grumbling and went in search of the rest of the family. She found Mercy, Sebastian, and Mrs. Ellington in the kitchen. Since none of them were likely to have killed Norman Saugus, she gave them a succinct account of what she knew and asked Mrs. Ellington to come with her to break the news to Belle Saugus.

"You poor thing," Mrs. Ellington sympathized. "What a grisly discovery."

Diana swallowed hard as the image of Saugus's dead face flashed before her eyes. She had a feeling it was going to be a long time before she rid herself of that ghastly memory.

ഇറോ

Ben returned to the hotel just in time to intercept Diana and Mrs. Ellington on their way to talk to Belle Saugus. "This isn't your responsibility," he told Diana. "I'll tell her."

"I am not some frail creature subject to fits of the vapors," Diana reminded him. "I am perfectly capable of getting through the ordeal. And Mrs. Saugus should have a woman with her when she hears her husband is dead."

Had Diana? Ben wondered. Had there been someone there for her when word had come that her husband had been shot to death in a barroom brawl?

"Besides," she added, just as he was about to relent, "I have a job to do."

"A *job?*" he echoed, unable to believe what he was hearing.

"Murders make headlines, Ben." A small frown creased her forehead. "We need to leave for Liberty as soon as we can after we talk to Mrs. Saugus. I have to send a telegram to Horatio Foxe."

She was still upset, he told himself. She was hiding behind her profession to keep from falling to pieces. Surely she was not as cold-hearted as she sounded.

"Shall I still accompany you?" Mrs. Ellington asked. Was she as appalled by Diana's statements as Ben was? That would not bode well for Diana's acceptance into the Grant family.

"Yes," Diana said, before Ben could answer. "We can't tell how Mrs. Saugus will react to the news. She may want the comfort of having other females around."

She did not.

"Get out!" Belle Saugus snarled when they'd told her that her husband was dead. She didn't even ask for details.

"But Mrs. Saugus—"

"Leave me be, Dr. Northcote! Haven't you done enough?" With tears streaming down her face, she seemed truly distraught. Ben might have been fooled if he hadn't caught sight of the skeptical look in Diana's eyes.

The door slammed in their faces.

"Well, that's that," Tressa Ellington said. "I'll go see about luncheon."

"Myron told them to leave by noon today, but I don't suppose he'll press the widow to go."

"I'm sure he won't," Ben agreed. "In the meantime, shall we do as she asks and leave her alone? She obviously needs to come to grips with what's happened."

"And at least we'll know where to find her," Diana murmured.

A few minutes later, back in their own suite, he turned to her with a questioning look. "You think Belle killed her husband?"

"I think she overdid her reaction to the news." She held her finger to her lips and listened. "I don't hear any weeping and wailing now."

"No maniacal laughter, either," he said in a dry tone.

"How was Saugus killed?"

His certainty it was the journalist asking made Ben frown, but he answered her anyway. "A blow to the head."

She looked at her hands and shivered. There was blood on one of her gloves. She tore off the stained one of the pair and threw it into a corner. "Blood dripped down his arm to his wrist."

"Yes."

She closed her eyes for a moment, collecting herself. "Someone hit Elly Lyseth on the head, too. It could have been the same person, Ben. Saugus's killer tried to hide this body, too."

"The same murderer? After all these years?"

"Why not?" She began to pace.

Just watching her made Ben tired. "This killer didn't hide the body. He put it on display."

"Before this happened we were building a case against Norman Saugus for arson, and possibly for Elly Lyseth's murder. There must be a connection."

"What kind of connection?"

"Maybe Saugus had his own ideas about who killed Elly. Maybe he got too close."

"You're grasping at straws, Diana. And the most logical person to have killed Norman Saugus is the most obvious—the same one who tried to kill him less than twenty-four hours ago."

"No. Not Uncle Myron. More likely Saugus's wife killed him, *thinking* she could put the blame on Uncle Myron."

"More people are murdered by their nearest and dearest than by strangers," he conceded.

She gave him a sharp look but didn't stop pacing. "I'm not going to ask how you know something like that."

He caught her arm on the next pass and held her still. "Can you really be saying you believe Belle Saugus killed them both?"

"Why not? Unless she murdered Elly, Belle would have no reason to do away with her husband."

"And if she was capable of murdering Elly—and she was on your list of suspects—she could certainly kill again to cover up the first crime. But, Diana, she'd have had to have help getting Saugus into that cornfield and up onto the cross that held the scarecrow."

"Never underestimate a woman's strength. Hauling water and beating rugs and doing other household chores builds as much muscle as wrestling trunks up flights of stairs or repairing a roof."

"I don't see Belle Saugus as particularly domestic." Ben didn't see that she'd had much reason to kill Elly Lyseth, either. The motive they'd speculated about had been jealousy, which presupposed an affair between Saugus and Elly. In light of what they'd learned from Howd and others, that seemed unlikely. At most, the young woman had flirted with him.

Diana frowned. "Perhaps she was not accustomed to hard manual labor, but I'll wager Belle Saugus has had plenty of practice handling a husband too drunk to put himself to bed."

The observation suggested that she spoke from personal experience, an idea Ben found distressing. "You're jumping to conclusions," he protested. "We have no evidence that Saugus was a drunkard. There are other reasons he might have stayed in his suite. He *might* have been ill. Or he could have been engrossed in planning his swindle."

Diana didn't seem to hear him. "The surrey is ready to go. Luke had already hitched up the horse."

"You still intend to go to Liberty? The coroner wants to speak with you. I expect him to show up here at any moment."

"The coroner can wait. Horatio Foxe cannot."

Handling the reins took most of Ben's attention on the drive into Liberty, but every time he glanced at Diana she was scribbling in her notebook. She'd overcome his objections about making this trip by the simple expedient of setting off on foot for the livery stable in Lenape Springs. He'd been left to stay behind or follow, as suited him. Since he'd had no doubt that she would attempt to make the short journey to the telegraph office, with or without him, he'd had no real choice but to accompany her.

When they'd passed the field, he'd noticed that Mr. Buckley had arrived, but the coroner didn't notice them slip past. Almost the entire village had gathered to watch him examine the body. Two more people at a distance made no impression.

Luke had been the only one in the livery stable, forbidden by his father to leave the premises. Castine was probably afraid he'd find a way to talk with Mercy Grant, Ben thought.

The young man hadn't gotten around to unharnessing Old Jessie and within minutes they'd been on their way. Ben doubted anyone had noticed their departure from Lenape Springs. Even the post office had a CLOSED sign hung on the door. Osmer Nicholls had joined the rest of the curious townspeople to watch the coroner at work.

Or perhaps he'd been called out to make up a coroner's jury, Ben thought, reconsidering. That might account for many of the men at the scene, but not for the women. Females couldn't serve on juries. Ben wondered how that rule had come about. As far as he could see, there was little need to protect the so-called "weaker" sex. After all, women were the ones who endured childbirth, and delivered most babies, too.

"Should I say 'bloodied and battered corpse' or just 'horrible sight of the murdered man?'" Diana asked, pencil poised.

"Must you use either phrase? Mustn't shock delicate sensibilities."

His sarcasm prompted a curious look. "Even if I avoid hyperbole, Horatio Foxe won't." She cleared her throat and began to read aloud what she had written: "A most terrible, cowardly, and cold-blooded murder was committed under cover of night in the tiny hamlet of Lenape Springs in upstate New York."

"This is hardly upstate. Sullivan County borders New Jersey."

"Don't be argumentative. Besides, to someone who lives in New York City, everything beyond Manhattan is upstate."

"Even Long Island?"

She ignored his mocking tone. "The horribly mutilated body of Mr. Norman T. Saugus was discovered in a field by a passerby. It had been dressed in the clothing of a scarecrow and put in the straw man's place. The authorities have been notified and are even now examining the remains. Coroner Buckley from Liberty, five miles distant, at once impaneled a jury. The post-mortem examination was made by Dr. Benjamin Northcote, visiting in the area from Maine. It was found that Mr. Saugus was battered to death with a blunt instrument."

Ben ground his teeth but said nothing. What did it matter if Diana wrote "horribly mutilated" and "battered to death" or not. She was right. If she failed to insert sensational descriptive details, Horatio Foxe would.

"Coroner and jury," Diana continued, "plan to search the rooms Mr. Saugus kept at the nearby Hotel Grant, a luxury establishment about to open for the season."

"Are you sure you want to mention the hotel by name?"

"If this is handled correctly, the publicity will benefit Uncle Myron's enterprise."

Ben wasn't so sure about that, but didn't argue.

"The murder victim was found at some distance from the hotel, which provides a safe and comfortable environment for guests. Since Mr. Saugus was not popular in the community, a number of suspects are being questioned."

"Will you mention his quarrel with Myron?"

"No. I may hint at trouble in his marriage. And I've remembered something. Yesterday, at the Lenape Springs Villa, I overheard Pastor Riker speaking to members of his flock. He was complaining about Mr. Saugus. He said they'd have gambling and horse racing and loose morals in Lenape Springs, worse than Saratoga, if Saugus wasn't stopped."

"Surely you're not going to suggest, in print, that a man of God ordered someone to commit murder?"

"Why not? What if one of Riker's listeners took his words as a suggestion that someone should get rid of Saugus? Permanently."

"Stick to one theory, Diana. I think it highly unlikely that anyone killed him just to stop the hotel from expanding."

"Perhaps not, but what if the killer heard what Riker said and tried to cover up the real reason for the murder by pointing the finger at a religious fanatic?"

"Pointing a finger? How?"

"The body was left on a cross." She was scribbling again. After a moment she sent him a sidelong glance just as he looked at her. "The best thing about this theory is that it eliminates both my uncles. They weren't at the Lenape Springs Villa to hear what Riker said."

"Someone else could have repeated it to them. And they have their own reasons for being angry with Saugus. The fight between your uncle and Saugus is going to come out, Diana. There's no way to avoid it."

"But I don't have to publicize it. And if I suggest other suspects to my readers, the authorities will have to take notice. Now, who else would want Saugus dead? Someone on my list of suspects in Elly Lyseth's murder would be best. What about Celia Lyseth? Given what we know of Mrs. Lyseth now, she probably thought her daughter's behavior immoral. Perhaps she did kill Elly. And if Saugus suspected her and she realized it, she could have killed him. *Or*, if she overheard the preacher, she might have taken it upon herself to carry out Riker's wishes."

"Next you'll be telling me Jonas Riker has mesmerized his entire congregation and turned them into assassins. Diana, listen to yourself. Your imagination is out of control. Those are wild speculations for a newspaper story, even one for the *Independent Intelligencer.*"

"It is an absurd crime. It may well have a fantastic solution."

She should be writing fiction, Ben thought, not for the first time, but what disturbed him most was her seeming indifference to the grisly discovery she had made. She had been shaken by her experience at first, but now . . .

"Murder is not an intellectual exercise, Diana."

"No, it is an abomination. And by writing about it, I may be able to impress that upon my readers."

"By creating rumors and spreading scandal?"

"Have you a better way?"

"Let the authorities deal with Saugus's death, Diana. There is no need for you to be involved."

"No need?" Her voice rose in pitch, making him wince. "I found him, Ben. That made it personal. And someone in my family may be accused of the crime. Am I to ignore that?"

"So you coldly state your version of the facts and—"

A small exclamation drew his eyes to her face. She looked hurt by his words and he was instantly contrite.

"If you wanted a frail, weepy sort of female, you should not have chosen me. Perhaps you would like to change your mind?"

She would not look at him and sat stiffly at his side, careful not to let her skirt touch his trousers.

"I don't want any woman but you, Diana," Ben said gruffly, "but there are times I wish you were less a newspaperwoman and more my intended bride. There is no need for you to write about this murder. Tell Foxe you are too closely involved. Better yet, let me tell him."

"I still have the other murders to cover for him. I may as well add this one. I am over the first shock. Indeed, I believe I will feel much less disturbed by what I saw if I write—"

She broke off when she saw his expression and winced when she realized what she'd just let slip.

"The other murders?" Ben asked in a deceptively calm voice. "What murder besides Elly Lyseth's are you investigating, Diana?"

"I intended to tell you. Horatio Foxe sent a second telegram asking me to write a piece on the Sailor Jack case. That's why I wanted to speak to Mr. Buckley." She aimed a too-bright smile his way.

The pulse in Ben's neck began to throb, a warning sign that his temper was coming to a boil.

"You knew what I did for a living when you asked me to marry you."

"I wanted to take you away from all that."

"Are you saying I must choose between you and my career?"

He hesitated a moment too long.

"No. Don't answer now. I don't want to hear it. I have a job to do, Ben. I need to do it or I *will* become one of those frail, weepy females."

Neither of them said anything more for the short distance that remained before they reached Liberty. Ben drove straight to the telegraph office. While Diana sent her news story to Horatio Foxe and a second telegram to Mrs. Curran, asking her to reply in a like manner rather than by post to the letter she had already sent, Ben composed messages to his mother and to the doctor caring for his brother.

He found Diana fuming when he finished.

"This is outrageous," she complained. "I am entitled to the privileges of the press."

"Nobody gets special privileges here, ma'am. This isn't Western Union."

"*That* is obvious. I've never even heard of J. & L. Telegraph."

The telegraph operator continued as if she hadn't spoken, and seemed unmoved by the content of her lengthy telegram. "The rates to all points on the line are ten cents for ten words. Messages to be transferred to the Western Union cost ten cents additional."

Diana turned to Ben. "I haven't enough money."

"I'll pay for all the telegrams." There was no advantage to him in trying to prevent her from contacting Foxe.

A few minutes later they were back out on the unpaved and dusty street. "I suppose it is pointless now to show that blank document to the constable."

"Probably," Ben agreed. "Shall we head back to the hotel? The coroner will have questions for us, and you did say you had a few for him as well."

When he'd first planned this drive into town, he'd also intended to tell Diana about her grandfather and suggest a visit to Isaac Torrence, but there was no sense in burdening her with such an announcement today. There wasn't time to pay a visit, and she had more than enough on her plate as it was.

He wasn't happy about the way she was dealing with finding a body, or that she had kept the contents of Foxe's second telegram from him, but she was right about one thing. He did not want a fragile female for a wife. He wanted Diana, flaws and all.

CHAPTER TEN

❦

They returned to Lenape Springs to find that Coroner Buckley had convened the inquest. Diana wasn't surprised. The fact that Norman Saugus's body was no longer in the cornfield indicated that a coroner's jury had already viewed it and moved on to the next stage of their duties.

"Mr. Buckley is not happy you two left before he could question you," Mrs. Ellington informed them.

Diana suspected he'd be even less pleased when he found out where they'd gone and why. She was sure it was only a matter of time before Mr. Buckley discovered that she was a newspaper reporter.

"They're in the main dining room," Mrs. Ellington added, leading the way. "With half the town crowding in, it seemed the best place."

Diana's steps faltered. "Does that mean I'll have to answer questions before an audience?" she whispered to Ben. Giving testimony suddenly seemed uncomfortably similar to being on stage. She hoped she wouldn't mumble her lines or, worse, forget what she'd meant to say.

"Just concentrate on Mr. Buckley," Ben advised. "Ignore

everyone else in the room."

That was easier said than done. Mrs. Ellington, who returned to her own duties once she'd delivered Diana and Ben to the dining room, had not exaggerated when she'd said half the town was there—the male half. Diana was the only woman present.

"Mrs. Northcote, I presume?" Buckley said.

Diana took an instant dislike to him. Spectacles perched on his long, thin nose, he reminded her of a pompous schoolmaster she'd once had. His attitude was equally annoying. Supercilious, she decided. Condescending.

Glaring at him, she felt her chin come up and her spine stiffen. When he indicated that she should take the makeshift "witness" chair, she obliged with a hauteur of her own.

"Now, then," Buckley said, "we'll try to keep this brief." After he swore her in, he asked, perfunctorily, "You are Mrs. Benjamin Northcote?"

Diana swallowed, struck not by stage fright but by a different kind of panic. Would she be breaking the law if she lied? And yet, how could she not? To reveal, here before all these people, that she was living in sin with a man not her husband, was impossible.

"Mrs. Northcote?" Mr. Buckley sounded impatient.

Diana cleared her throat. "I prefer to be addressed by the name I use professionally," she said. "As Diana Spaulding I write a column called 'Today's Tidbits' for the *Independent Intelligencer.*"

She heard a startled gasp and a few mutters as previously unenlightened spectators absorbed this information. The coroner looked as if he'd stepped in something nasty and moved a bit farther away from her. "Very well, Miss Spaulding, I—"

"Mrs. Spaulding. I was a widow when I met Dr. Northcote."

"Very well, *Mrs.* Spaulding, will you tell us, please, how you came to discover Mr. Saugus's remains."

She kept the account factual and brief, having no desire to revisit the unpleasant details. She breathed a sigh of relief when he seemed satisfied. In spite of the mistrust she'd generated by revealing her profession, Mr. Buckley was clearly a gentleman who'd been brought up to treat ladies courteously. She took ruthless advantage of this weakness by feigning a need for Ben's support when she left the witness chair.

Once Diana's testimony had been recorded on paper, she was dismissed. If she *had* been a proper lady, she'd have taken her departure at once. Instead, she remained at the back of the dining room, trying to make herself as inconspicuous as possible, while Ben took her place to answer questions.

"You examined the body?" Mr. Buckley asked, after he'd established Ben's identity and credentials.

"Yes, I did. I estimate he'd been dead for several hours."

"Killed during the night then?"

"Yes."

"Dr. Northcote, keeping in mind that mere matter of opinion is not legal testimony, do you have any more to add about the circumstances of Mr. Saugus's death?"

"He was killed elsewhere and brought to the cornfield. I observed signs that a wagon had been driven into the field and that a heavy object—the body—had been dragged from those tracks to the scarecrow."

Diana stifled a gasp. Ben hadn't shared that tidbit with her.

"So he was moved under cover of darkness?" the coroner asked.

"I'd say so, yes."

Buckley nodded, as if to himself. "Well, then. That should do it."

When the coroner turned to address his jurors, Ben joined Diana by the door. "Shall we go?"

"I want to hear what they decide."

"They have little choice. This time the death is clearly murder. And just as clearly, there is no suspect who can be charged."

"We missed earlier witnesses, if there were any. I want to hear what the jury has to say."

Yielding, Ben propped his shoulders against the doorframe,

crossed his arms in front of his chest, and waited while Mr. Buckley reminded the jurors of their choices.

"Murder is the killing of a human being, without the authority of law, by poison, shooting, stabbing, or any other means, or in any other manner. It is either murder in the first degree, murder in the second degree, manslaughter, excusable homicide, or justifiable homicide, according to the facts and circumstances of the case. The charge shall be murder in the first degree when it is perpetrated from a pre-meditated design to effect the death of the person killed, or of any human being."

Buckley paused to let that sink in, then rattled off the remaining definitions, seemingly just to get them out of the way.

"It is murder in the second degree when perpetrated by any act imminently dangerous to others and evincing a depraved mind, regardless of human life, although without any premeditated design to effect the death of any particular individual."

"Not that," Diana murmured. Not in Saugus's case, at any rate.

"It is murder in the third degree when perpetrated in committing the crime of arson in the first degree."

Diana and Ben exchanged a glance. She wondered if she should investigate more thoroughly the laws on arson. They might prove relevant even now.

"The killing of one human being by the act, procurement, or omission of another, in cases where such killing shall not be murder under the statute is either justifiable or excusable homicide or manslaughter," Mr. Buckley continued.

He'd obviously memorized the statutes, and went quickly through manslaughter in the first, second, third, and fourth degrees. The latter, Diana thought, would apply if Elly Lyseth had been struck down during a quarrel. This was deemed "excusable" homicide, "justifiable" being an adjective reserved for homicides committed by public officers and those acting by their command in their aid and assistance.

Mr. Buckley had barely finished his list of options before the jurors agreed that murder in the first degree had been done by person or persons unknown. He dismissed them, with his thanks, and waited until the room had cleared before turning his attention to Diana and Ben. "You will be required to appear and testify at the next criminal court at which an indictment for this offense can be found."

"And when will that be?" Ben asked.

"Hard to say. Depends on whether the villain who committed this heinous crime can be identified. You wouldn't have any ideas on that, would you?" With a deliberate motion, he put his transcript of the proceedings away, indicating that he was not asking the question in his official capacity.

"None at all," Diana said.

"A pity. I'd have thought a journalist would be snooping already."

"I am also a guest at this hotel, Mr. Buckley, vulnerable to the same kind of attack that ended Norman Saugus's life. Until the local authorities discover who killed him and arrest that person, I fear for my own safety. Indeed, I fear for my very life."

"Very melodramatic, Mrs. Northcote, but hardly relevant."

"My wife has a point, Buckley," Ben interrupted. "Will you extend the professional courtesy of keeping me appraised of your progress in—"

A crack of laughter cut short his request. Buckley looked first at Diana, then at Ben, shaking his head and chuckling to himself. "Professional courtesy," he repeated. "Because she fears for her life!"

Diana slanted a glance at Ben and found a slow smile tugging at the corners of his mouth. "What is so funny?" she hissed at him.

"I think you have to be in medicine or law enforcement to understand this type of humor," he whispered back.

She felt like a child who'd been patted on the head and told to let the grown ups worry about it. All that stopped her from snapping at the coroner was the level look he gave Ben when he stopped chortling.

"All right, Dr. Northcote," he said, pulling out chairs at one of the tables for them. "I'll tell you and your reporter what I think, but only because I want your ideas. No holding back, eh? After all, you've got no personal stake in this. These people are all strangers to you."

"That's right. Or rather, they were strangers until last Friday. But I have had time since to get to know a few of them." Ben settled Diana at the table before seating himself.

"Three days?"

"Some men inspire instant dislike," Ben told him. "Others radiate honesty."

"Very true," Buckley agreed, taking the third chair and leaning forward on his bony elbows. "What's your opinion of Howard Grant?"

"He's not a killer." Ben spoke up before Diana could.

"Odd, though, that he's disappeared."

"Do you plan to send someone after him?"

"I don't know yet."

"Howd Grant wouldn't hurt a fly," Diana protested, tired of being ignored by the coroner.

Buckley looked skeptical.

Outraged on her uncle's behalf, Diana found herself telling Mr. Buckley their suspicions about Saugus's business practices. "The man must have left a trail of fraud victims in his wake," she concluded. "Any one of them could have followed him here to take revenge."

She was about to advance her alternate theories, especially the one that involved local opposition to expanding the hotel as a motive, when the coroner cut in.

"But his most recent victims have the best motive, don't you think, Mrs. Northcote? Especially since Mr. Saugus quarreled with Myron Grant only hours before he was murdered."

"How—?"

"Did you think I wouldn't notice that the corpse had a black eye? When I asked her about it, Mrs. Saugus reluctantly admitted there had been a fight in their suite. She said you were both there, together with Howard Grant. She made no accusations, and claimed not to know what it was that provoked the fisticuffs, but it is obvious Myron Grant was angry at Mr. Saugus. Perhaps angry enough to kill?"

"He calmed down," Diana protested.

"And Howd Grant was with his brother afterward," Ben put in.

"Not all night. Either one of them could have met up with Saugus again before dawn. His wife tells me that when he couldn't sleep he often went out for a breath of air."

Diana frowned. Why *hadn't* Belle Saugus accused Uncle Myron outright? Much as Diana hated to admit it, he *was* the obvious suspect. If Mrs. Saugus had come forward as a witness, claiming Myron wanted her husband dead, the coroner's jury would probably have ordered his arrest. A word from her even now and he'd be on his way to the county jail.

That meant *she* had something to hide, that she didn't want to call attention to herself. Because she'd murdered her husband? Or was she afraid of being charged with another crime?

"What is arson in the first degree?" Diana asked abruptly.

Buckley, who had been speaking to Ben in quiet tones, blinked at her in surprise. He removed his glasses and wiped the lenses, then returned them to their proper place. "Arson in the first degree consists of willingly setting fire to, or burning in the night time, a dwelling house in which there shall be at the time some human being."

"Does that include hotels?"

"A dwelling house is any building occupied by persons lodging therein at night."

His precise recitation annoyed her. "Do you have the statutes memorized?"

"Yes. Would you care to hear the section on duels?"

Almost against her will, a tiny smile blossomed on Diana's lips. Friend or foe? She just couldn't decide about Coroner Buckley. But she supposed they had no choice but to work with him. At this stage, he was the one in charge of the murder investigation.

"We think Saugus set the fire here ten years ago, and that there is a connection to Elly Lyseth's death." She repeated what they'd overheard in the quarrel between Saugus and his wife that first night at the Hotel Grant and explained the reasoning behind their deductions.

Buckley listened attentively, but he was shaking his head when she finished the tale. "Nothing you've told me convinces me of a need to look outside the Grant family for a killer. In fact, this new information gives Myron Grant an excellent motive for killing Saugus."

"Because he tried to burn the hotel down."

"That, yes. But if I follow your logic, Saugus thought he knew who killed Elly Lyseth. What if he had proof it was Myron Grant?"

"You can't believe that!"

"I can and do, and I intend to prove it."

Buckley's smug expression was the final straw. Diana rose in a flurry of skirts and stalked from the dining room.

She'd tried to be a good citizen, and what had it got her? A pat on the head. A condescending look. And the knowledge that she'd just driven one more nail into her uncle's coffin.

She returned to the tower suite and retrieved her lists, but she did not reread what she'd written. Instead, the papers clenched in her hand, she paced, fuming as she stomped across the soft carpet in one direction, then reversed course. She'd have welcomed finding some small object in her way. It would have relieved her frustration to have something to kick across the room.

So much for getting information out of the coroner! Instead he'd taken what she and Ben knew and turned it against her family. And just where was Ben? Still in the dining room with Mr. Buckley, swapping coroner stories, no doubt!

It was left to her to find the real killer. She already had an obligation to Horatio Foxe to investigate the murders, although she had lost most of her enthusiasm for writing about crime. But producing a newspaper story was not her primary motivation. She had to solve the mystery of Norman Saugus's death—and Elly Lyseth's—if she ever hoped to be acknowledged by her mother's family. Failure might mean she'd lose one of her new found uncles. If that happened, she'd never have the chance to tell him who she really was.

෯෬

Your wife seemed upset," Mr. Buckley remarked as he and Ben adjourned from the dining room to the gentlemen's parlor, settled into comfortable chairs, and helped themselves to cigars.

"Finding a dead body can do that to a person." And whatever Diana was up to right now, it was best to leave her to it until she'd calmed down. Ben didn't think she could get into too much trouble here at the hotel in broad daylight.

"She is unaccustomed to violent death," Buckley mused. "I hope I was not too hard on her."

"She's resilient."

Buckley inhaled deeply and blew out a cloud of smoke. "I had an interesting case last fall."

A pleasant half hour passed while they exchanged war stories. Buckley told Ben about the Sailor Jack case. Ben recounted the details of a recent murder in Bangor in which the deceased had been struck down by a peavey, a tool used by woodsmen to steer timber down river during the spring log drive.

"I suppose I must speak with the widow again before I leave," Buckley remarked when their cigars were down to stubs.

Ben stood when he did. "Do you mind if I accompany you?"

"Not at all. To be truthful, the woman terrifies me."

Buckley's knock was followed by a long silence before Mrs. Saugus opened the door. As soon as she recognized the coroner, she burst into tears. She didn't seem to notice Ben.

"I'm sorry to intrude, Mrs. Saugus, but I hoped you might have remembered something."

With her voice muffled by sobs, her words were difficult to understand. but Ben gathered that she had slept soundly on the night of the murder and had no idea what had happened to her husband. Saugus had still been in their parlor when she'd retired. He'd been gone when she awoke.

"Did he go to bed at all?" Buckley wanted to know.

"I don't think so," the widow said, sniffling.

"Was he still fully dressed when you saw him last?"

She nodded and her tears became more copious still.

Buckley tried gamely for several more minutes but learned nothing new. With a few standard platitudes, he assured her that the authorities were doing all that could be done and bade her good day.

Ben was right behind him, but at the door he glanced back. Hunched over in her chair, Belle Saugus had her back to them. She appeared to be devastated by her loss. But in the mirror opposite, Ben caught a glimpse of her face in profile. Tears no longer flowed down the cheek he could see, and the widow's lips were tightly compressed. In that unguarded moment, he'd have sworn the emotion making her shake was not grief, but anger.

Thoughtful, he accompanied Buckley back to the lobby. Belle Saugus might be furious at the coroner for failing to arrest her husband's killer, but if Diana was right that she'd once been an actress, then it seemed possible to Ben that Belle was livid because all the plans she and Saugus had made were now in ruins because of his death.

Such instability could be dangerous, especially with Buckley convinced that Myron Grant was the most likely suspect in Saugus's death.

"You're barking up the wrong tree," he said as the other man put on his hat.

"Find me a better one, then."

"Howard Grant can confirm his brother's whereabouts for most, if not all, of last night." They didn't know exactly when Howd had left the hotel.

"Then get him back here to do it. The sooner the better."

Ben agreed to try, and as soon as Buckley left he went to the check-in desk. "I need directions to Sundown," he told Mercy Grant.

Diana had been pacing in their suite for at least an hour when Ben came to collect her and hustle her outside. He stopped in the lobby only long enough to fill his pockets with nuts, then whisked them across the expanse of lawn to a stone bench in the shade of a horse chestnut tree.

"What's going on?" Diana demanded as he held out a treat towards a lurking squirrel. It scampered forward, tame as you please, and took the offering from his outstretched hand.

"I couldn't convince Arthur Buckley that he should look beyond Myron Grant for Norman Saugus's killer," Ben said, watching the squirrel's equally rapid retreat with its prize. It paused atop a stump to sit on its haunches and take a nibble.

"I was afraid of that," Diana said. "Well, then, it's up to us to sort things out."

"I'm afraid so." He held out another tempting tidbit. The same squirrel dropped the first nut and raced in his direction, not only quite tame, but greedy as well. "He'll probably arrest your uncle unless we find evidence to clear him."

"What can we do?"

Drawn by the presence of food, Tremont the goat left off chomping grass and joined Diana and Ben beneath the tree. When she butted Diana's elbow with her head, Diana absently began to pet her.

"I'm going to Sundown to bring Howd back," Ben announced. "He was with Myron a good part of the night. He needs to say so to the authorities."

"I'll come with you."

"No, you won't. I'll have to go on horseback at least part of the way. It will be quicker if I go alone."

Diana started to assure him she could ride, then closed her mouth, pursing her lips. It made more sense to separate. They could accomplish twice as much if she stayed behind. That did not mean, however, that she liked having him tell her what to do. "You're being high-handed again."

"I'm being practical." He left the remaining nuts on the ground as he rose and dusted off his trousers. "I'll leave within the hour. You stay here and—"

Springing to her feet beside him, Diana caught hold of Ben's lapels. "If you say 'be careful' or 'stay out of trouble' or any other such unnecessary words of warning, I will kick you quite hard. I don't take marching orders from you, Ben Northcote. If I stay here, I make my own decisions about how to spend the time. You won't be around to tell me what I can and cannot do."

"For God's sake, Diana, I don't want to control your actions. I want *you* to control them. Think before you act. Yes, *stay out of trouble.*" He stepped back quickly, avoiding her foot. "You have an affinity for it. I'll be back as quick as I can."

"You don't trust me to investigate on my own."

"Admit it, Diana. You tend to rush into things without thinking them through first. I just want you to be care— I want you to protect yourself, since I won't be here to do it for you, especially if you decide to ask impertinent questions of people you suspect have committed murder."

"I can be subtle, you know."

"You haven't a subtle bone in your entire body. You always *confront* people."

They were nose to nose, all but shouting at each other, when Ben suddenly fell forward, bumping hard against Diana and nearly sending both of them tumbling to the ground.

"What the—?"

As Diana righted herself she craned her neck to see around Ben's imposing bulk. She thought someone must have pushed him, but that was not the case. Tremont stared back at her with slightly crossed eyes. She could have sworn the goat was smiling.

"I guess she doesn't like loud voices." Diana was unable to restrain a giggle.

"Either that or she's taken a shine to you and wants to protect you," Ben said, ruefully rubbing the back of his thigh. "That's one hard-headed goat."

Diana tried to avoid meeting his eyes, but it was impossible. The moment their gazes locked, they both burst out laughing.

"Hard-headed goat, hard-headed woman," he muttered when the mirth had subsided.

"High-handed man," she shot back. "I promise I'll be careful if you will."

"Done." He offered her his hand and they shook on it.

That evening, the Grant family and Mrs. Ellington once again gathered for a meal. Diana was their only guest, since Ben had left right after the incident with Tremont to fetch Howd back from Sundown. Sebastian Ellington had accompanied him. Diana was not certain why. According to Mercy, Sebastian had never visited Howd's mountain retreat before and would be no help finding the place. There was, to quote Mr. Lyseth, "no mortal reason" for him to have gone . . . except, perhaps, to get away from the scene of the crime for a while.

"You have outdone yourself with this meal, Mrs. Ellington," Diana said, savoring a bit of tender beef.

"Cooking soothes the soul," Tressa Ellington replied.

"We should expect to eat well, then," Mercy quipped.

Uncle Myron scowled at her. "This will all blow over. Wait and see."

"Uncle Myron, the coroner thinks you killed him."

"Nonsense, girl." But he didn't look as confident as he sounded.

Mashed potatoes turned to paste in Diana's mouth. She swallowed the lump and set down her fork. "We need to discover an alternate suspect." She gave Myron Grant a hard look. "You knew him best. Who would hate him enough to do that to him?"

"Don't know his enemies. His friends, either. If he had any."

"What about his backers?"

"Never met them."

"Perhaps they don't even exist," Diana murmured.

"They must," Myron insisted. "How else could he have hoped to turn Lenape Springs into another Saratoga? That's too big for one man to manage."

"Was that Saugus's idea or yours?" Diana asked.

"Mine," Uncle Myron said.

At the same time, Mercy said, "Sebastian's."

They all stared at her.

"You never talked so big before he came here, Uncle Myron."

A sheepish expression on his face, Myron avoided Mercy's gaze. "Seemed like it was worth a shot. *My* idea," he insisted, "but Sebastian thought it was a good one."

"Sebastian is an egotistical young idiot!" Mercy banged down her glass, sloshing water onto the lace tablecloth.

"He's older than you are, missy, and he knows more about hotels."

"He knows what's likely to make one fail!"

A painful silence fell, broken only by the scrape of Mrs. Ellington's fork against her plate.

"I . . . I didn't mean that the way it sounded." She shot a covert glance at Diana. "Sebastian's family, after all."

"If you overextend yourself with the renovations and

expansion," Diana asked Myron, "is Sebastian in a position to step in and take over?"

"That's family business, Mrs. Northcote," Myron snapped, "and it has nothing to do with Norman Saugus's murder. Sebastian didn't kill him. That's for sure. He had no reason. He didn't know about the arson."

Mercy jerked in her chair with an audible thump. "Arson? What arson?"

"It's not important now," Myron told her. "Don't worry your pretty little head about it."

"On the contrary," said a soft, feminine voice from the doorway. "Burning down this rattletrap was the point of the exercise."

Belle Saugus sauntered into the dining room, resplendent in mourning black. The impact would have been greater, Diana thought, had she covered that red hair and abstained from putting artificial color on her cheeks and lips.

Belle oozed close to Mercy and leaned down so she could look the younger woman in the eye. "You want to know about arson, dearie? My late husband planned to burn this hotel to the ground for the insurance." She glanced up at the rest of them and smiled. "I admit it freely. I even admit that Norman set that other fire, the one ten years ago that destroyed the west wing. The entire place should have gone up in flames then. As it was, we barely made enough from the insurance to live on for six months."

"Why are you telling us this now?" Diana asked her. "Aren't you afraid we'll repeat your confession to the authorities."

She seemed to consider this, then grinned. "No. Shall I tell you why? Because, naturally, I had no part in any of it. I'm an innocent victim myself, deceived by a conniving husband."

Diana waited for the other shoe to drop.

"But you, Myron Grant—" Belle left Mercy to glide to Myron's side and tap him lightly on the shoulder. "—you knew all about his plans."

A formidable glower accompanied his denial, but it didn't seem to bother the new widow one whit.

"Think, Myron dear, what would happen if I told the coroner—or better yet, the sheriff—that you were in on the arson scheme from the beginning. I'll do it if I have to. And I can also put the blame on you for Norman's murder . . . unless you give me what I want." She trailed her fingertips across his back and moved on to stand next to Diana's chair.

"What *do* you want?" Diana asked her.

"For the moment, to remain here. Oh, yes . . . and to have Norman's funeral taken care of."

"Meaning?" The thunderous look in Myron's eyes would have made a lesser woman quail.

"Run along down to Castine's Store like a good fellow and buy a casket, will you, Myron? Pay to see that he's properly laid out." She grinned. "Arrange for Pastor Riker to say a few words for the good of his soul."

"He didn't have one," Myron muttered.

"Now, now! Did no one ever tell you not to speak ill of the dead? I believe that's all I require for the moment. Later, after things settle down, I'm giving some consideration to carrying out Norman's original plan. The insurance money will provide me with a comfortable nest egg."

"You mean to burn down my hotel?" Myron's face turned an unhealthy shade of crimson and he started to rise from his chair. Only Tressa's hand on his arm stopped him.

Belle Saugus sent an approving look his way as she completed her circuit of the dining room table. "Now you're catching on. Better to lose the hotel than your life, don't you think? A word from me and you'll be arrested for murder. Think about that, Myron Grant. You'll soon see which course is the lesser of two evils."

"She does know how to make an exit," Diana murmured after the other woman had swept out of the room.

"She's unstable! Insane!" Myron's color had changed to ashen and his big hands were shaking. "She can't prove a thing."

"No, but she can make life difficult for you." Belle Saugus's low-key, calculated demand had been more unsettling than any hysterical threat.

"She probably killed him herself," Mercy muttered. "I wouldn't put it past her."

"Neither would I," Diana agreed, "but how do we prove it?"

"They weren't the most pleasant couple, but they always seemed to get along," Mrs. Ellington said.

"Not always. Ben and I heard them quarreling that first night. Their rooms are right below our suite."

"Well, all couples quarrel sometimes," Mrs. Ellington said.

"We couldn't make out all the words, but a few were clearly audible. They mentioned Elly Lyseth. Or rather Mrs. Saugus referred to *that girl.* She also used the words *crimes* and *scoundrel.*"

"There seem to be plenty of crimes to choose from when speaking of Norman Saugus," Mrs. Ellington said. "And there's no doubt he was a scoundrel. But I don't see—"

"We heard him say a few words, too. *Whore.*" She felt her face color, for a number of reasons, but she knew her listeners would assume it was only because that was not a term a lady ordinarily used in mixed company. "Then he said *stage,* which I now suspect means his wife was once an actress. And finally, he said the word *murderer.*"

"Stage could also refer to the Tally-Ho line," Myron said. "The stage that runs from Liberty to Jeffersonville."

"And what more natural to refer to Elly and her murder when her bones had just been found a few hours earlier?"

Diana looked from Mrs. Ellington to Myron and back again. "Are you trying to find excuses for her? She's planning to burn down the hotel."

"But murder? Of her own husband?" Mrs. Ellington looked aghast at the very idea. "And do you mean to suggest that she had something to do with Elly Lyseth's death, too?"

"That's exactly what I mean. At first I thought Belle Saugus might have killed Elly Lyseth because Elly was Saugus's mistress, but what if it was much simpler than that? What if Elly stumbled onto that first arson scheme—I have no doubt Belle was part of that, no matter what she claims now—and Elly was murdered to keep her quiet."

"Saugus murdered her?"

"That was my suspicion for a time, but it makes as much sense to think Belle killed her, and for the same reason—to keep her from revealing their plans. Perhaps Saugus didn't know about Elly's murder at the time. Perhaps he only put two and two together after Elly's bones were found. That's why they quarreled that night. That's why he spent the next day drinking. And that's why Belle had to kill him, too."

Diana's newest theory even made sense of the fact that the fire had been set several days after Elly disappeared. Belle could have killed Elly and hidden her under the floor, assuming the blaze would cover up her crime. With that wing of the hotel closed for the season, there had been little risk that anyone would discover the body in the interim.

"Can you prove any of this?" Myron asked.

"Not yet."

His expression bleak, Myron toyed with the food remaining on his plate. Belle's ultimatum had killed everyone's appetite. "If I survive the next few weeks," he muttered, "I vow I'll be content just being an ordinary innkeeper." He speared a Brussels sprout. "Though I do still think I can make something out of the mineral spring."

CHAPTER ELEVEN

ଧଠର

In June, July, and August, midday is usually hot," Sebastian proclaimed, "but the summer nights are cool. There are almost daily showers, but they don't last long."

Ben grunted and turned up his collar. Between that and the broad-brimmed hat he wore, only a few of the cold, wet drops found their way to his skin, but he was not accustomed to traveling long distances on horseback. He was heartily sick of the journey that had begun the previous afternoon by buckboard and had included a restless night in a hotel in Grahamsville, where he'd been obliged to share a room with Sebastian, who snored as loudly as a steam engine but with a less regular rhythm.

At least it had not been a wholly unproductive break in the journey. He'd seen a house in Grahamsville, built in a style that would suit Diana well. The entrance was by a neat and artistic porch, which was divided from the front veranda by a gothic arch. There were plenty of long windows, two towers, and a second floor balcony. He wished he'd had the opportunity to see the inside, but the outside alone had been enough to start him thinking about where they would live after they were married.

Before they'd left Denver, Diana had agreed to a June wedding, but they hadn't made any definite plans for the future. Perhaps Diana assumed they would live with his mother and brother, but Ben had reservations about sharing an abode with his eccentric family. He'd considered moving into the house that served as his office, but he liked this new idea better. He'd build Diana a house just like that one. He knew the perfect location for it, too.

Absorbed in his thoughts, Ben did not at first notice that Sebastian had veered off the main path. They'd been riding since sunrise, their pace excruciatingly slow since they'd left the hamlet of Eureka on a little-used, overgrown trail.

Sebastian stopped to consult a map, but it was not the one Myron Grant had drawn for them. That was currently in Ben's possession. This one was considerably older, and had been much folded.

"The missing map to the Indian lead mine, I presume?"

"Silver mine," Sebastian insisted with an unrepentant grin. "It's near here. I'm sure of it."

"If it still exists, and is worth anything, don't you think Howd would have discovered it by now?"

"It won't hurt to look."

"We're short on time. The sooner we find Howd and get him back to Lenape Springs, the sooner Myron will be exonerated." He hoped.

"Feel free to go on without me. I intend to search for the mine."

Ben didn't argue. It was clear to him now that this was the only reason Sebastian had volunteered to be his guide. Ben turned his horse around and soon regained the road that led to Howd's rustic retreat.

According to Myron's map, he had only another mile or so to go. Ben squinted through the drizzle, trying to see up ahead. Even below Sundown, where the country had been low and flat, groves of fern had grown out onto the trail. Here the woodland path was only wide enough for a single horseman and wound through the forest in serpentine loops that obscured his view of anything more than a dozen feet ahead.

It became even more rutted and winding as he rode higher, following the course of a creek off to his left. Ben suspected he'd make better time on foot. He was tempted to dismount and go the rest of the way by shanks' mare. The only thing that stopped him was his knowledge that here in New York State, in contrast to Maine, some of the snakes were poisonous. It would be far too easy to step on one in this rough terrain.

Without warning, the rain stopped and the sun broke through the clouds, revealing a glistening green world alive with small creatures. Ben watched as a red squirrel dashed up a nearby locust, came down again next to a cedar, and finally jumped to its home in a woodpecker's hole. A porcupine, disturbed by the passage of a human through its domain, chattered shrilly, setting Ben's teeth on edge. Small as it was, the porcupine was one of the few animals he feared encountering in the woods. The damage it could do to him, and his horse, didn't bear thinking about. Fortunately, he did not catch sight of the creature, though he did notice a hemlock it had stripped of its bark.

Rounding the next bend, he came suddenly upon a substantial dwelling and recognized it from the description he'd been given as what had once been the first Grant venture into innkeeping. The former hostelry and trading post had a dilapidated appearance, having been built at least a hundred years earlier, but it looked structurally sound.

In the old days, Ben supposed, this obscure track had probably passed for a highway. Surrounded by wilderness, the old Indian trails had provided vital links to civilization. Only later, when villages and hamlets sprang up closer to substantial bodies of water, would a place like this have been bypassed.

"Howd Grant?" Ben called. "You in there?"

Ben had not allowed himself to consider that he might have made this trip for nothing, that Howd might have taken off for parts unknown to avoid arrest for murder. Still, he was relieved when Grant came around the corner of the building, blinking in surprise.

"Why, Dr. Northcote." Howd looked puzzled to see him, as well he might. "I was just examining some tracks. Mink, I suspect. The creature leaves a rather distinctive five-toed footprints." He blinked owlishly. "Is something wrong?"

"You could say that," Ben answered, dismounting. "Norman Saugus has been murdered."

Blanching, his expression alarmed, Howd had trouble getting his next question out: "Who k-k-killed him?"

"We don't know. We're hoping you can help eliminate one or two possibilities."

"You'd better come in," Howd said, and led the way into the house.

Ben had expected it to be rough, and it was, with no running water and only oil lamps for light. He was unsurprised to discover that large windows had been cut in both the back walls and the roof to create an artist's studio. What did take him aback were the objects decorating the place. In among the sketchpads full of drawings and easels holding half-completed water colors, were dozens of stuffed animals and birds. On one wall a huge, glass-fronted case held a butterfly collection.

"Do you do the taxidermy yourself?" Ben asked, indicating a perfectly preserved hawk, wings outstretched.

"Yes. Beautiful, aren't they? They help me with the fine points when my preliminary sketches in the wild don't show enough detail."

Ben nodded agreeably, but he studied Howd with new eyes, as the naturalist heated coffee on a wood stove and served it up in chipped china cups. Perhaps he'd been too hasty to rule out Howd Grant as a suspect. Elmer Castine had said he had a temper, but Ben had taken Grant for a mild-mannered fellow because of the art he produced.

He should have remembered that naturalists were also scientists, a breed that, as a whole, put gaining greater knowledge of their subjects above any suffering those subjects might endure. Ben had first-hand experience of the way supposedly humane physicians, in the name of research, treated patients in insane asylums.

He accepted the coffee and drank half the contents of the cup. He hadn't realized how chilled he'd become on the ride.

"That one's a coon that used to live in a hollow beech near here," Howd said, pointing to a specimen, "and those are snowshoe hares from the willow swamp. There was a pine marten up in the trees I was hoping to trap. That's a big weasel with a spot of yellow on its brown throat."

"I'm familiar with the creature," Ben assured him. "Although Bangor is a city, it is surrounded by farms and forest. My medical practice regularly takes me out into the countryside." In addition, in years past, he had climbed mountains for recreation. "Ever have a problem with wolverines?" he asked.

"Neither wolverines nor fishers ever lived in the Catskills in any numbers."

"What about bobcats?"

"Wildcats, do you mean? I've never seen one but I've heard them. A shrill scream, and then a sobbing noise, like a baby after being spanked."

Ben would have said it was more of a rasping noise, but the description was close enough. "A sound to lift the hat right off your head," he agreed.

"Especially if you're alone in the woods at night at the time." Howd grinned. "I was coming home from visiting a lady friend first time I heard it, and the only thing I could think was that wildcats sometimes get as big as thirty pounds. Animal that size can pounce on a deer's head, bite down on the jugular vein, and have venison for a week. I sure didn't want him chomping on me!"

Grant's collection also included a fox, a gray squirrel, and a woodchuck that, incongruously, was wearing a hat. Ben honestly didn't know what to make of that.

He shifted his gaze to one of the paintings, a water color that showed a bird clinging to the underside of a limb. Butterflies drifted through one corner of the painting, and a squirrel peeked around the trunk of the tree.

"Nuthatch?" Ben asked, studying the bird.

"Red-breasted. Less common than the white-breasted nuthatch, but there are plenty of both around. They make a squeaky little cry. It's as impossible to mistake as the harsh scolding of a blue jay, or the warbles of the purple finch, or the arpeggios of the hermit thrush or the chip chip sound of a junco. Now, this is what I've been working on today." He indicated a half-completed painting. "That's a hairy woodpecker. Rarer and bigger than the downy woodpecker."

As he prattled on, Ben looked at the butterflies again, caught and pinned in place, dying so that they could become subjects of Howd Grant's art. Ben's brother studied subjects just as intently before he painted them. The difference was that Aaron used human models.

Ben frowned. Although Aaron kept them alive, the girls were just objects to him, bits and pieces to be used and discarded when the painting was complete. What was at first almost an obsession, accompanied by flattery and kindness, was later replaced by indifference, even cruelty, when he was ready to move on. Ben had heard him tell a girl she was too ugly to model for him anymore, simply because he'd found a new subject. Her tears had not moved him in the least.

Did Howd ever paint people? Ben wondered. In particular, had he ever painted Elly Lyseth? His water colors of animals, so beautiful and serene, gave no hint that living creatures had been killed to produce them.

Grant was still going on about woodpeckers when Ben interrupted him. "At what hour did you leave Lenape Springs?"

"I'm not certain, though it was in the middle of the night. The night Myron tried to kill Saugus. I was with my brother for awhile, then I went to my room, but I couldn't sleep." He shrugged. "It seemed like a good time to get away for a few weeks, so I left a note and came up here. Sometimes a man needs to be alone."

"Did you see Saugus again after the fight with Myron?"

"No. I didn't see anyone. It was quiet as a tomb when I left the hotel."

"How did you get up here?"

"I walked the five miles to Liberty."

"At night?"

"The moon was nearly full. Besides, I like to walk at night. I see well in the dark."

"And then?"

"I found rides with travelers driving wagons to get from Liberty to Neversink Flats and then from Neversink Flats to Grahamsville. I walked the rest of the way here."

"You need to come back with me," Ben told him.

"Why? Myron was still up when I left him. I can't prove he didn't kill Saugus." It apparently didn't occur to him that he could lie to help his brother.

"If you don't, suspicion may fall on you instead," Ben told him bluntly.

"Me? Who'd think I'd do such a thing?"

An hour ago, Ben would have said "no one." Now he wasn't so sure. You could never tell about the quiet ones.

By Tuesday afternoon, some twenty-four hours after Ben had left for Sundown, Diana was beginning to think that there must be secret passages in the Grant Hotel. Not only had she been unable to run Mercy to earth, but she couldn't seem to find Mrs. Saugus, either. Perhaps they were together in a hidden room somewhere. That theory made as much sense as any other!

Why on earth did her cousin continually find excuses not to talk to her? Diana had briefly entertained the notion that, as a child, Mercy might have known more than people thought about her father's romantic adventures, but she hadn't seriously considered Mercy a suspect in Elly Lyseth's murder. Perhaps she should have. Certainly the young woman was acting in a suspicious manner.

Diana continued along another hallway, stopping when she came to a alcove with a window offering a panoramic view. She could see the road from here, but there was no sign yet of Ben returning. She hoped he'd be back soon. She missed using him as a sounding board. She missed him in other ways, too, but in particular she liked being able to talk about anything and everything with him. Even when they quarreled, they ended up further ahead. He had a way of sparking insights in her. Sometimes it took her awhile to accept them, and even longer to be grateful to him for forcing her to look hard at some aspect of the situation, but Diana had long since accepted that she and Ben made a good team.

Did he feel the same way? She thought so. Sometimes. At others, she knew his protective instincts took over and he let his concern for her safety interfere with treating her as an equal partner.

With a sigh, she left the alcove and continued along the corridor, opening doors as she went to reveal bedroom after bedroom, each furnished and ready for the season. None of them contained Mercy Grant or Belle Saugus, but the last on this floor was occupied. Diana surprised Celia Lyseth putting fresh linens on the bed.

"You!" Mrs. Lyseth exclaimed, glaring at her.

"I beg your pardon. I was looking for Miss Grant." She retreated as Mrs. Lyseth advanced, hands curled into fists at her sides.

"I know about you! Spawn of the devil!"

"I beg your pardon?"

"Newspapers!" Mrs. Lyseth grimaced as she spat out the word.

"Yes, I am a journalist, Mrs. Lyseth," Diana said in her most placating voice, "and I have been assigned to report the facts concerning—"

"Hah! I know what you're up to!" Step by step she backed Diana towards the stairwell.

The temptation to turn and flee was great, but Diana withstood it. She stopped, her back literally against the wall beside the door to the stairs, and attempted to reason with the woman. "I mean you and yours no harm."

"No harm? No harm!" The second time the words were uttered in a screech that made Diana's ears hurt. "I know your sort."

"My . . . sort?" Diana was beginning to become alarmed for Mrs. Lyseth's health. The woman's face was a dangerously purple red and beads of sweat glistened on her upper lip. As her ample bosom rose and fell with ever increasing rapidity, she began to pant.

"What the newspapers did to Pastor Riker was a crime. He should have sued that scandal sheet! That's what Lida May says. All vicious lies. Tried to crucify him, they did."

Only the wild look in Mrs. Lyseth's eyes kept Diana from asking for details. Deciding it would be the better part of valor to unearth them from some other source, she posed a different question instead. "What is it you think I mean to do, Mrs. Lyseth?"

"Defame us." Without warning, Mrs. Lyseth grasped Diana's wrist, squeezing it so tightly that Diana was certain she'd have bruises. "Make us laughing stocks."

"There's nothing funny about the death of a young woman."

For a moment, Mrs. Lyseth looked confused. Her grip loosed, and Diana was able to pull free. "You mean Elly?"

"Of course I mean Elly. What else have we been talking about?" She rubbed her sore wrist, and inched closer to the door.

Diana had to admit, if only to herself, that she was of two minds about badgering the families of victims of crimes. She hadn't had to question grieving relatives when she'd reported on those few murders in Manhattan. There had been enough juicy details available without resorting to such low behavior.

"You can say what you like about Elly," Mrs. Lyseth announced.

"She was no better than she should be. But I won't have you casting aspersions on the righteous. We've a fine upstanding congregation. The chosen of God."

And who am I to argue with God? Diana prudently kept that thought to herself.

"Repent your evil ways!" Mrs. Lyseth's shrill voice rose to a new level, and she took another threatening step towards Diana.

The door behind Diana opened, and Floyd Lyseth stepped through. "That's enough, Celia. They can hear you all over the hotel."

"Stay out of this, husband. I am on a mission from God."

"You're a crazy old woman, that's what you are." He brushed past Diana and seized his wife by the shoulders, giving her a rough shake.

Celia Lyseth promptly burst into tears.

"Mr. Lyseth—"

Lyseth turned his scowl on Diana. "I've nothin' to say to you. We know why you're here."

Diana could see that both the Lyseths were upset. She told herself that they would naturally resent questions from the press. Elly had been their daughter, no matter that harsh words had marked their relationship with her.

"I have no intention of causing you further distress, Mr. Lyseth. If anything, I hope to alleviate your grief by revealing what really happened to your daughter."

"She died. That's enough." He enfolded his still sobbing wife into his arms and awkwardly patted her back. "She died the night she left us, the night her poor mother sobbed till dawn because that ungrateful child had said such terrible things to her." His eyes unfocussed, he stared past Diana. "Sat up all night, the both of us, and never knew she was lyin' there dead. We still thought she'd come back in the morning." He gave a short bark of mirthless laughter. "We'd have thrown her out if she had."

"I thought Elly packed up all her belongings and left town."

Wasn't that what Celia Lyseth had claimed? Diana wondered when Celia had made that discovery. Or had she made it? For all Diana knew, Elly's things were still in the Lyseth house. After all, Mrs. Lyseth's grasp of reality was tenuous, to say the least.

The Lyseths walked away from Diana before she could ask any more questions. She thought better of following them and instead retreated in the opposite direction, heading down the stairs.

The Lyseths, she decided, were bad-tempered and self-involved. They'd probably made Elly's life a misery. And it was possible they were more than that. Thoughtfully, she reconsidered Celia and Floyd Lyseth as suspects. Certainly each had demonstrated the potential for violence and passion and irrational behavior. In addition, Celia had come under Pastor Riker's influence this past year. She *might* have seen fastening an enemy to a cross as some sort of poetic justice. Especially if she thought that enemy had killed her daughter.

Frowning, Diana pushed open another door and entered the passage to the lobby. There was a flaw in her logic—Celia Lyseth didn't seem to care that her daughter had died. Did that make it more or less likely that she'd murdered the girl herself?

In addition, her husband appeared to have given her an alibi. She might have slipped out of the house after he'd fallen asleep. She might have known where to find Elly. But had the murder occurred at night?

Diana stopped in her tracks. She had meant to ask Uncle Howd where he'd last met with Elly and at what time of day. She needed to find out if anyone had seen her after that and, if so, whether she had been alone. People would have had no reason to remember, not when they'd all thought she'd run off with a peddler, but now that they knew she'd never left Lenape Springs . . . .

She needed to trace the drummer, too, Diana decided. Who knew what he might remember of events from that long ago autumn?

Oblivious to everything and everyone else, Diana headed for

the writing room. She seemed to do her best thinking there. Why, she wondered, had Sebastian told her to keep Mercy and Celia Lyseth apart after Elly's bones were discovered? She'd assumed at the time that it was because Mrs. Lyseth was so unpredictable in her behavior, but Mercy had been angry that day—at her father in particular. Why? Had it only been because she'd discovered he'd given Elly that locket? Or had there been more to it?

"Diana?"

Diana jumped, startled out of her reverie by Mercy's voice.

"I understand you've been looking for me."

Turning, Diana caught her cousin by the wrist, employing Mrs. Lyseth's tactic to keep hold of her quarry. "Come with me," she said, and led the way to the writing room.

When the door was firmly closed behind them and both women were seated on the comfortably upholstered wicker chairs that furnished the room, Diana looked her cousin square in the eyes. "Why have you been avoiding my questions?"

"I've been busy. The hotel—"

"No, Mercy. You've been avoiding me. You've never given me a chance to interview you about Elly."

"That's not true!" Mercy protested. "I told you I barely remember her."

"And I don't believe you. What are you hiding?"

Mercy was out of her chair and on her feet before Diana could stop her. She all but flew from the writing room, slamming the door behind her.

With a sigh, Diana pulled her list of suspects from the pocket of her skirt. She stared at it, her expression bleak. There wasn't anyone she could cross off . . . except Norman Saugus.

When an hour in the writing room resulted in no new inspiration, Diana returned to her suite and took a nap before the evening meal.

Well-rested, well-fed, and determined not to let Mercy out of her sight, Diana cornered her cousin the moment Mrs. Ellington began to clear the table. "A word with you," she said in an undertone. "Now, and in private. Or would you prefer I ask your uncle to insist on your cooperation and remain with us while you answer my questions?"

They adjourned to the veranda. Dusk was upon them, and in the dimness Diana could hear the hum of insects. Mercy plucked up two fans from a table and handed her one.

"Did you kill Elly Lyseth?" Diana asked.

Mercy's gasp could have meant anything. When she tried to turn away, Diana caught her forearm, forcing her to continue their conversation face-to-face.

"You were not an infant, and you were close to your father. You knew he was courting Elly Lyseth."

"I knew she'd seduced him!"

Diana let that go. "You resented her. You feared she might become your stepmother. You were jealous."

In the fading light, Diana could see Mercy's stricken expression. Finally, she nodded. "She wasn't good enough for him."

"Would any woman have been?"

That surprised a short bark of laughter out of Mercy. "No, I suppose not, but Elly Lyseth was the . . . the . . . town pump!" She blushed at using such a vulgar term, but shot Diana a defiant look.

"Did you know your father had given her the locket?"

"No. Not until it was found with her bones."

"Did you know the bones were there?"

"No! Diana, you must believe me. I had nothing to do with her death. I was heartily glad when she disappeared, but I didn't kill her. Nor do I know who did, except that it wasn't my father. He, poor fool, seems to have loved her."

"Then why on earth have you been avoiding my questions?"

"I was . . . ashamed."

"Of what?" They stood in shadow, and Diana hoped that would make it possible for Mercy to answer her at last. "Of what?" she repeated in a gentle but insistent tone of voice.

"I doctored a box of sweets with a purgative. If she ate them, they'd have made her terribly ill. But they wouldn't have killed her."

"When was this?" Diana had a feeling she already knew.

"The day before she disappeared."

Hearing the hitch in Mercy's voice, Diana patted her hand. "You're right. They wouldn't have killed her. And if you're thinking she might have become ill enough to fall and hit her head, I can assure you that she'd not have landed that hard without help. Either someone struck her down, or they thrust her away from them with sufficient force to crack open her skull."

She did not have to add that Elly's weakened condition, had she eaten the adulterated candies, might have made it easier on her killer. That was something they'd never know.

What's wrong with Sebastian?" Diana asked when she and Ben were alone in the elevator. It was after midnight, but she'd been back in the writing room, making a new list and trying to make sense of the old ones, when the weary travelers returned.

"Nothing an oatmeal bath and a good night's sleep won't soothe," Ben replied. "He went off on his own with the map to the Indian lead mine."

"Did he find it?"

"No, but he wandered into some swampy ground and a swarm of mosquitoes found him. He arrived at Howd's place just as the two of us were about to leave, one eye almost swollen shut and red spots all over his neck." They stepped out of the elevator and started down the corridor towards their suite. "I'm afraid I did not precisely uphold my oath as a physician."

"You refused to treat him?"

"Oh, I applied a salve for the worst of the itching—Howd keeps adequate medical supplies—but on the ride back I made sure he knew that mosquitoes spread malaria. I was quite graphic about the symptoms of that."

"Ben," she admonished him. "That's terrible. Did he believe you?"

"I think he did. He knows part of the reason people take summer vacations is to get away from summer diseases—malaria, yellow fever, and cholera in particular—and that there are fewer cases of those diseases, and fewer mosquitoes, for that matter, at higher altitudes and in temperate climates."

"I don't suppose you mentioned any of the opposing theories?"

"That such diseases are caused by phases of the moon, or perhaps by electricity? No, I did not. Don't tell me you believe such nonsense?"

Diana entered the suite ahead of him. "It was only last year that an authority on malaria said so, ridiculing the mosquito idea. It made headlines in the *Independent Intelligencer.*"

"It would," Ben muttered, and yawned. "Don't tell Sebastian. He deserves to worry. After all, he stole that map."

"Mercy will not be surprised."

"Howd has it now. He's going to have it framed, as you suggested."

When Ben had stoked the fire, they settled down on the sofa in front of it, and he gave Diana a brief summary of his adventures. The account reflected poorly on Sebastian.

By the time he'd finished, his eyes were drifting closed. "I want to tell you about our stop in Grahamsville," he murmured in a sleepy voice. "I hope it will interest you, but it has nothing to do with Saugus's murder."

Diana nudged his arm. "Can you stay awake a bit longer? I have a few things to tell you."

He yawned several more times during the recitation, but seemed to be paying attention. "Any conclusions?" he asked when she finished up with Mercy's confession.

"I've made a new list." She didn't bother to produce it from the pocket of her skirt. She had it memorized.

"Is it any shorter than the last one?"

She made a face at him, but he didn't see it. His eyes had closed again. She didn't have the heart to make him listen. She got him up and into the bedroom, out of his travel-stained clothes and into his muslin nightshirt, and into the big, sinfully soft bed. He was asleep almost as soon as his head hit the down pillow.

Diana stood smiling down at him. She tucked the blanket in under his chin, laid out his brocade dressing gown and embroidered slippers for the morning, and went back out into the parlor to bank the fire.

She'd tell him tomorrow about her new list. Maybe he could make some sense of it. As it stood now she had two possible motives for Saugus's murder—either Saugus had figured out who had killed Elly and had been murdered to keep him quiet; or, he'd killed Elly himself and someone else had realized it and killed him to avenge her death.

Determining *who* had murdered Saugus was harder. Her list of suspects was crowded, even after she left off family members. At the moment, Belle Saugus was at the top, followed by Celia and Floyd Lyseth. Diana had added Jonas Riker's name, at least until she discovered what he'd done to cause newspapers to "persecute" him. And last but not least, her list concluded with the ever-popular "person or persons unknown." The elusive drummer, perhaps?

CHAPTER TWELVE

❧∞❧

Diana flipped through a recent copy of *Good Housekeeping* while she waited for Ben to wake up, idly trying to decide whether to skim an article titled "Sending for the Doctor" or read the next installment of Helena Rowe's "Family Fashions and Fancies." Ben deserved to sleep in, but she was impatient to . . . do something.

A pity she did not know what.

She had been frustrated in her attempt to arrange a trip to Monticello, the county seat. When she'd first inquired about transportation, Uncle Myron had said flatly: "There's a murderer on the loose. You mustn't go alone."

"You could come with me," she'd suggested.

"Haven't got the time. Can't spare Lyseth to drive you, either."

And when she'd tried to hire the surrey, she'd been put off with the feeble excuse that Old Jessie needed shoeing. Luke Castine's look of surprise at his father's claim had convinced Diana that the blacksmith was just being contrary. And trying to protect "the little lady," of course. The effort was no doubt well-meant, but extremely annoying.

Arranging a visit to the county seat should have been a simple matter, but apparently it was not that easy to get there, even with an escort. There was no train that ran directly from Liberty to Monticello. For some inexplicable reason, Monticello was on a different line. The quickest route was to drive the five miles to Liberty, board the train that went to Weehawken but get off at Fallsburgh, and then take one of Royce's stages the rest of the way, an additional five miles.

Was it worth it, she wondered, just to talk to the sheriff? There was no guarantee he would agree to let her interview his prisoner, the notorious Sailor Jack. As for questions about the progress of the investigation into Norman Saugus's death, that, too, could be a waste of time and effort. The sheriff was not personally involved in the matter, although he was the one to whom any person arrested would be sent for incarceration in the county jail. Still, Diana had hoped he'd be inclined to share what he knew, that he might let some vital piece of information slip. People did tend to confide in her.

With a sigh she set the magazine aside unread. In spite of his dislike of her assignment, she could probably persuade Ben to take her, but first he had to wake up. She didn't begrudge him his need for sleep. It had been very late indeed when he'd returned. On the other hand, Uncle Howd had been up at the crack of dawn, anxious to talk to the coroner and provide at least a partial alibi for his brother's whereabouts on the night Norman Saugus was killed.

Perhaps she should have gone into Liberty with Uncle Howd. Instead, here she sat, twiddling her thumbs as the day slipped rapidly away from her. It was already after two.

She'd wanted to talk to Belle Saugus, but Belle had locked herself in her suite and refused to answer the door. Diana had just decided to walk to Castine's store and ask Mrs. Castine about the peddler with whom Elly had supposedly eloped, when the door to the writing room was flung open and a whirlwind entered.

"There she is!" a familiar voice cried. "And it's good it is to be seeing her at last."

"Mrs. Curran?" Diana blinked, unable at first to believe her eyes. What on earth was her landlady doing here?

Mrs. Curran was a small woman, but years on the stage had given her presence. She'd acted all the great Shakespearean heroines, losing every trace of her native Irish accent when she spoke the words of the bard. She'd toured throughout America and abroad. Diana sometimes thought Mrs. Curran knew *everyone* in the theater.

When she'd retired, the actress had purchased a small house on Tenth Street in Manhattan and opened the premises to female boarders. She'd made one stipulation—they must have a theatrical connection. At present the residents were two actresses, a dresser, and a seamstress who made theatrical costumes. That Diana was the widow of an actor had allowed her to join their ranks; that she'd included theatrical news in her column for the *Independent Intelligencer* had kept her there . . . and very nearly resulted in her eviction when Horatio Foxe had started adding scandal and innuendo to what Diana had written.

"Well, Mrs. Northcote?" Mrs. Curran demanded. "What have you to say for yourself? A fine thing it is to discover you've gone and married again and never so much as a word about it when last you wrote to me!"

Aware of Mercy standing in the background, ears flapping, Diana flushed. "It was . . . that is, I—"

"No! Don't bother to apologize. What's done is done. Though I was looking forward to attending a wedding. It's been many a long day since I've toasted a bride and groom." She came the rest of the way into the room and closed the door behind her, shutting Mercy out.

"Sit down, please," Diana said.

Mrs. Curran settled herself in a chair and put her feet up on the small footrest in front of it. "Ah, me. I'd forgotten how many stops trains make, and I had to be at the ferry before eight o'clock this morning!" Like most theatrical people, she was accustomed to sleeping somewhat later than that.

"You must be exhausted. Shall I send for refreshments?"

But Mrs. Curran waved off the offer and proceeded to give a full account of her journey. The first stop had been at Middletown, sixty-nine miles from New York. It had taken only two hours to go that far. From then on, however, stops had been more frequent, and she estimated it had taken five full hours for the entire trip from Weehawken to Liberty.

"I feel dusty and disheveled," she declared. "And stiff and sore, as well, though the reclining chairs were comfortable."

"You look remarkably fresh," Diana assured her. "Is that a new gown?"

"Do you like it?" Mrs. Curran preened. She was a skilled seamstress. With the help of her lodger, she managed to make clothes that were the latest stare in fashion. Pattern catalogs and copies of *La Mode Illustrée* were strewn all over her little sewing room on Tenth Street.

"Exquisite."

"I brought your trunk and boxes."

Taken by surprise, Diana gaped at her. "You brought my—"

"Yes. Good gracious, girl! Close your mouth. You'll catch flies."

"But I don't understand. Is that why you're here? I thought you'd come to answer my question about Belle Saugus. To be truthful, I expected you to send a telegram."

Mrs. Curran sniffed. "And why should I miss all the fun, I ask you? Is she still here?"

"Belle Saugus? Yes."

"Good. Then the trip's been worthwhile." She took a moment to survey her surroundings, looking more than ever like one of the birds in Howd's water colors as she turned inquisitive eyes this way, then that. "Not bad. Well, as I was saying, then, I received your letter and the sketch. It's a good likeness. I hadn't seen that woman in twenty years, but I recognized her at once. She was on the stage, as you guessed, but that wasn't how she made her mark.

She did that by being a notorious hotel thief."

"How do you—"

Mrs. Curran grinned at her. No one knew the little Irishwoman's precise age, but at the moment she looked more like a mischievous three-year-old than an aged crone. "I had my suspicions, but no proof, so I took your sketch to the 15th Precinct and showed it to that nice young Officer Hanlon. He took me to see Captain Brogan, and Captain Brogan had a book."

"The one Inspector Byrnes wrote?" Thomas Byrnes, Chief of Detectives, was the author of a volume called *Professional Criminals of America.* "Mr. Foxe owns a copy. He loaned it to me a few months ago. That was how I—"

Mrs. Curran cut her off. "So I discovered. And it's that man's copy I brought with me to show you."

Diana didn't know which astounded her more, that Belle Saugus was apparently included in Inspector Byrnes's book or that Mrs. Curran had voluntarily contacted "that man"—Horatio Foxe. She held him responsible for putting Diana's life in danger back in March and blamed him, too, unfairly, for interfering with Diana's plans to return to Maine, and Ben, in mid-April.

"Fascinating reading," Mrs. Curran declared. The heavy book took up almost all the space in the gripsack she'd brought with her into the writing room. "I'd no idea there were so many ways to break into a hotel room. You should warn the good folks here, especially as they're harboring a viper in their midst."

Diana tried to remember what she'd read about hotel thieves, but when she'd consulted the volume before, she'd been interested in a different type of criminal.

"Look here," Mrs. Curran said.

And there was Belle Saugus—Belle Rhymer according to the caption. She'd been arrested and sent to prison in 1874 at the age of twenty-five. She'd been released after serving two and a half years, but according to the text she'd not mended her ways. She was wanted for several more robberies. Her whereabouts in 1886, when Inspector Byrne's book was published, had been unknown.

"I remembered her because she was acting with a touring company when she was caught. She combined her professions, you see. At least, she did at first. She must have married your Mr. Saugus after she got out of prison. Perhaps she mended her ways." Mrs. Curran sounded doubtful.

"And perhaps she just took a partner," Diana mused, "and expanded into insurance fraud."

"You're not to bring the police in until you've interviewed her," Mrs. Curran warned. "That man wants his story in return for the loan of this book."

"I'm surprised he didn't bring it himself."

"Oh, he wanted to, but I think he's a bit intimidated by Dr. Northcote." She gave Diana a sly look from beneath her lashes. "It will be quite a surprise to him when he learns you've already married him. I could hardly believe it myself when that young woman at the reception desk told me that Mrs. Spaulding was registered as Mrs. Northcote. I thought you intended to wait until you returned to Maine to marry. I was quite looking forward to a trip to New England. Oh, well. I've treated myself to a visit here instead. It seems a nice enough place for a holiday. I've been assured I'll have a room with a view."

"It is an excellent hotel," Diana said, "but they aren't really open for the season yet."

"So I'm told, which accounts for the excellent rate the young lady offered. Don't look so concerned, Diana. I can afford a holiday. And I am looking forward to meeting Belle Rhymer again. Shall we go and talk to her now?"

"There's something you should know," Diana said. "Something happened after I wrote to you. Her husband was murdered."

The bright little eyes gleamed. "Well, now, that changes things. Did she kill him?"

"I don't know. It's possible. I'd rather she be guilty than my . . . host. The owner of the hotel, Myron Grant, is the one the coroner suspects."

"There's something you're not saying, but never mind that now."

"Mrs. Curran, you can't come with me. You'd be a distraction."

'You promise I can talk to her later?"

"I promise."

"Then I'll wait my turn, but tell me what you mean to do when you confront her."

"Only talk to her. Show her the book. See if I can get a reaction out of her."

"Hah. Be careful what you wish for. If she's a murderess, why should she hesitate to kill you, too?"

Diana brushed aside the suggestion. "I'll be safe enough. If she did kill her husband it must have been in the heat of passion. She can hardly have such strong feelings about me."

Mrs. Curran did not look convinced. "Take Dr. Northcote with you," she suggested as they left the writing room.

"No need."

Tressa Ellington, crossing the lobby, overheard. "You've just missed him," she said. "He was on his way to find you when Myron waylaid him, The two of them are closeted with Howd in the family parlor."

"Howd's back from Liberty?" And Ben was awake.

Mrs. Ellington nodded. "He says he talked to the coroner, but he doesn't look happy. I think Myron's still under suspicion."

"Well, we'll see about that," Diana said, and stalked off in the direction of the elevator.

"Where is she going?" she heard Mrs. Ellington ask Mrs. Curran. "The family quarters are the other way."

"It's a long story," Mrs. Curran replied, "but if you could see your way to providing a cup of tea, I'd be happy to tell it to you."

෨෬

Belle did not acknowledge Diana's first knock.

"Mrs. Saugus!" she called. "We need to talk."

When she still received no answer, she raised her voice, and the ante: "Let me in, Miss Rhymer, or the next person to come calling will be the sheriff."

"What do you want?" Belle demanded, flinging wide the portal and stepping back so that Diana could enter.

"So gracious," Diana murmured, accepting the invitation.

Belle ignored the sarcasm. "Say your piece and get out."

"I've heard it said that a picture is worth more than ten thousand words. An old Chinese proverb, I believe." She held out the book, open to the appropriate page.

"I don't—" Belle froze, a stricken expression on her face. She stared at her own likeness, which was grouped in a rogues' gallery with five other felonious females. "Dear heavens!"

"You didn't know you were included here?"

"I didn't even know such a thing existed." Taking the volume from Diana, she glanced briefly at the title page, saw Inspector Byrnes's name, and winced. Then she returned to the page with her photograph. "How dreadful I look! I remember now how they made me pose for it. Face forward. No expression. They were determined to make me look as ordinary as possible."

In fact, Diana recalled, they were attempting to prevent her from distorting her face and confounding recognition. Inspector Byrnes had written that prisoners often tried to present a false physiognomy for the camera, although he claimed that their grimaces were always in vain and that there was not a portrait in his book that did not have some marked characteristic by which one could identify the person who sat for it. Mrs. Curran's keen eye and excellent memory had easily made the connection between a young actress, an old photograph, and an amateur artist's pencil portrait.

"You're a hotel thief," Diana said. "The police in several cities have outstanding warrants for your arrest."

"I've not stolen a cent in years," Belle was reading her case history and did not look pleased.

Diana drifted close enough to see the text over her shoulder: "Thirty-seven years old in 1886," Inspector Byrne had written. "Medium build. Height, 5 feet 4 ½ inches. Weight, about 135 pounds. Red hair, hazel eyes, light complexion. Her nose has been broken."

Diana gave Belle a sideways glance. The bump that signaled an old break was barely noticeable unless one were looking for it.

"Belle Rhymer is a well known female hotel thief," Inspector Byrnes's text continued. "She is considered a very clever woman and is known in all the principal cities East and West. She was arrested in New York City for an attempt at grand larceny and tried, found guilty, and sentenced to two years and six months in State Prison, by Judge Sutherland, on April 6, 1874. She was released in October of 1876 and is believed to have resumed her career as a hotel thief. Her picture is a good one, although taken twelve years ago."

"Fourteen years ago now," Belle grumbled, "and the man is mad if he thinks that is a good picture. Look at my hair! Look at that dress!"

"Did your husband know you had been in prison?" Diana asked.

"What are you really after?" Belle demanded. "If you meant to have me arrested, the sheriff, or more likely the local constable, would already be here."

"First," Diana said, "you will stop making threats against Myron Grant. If you accuse him, I will tell the authorities about your past. They're not likely to believe anything you say once they know you've been in prison."

"I suppose you want me to leave here, too?"

Diana hesitated. She did not. How could she prove this woman had killed both Elly Lyseth and Norman Saugus if Belle left Lenape Springs? "Has anyone told you I write articles for a newspaper?" she asked.

"Which one?"

"The *Independent Intelligencer.*"

Belle's eyes went from one stock theatrical expression to another in an instant, first suspiciously narrowed, then widened in surprise. "Didn't think they had *ladies* working there."

Diana ignored the implication. Indeed, she hoped to play on Belle's assumption that she lacked scruples. "I want an interview, Belle. A confession of *all* your crimes. In return, I might be prepared to help you . . . relocate. If the authorities arrive after you've left, it will hardly be my fault."

When Belle looked doubtful, Diana sweetened the pot with the possibility of a bribe. "I don't have much money here, but —"

"I'll take your ring," Belle interrupted. "And any other jewelry you've got. And Dr. Northcote's gold pocket watch."

Inwardly, Diana winced. In spite of her qualms about wearing it under false pretenses, she'd sooner part with her entire wardrobe than the tourmaline wedding ring Ben had bought for her. Still, this was no time to quibble. She didn't mean to honor the bargain in any case.

"Done. Now—your confession?" She whipped out her little green, leather-covered notebook and a pencil.

Belle settled herself comfortably, waving Diana into a chair, and launched into an account of her days as a hotel thief. "There's a thrill to it," she confided. "You risk being caught at any moment. There you are in the hallway, inserting a pair of nippers into the keyhole to catch the end of the key. Anyone could come by. And inside, the unwary victim is in his bed, asleep, but likely to awaken if he hears a noise."

"I thought hotel thieves preferred empty rooms."

"Where's the excitement of that? Small nippers, a bent piece of wire, and a piece of silk thread are sufficient to unlock almost any door. I always took the time to lock the door behind me again, too."

"What about locks with thumb bolts?"

"Well, those do have to be fixed in advance to open. Means a lot of waiting, sometimes even months. Have to go away and come back again."

"But there's a way to do it?" Diana was genuinely curious to hear what Belle would say.

"Oh, yes. First you take the room yourself and file a slot in the spring bar of the thumb plate. Then later, you stay in another room at the hotel and keep an eye on the hotel register until a likely prospect occupies one of the fixed rooms—someone in the habit of wearing costly jewels, for instance. That's the time to strike."

"Did you sometimes have several rooms 'fixed' at the same time?"

"On occasion, yes. The real trick is to be aboard a train, on the way to another town, well before the crime is discovered."

"Did you go back to doing that after you got out of prison?"

"And other things." Her lips tilted up in a reminiscent smile. "Norman dreamed up one particularly delightful swindle. Shall I tell you about it?" She didn't wait for confirmation. "We would visit a bookstore and he would pretend to order books. While the sales clerk was occupied, I'd steal letter paper or bill heads from the business. Then we'd forge orders for books and sell them at about half the trade price. Pure profit, since the book store got the bill."

There were other tales in a similar vein, and Belle gave every appearance of candor as she confided story after story. Diana found herself almost liking the woman—for her enthusiasm, if not her moral character. With an effort, she reminded herself that Belle Saugus was not some charming female rogue. She was quite possibly a murderess, and definitely a liar. It would be a foolish reporter who believed everything she was told.

"You and Norman made quite a team," Diana said, letting admiration creep into her tone, "but you quarreled when you came here. We heard you the night Elly Lyseth's body was found."

Belle's hands, which had frequently been in motion as she talked, stilled in her lap. She lowered her eyes, hiding her expression. "I think he might have killed that girl," Belle said. "I know he was the one who set the fire. I knew nothing about it at the time, of course. And it was an empty threat on my part to set another one. I am a peaceable sort. I don't hold with arson. Or murder. I was just trying to up the ante before I asked Myron for money. He'd have paid, too, to get rid of me."

Diana leaned eagerly forward. "Have you any proof your husband killed Elly?"

"Only my instincts. He was extremely upset that she'd been found." She, too, leaned forward. She spoke in a whisper. "You must know the look a man gets when he's feeling guilty about something. Norman had it that night. And when he holed up in this suite the next day . . . well, you'll have guessed, I suppose. He was drinking heavily."

"But he seemed so cheerful when I first met him," Diana protested. "And that was right after Elly's bones were found."

"All an act, my dear. All an act. Why do you think we fought later that night? He'd been holding his emotions in check. He was drawn tight as a bowstring by the time we returned to this suite."

Diana wasn't sure she believed Belle but did not say so. Instead she asked, *"Why* did he kill Elly Lyseth?"

"I assume she was in the wrong place at the wrong time and somehow learned about his plans to burn down the hotel."

"Then who killed your husband?"

"Why, someone who knew he murdered the girl, of course. He was afraid he'd been found out. That's why he got so drunk." She looked pleased with herself at this deduction. Too pleased.

It was a plausible tale, Diana supposed. But it was also most convenient for Belle. Successfully blame everything on Norman, who was no longer around to defend himself, and she would get clean away.

"I want to go through your husband's papers," Diana said.

Belle's eyes narrowed. "Why?"

"Why do you think? To find out if he left some evidence behind. Of fraud. Of arson. Of murder. You don't get paid until I've seen all there is to see."

"Fine! If that's the way you want it, help yourself." She waved Diana towards the bedroom.

Diana was appalled when she saw how many more boxes of papers there were in the inner room. Some contained blank documents, like the one she'd filched the night of the quarrel between Saugus and Uncle Myron. But others had been used. Apparently Saugus had defrauded a great many people over the years.

She caught Belle's sleeve as the widow tried to retreat into the parlor. "You'll have to earn your freedom, Belle. Go through everything. Make an inventory. Fill in any details you know that aren't contained in your late husband's notes. When you've done that to my satisfaction, I'll pay you. Not before."

Belle's response was a profane tirade including a pithy suggestion about what Diana could do with herself, one Diana had never heard pass a woman's lips before. She ignored both the words and the venomous tone.

"Your choice." She swept out of the suite, taking *Professional Criminals of America* with her.

Diana had no intention of giving up her wedding ring, no matter how good a job Belle did. In fact, she rather hoped Belle would renege on the deal and end up in jail. Diana was resolved to return later and look for evidence herself, but for now she'd had enough of Belle Saugus . . . and of the stifling smell of Belle's patchouli sachets.

⁂

Ben was not in a good mood. He'd overslept, then been rushed into a meeting with Myron and Howd. By the time he was free to look for Diana, it was nearly four in the afternoon and she was nowhere to be found.

He opened the door to the kitchen and found Tressa Ellington entertaining a small, birdlike woman of indeterminate age. "I beg your pardon. I was looking for my wife."

"She's talking to Belle, Dr. Northcote," the woman said.

"Mrs. Curran?" Ben had only met Diana's landlady once, but it was undoubtedly she.

"I brought Diana's trunk, and a few other odds and ends."

"She expected you'd reply by telegram," he blurted.

She laughed at his embarrassment and graciously accepted his apology for rudeness. "Surprised you, I expect. But once I recognized Belle, I—"

"You did know her, then?"

"I did, yes. And more." She gave him a succinct summary of what she'd told Diana. Mrs. Ellington's lack of surprise indicated she'd already heard the tale. "I wanted to go with Diana to question her, but she said she'd do best on her own."

Ben bit back a curse. Diana thought the woman was a murderess and she'd gone to confront her alone. Madness! "How long ago?"

"Oh, an hour at least."

He took heart in that he'd heard no screams, no gunfire, no explosions. But he still didn't like leaving Diana alone with Belle Saugus. "Excuse me, Mrs. Curran, Mrs. Ellington. I believe I will join the ladies upstairs."

Mrs. Ellington blocked his retreat. "Are Howd and Myron still at it?"

"They're trying to think of a safe way to deal with Belle's threats," he replied. When he'd left them, they'd just broached a fresh bottle of dandelion wine.

"I believe your wife may have solved that problem," Mrs. Ellington declared.

"I'll just go and see, shall I?"

"I'll come with you," Mrs. Curran declared. "I've a few things to say to Belle Rhymer."

"Not without me, you won't," Mrs. Ellington declared. "Just let me make one stop first. We can't be too cautious if she's all you say she is."

Mrs. Ellington headed for the lobby at a fast clip. Since that was also the way to the elevator, the quickest route to Belle's suite, Ben followed her. She'd already reached the little room behind the check-in desk by the time Ben and Mrs. Curran caught up, but she'd stopped dead in the doorway. Although her body blocked Ben's view, he could hear every word she spoke.

"You ungrateful wretch! Put those papers back where you found them."

"No harm done, Aunt Tressa. I was only curious."

"I've no patience with you, Sebastian. Not anymore. I'm tired of your lies and your conniving. I think it's time you went back to your parents." At last she moved, stepping into the room and going directly to the roll-top desk. She opened a bottom drawer and withdrew a pistol.

"Good God, Aunt Tressa! There's no need to overreact."

Ben reached the door in time to see Tressa Ellington's startled expression. It was clear to him that she'd been after the gun to take along on the visit to Belle Saugus, possible murderess, and equally obvious that Sebastian read a different intent into her actions. Mrs. Ellington studied her nephew's face. Then she lifted the gun and pointed it directly at Sebastian.

"Don't make me resort to desperate measures," she told him. "They say confession is good for the soul."

Sebastian swallowed hard, his eyes glued to the barrel of the pistol. It was a scant foot from his head as he knelt on the floor beside the desk. Scattered around him were several legal-looking documents.

"Well?" Mrs. Ellington's voice brooked no argument.

"Fine! Have it your way. I came to Lenape Springs to worm my way into Uncle Myron's confidence. He doesn't have a son. Why not make me his heir?"

"He has other nephews."

"Oh, believe me, I know it. That's why there's no chance my father will leave me *his* hotel. My oldest brother gets that." The bitterness in his tone matched the sour expression on Sebastian's face. "But I always intended to have a place of my own someday. Why not this one? Why not now?"

"Got impatient, did you? Maybe you've been helping things along a bit? Planting ideas in Myron's head? Bad ideas? What were you looking for in Myron's papers?"

When she gestured with the pistol, Ben's heart leapt into his throat. Few things were as frightening as a woman holding a gun that, in all probability, she did not know how to use.

Sebastian rose slowly to his feet and backed up a couple of steps. When she waved the gun at him again he prudently raised his hands. "This hotel was left to *all* Grandfather Grant's children. The others signed their shares over to Uncle Myron, but without that paper, any of his siblings could make a claim. My mother, for example."

Mrs. Ellington glanced at the documents on the floor. "Did you find it?"

"No."

"Empty your pockets."

The gun convinced him to obey. His breast pocket yielded an envelope of the sort lawyers used.

"Dr. Northcote, if you would be so kind?"

Ben made short work of opening the envelope and skimming its contents. "It's the agreement to give Myron the hotel," he confirmed.

"You young fool." Mrs. Ellington's tone left no doubt of her disgust with her nephew. "What good did you think it would do to steal this? Even if it's the only copy, which I doubt, destroying it would result in all the Grants having a say in what happens to the hotel. You might persuade Sally Ann to sign over her share to you but the other Grants would simply outvote you when you tried to take over."

"There are four sisters and two brothers. I've already convinced three of the sisters to back my plans for the hotel, and I've got a line on the fourth. Seems Aunt Elmira has a score to settle with Uncle Myron. She's not going to stand in my way."

Ben decided it was time to step in. He relieved Mrs. Ellington of the pistol, discovered with some relief that it was not loaded, and slipped it into his pocket. Then he turned to face Sebastian. "Did Mrs. Torrence contact you, or was it the other way around?"

"Why should I tell you?"

"Because I asked so nicely?" Ben seized Sebastian by the shirtfront and gave him a shake. "Answer the question."

"It wasn't Aunt Elmira. Not directly. It was Ed Leeves who got hold of me, about six months ago. He used to live in this town. Guess he doesn't much like the Grants, either."

Ben released his prisoner. Ed Leeves. Lida Rose Riker's older brother. The man who was trying to convince Diana's mother to marry him.

"I'll take care of this," he said to Mrs. Ellington. "I'll send Leeves a telegram tomorrow."

"You can make him back off?"

"Yes." He hoped he could. If not, he'd have to warn Myron what was afoot, and that would mean a premature end to Diana's deception.

"What's going on in here?" Mercy burst into the small room, took one look at the scattered papers and the document now in Mrs. Ellington's hands and gasped. "Oh, Sebastian. How could you?"

"How could I what, cousin? Look out for myself?"

"He set Myron up," Mrs. Ellington cut in. "Encouraged him in his foolishness. Saugus alone would never have persuaded Myron that Lenape Springs could be another Saratoga. It took Sebastian to convince him of that, and all so he could look like he was saving the hotel when he took over."

"Were you behind murder and arson, too?" Mercy hurled the harsh accusation at her cousin, then launched herself, pummeling his chest with her fists. "Villain! Traitor."

"Stop it, you little vixen!" He pushed her away. When she came right back at him, he hit her across the face with the back of his hand.

The blow sent her spinning into Ben. They both crashed to the floor, and Sebastian leapt over them.

"Are you all right?" Ben asked Mercy, righting himself and pulling her up after him. She looked stunned, and the print of Sebastian's hand was livid on her cheek.

"We'll look after her," Mrs. Ellington said. "You catch Sebastian. Don't let him get away."

Sebastian was still on the veranda when Ben overtook him, caught him by the shoulder, and swung him around. Sebastian reacted with a right hook that clipped Ben's jaw.

"Damnation," Ben swore. "I don't want to fight you."

"Then don't," Sebastian shot back, following the words with a roundhouse punch that once again connected with Ben's face.

The burst of pain was so intense it made his eyes water, and all the frustration he'd been feeling exploded. Mindless rage took over, egging him on as he fought back. He ducked in time to avoid being hit again, but he had gone beyond merely defending himself now. He was aware of nothing but the blazing agony in his jaw and the need to inflict equal pain on his opponent as the two of them grappled at the top of the veranda stairs.

He didn't know how many blows they'd traded before Sebastian's foot slipped and sent them both tumbling down the short flight of steps to the ground. Tremont the goat, munching grass nearby, bleated indignantly and sidled farther away.

The incongruous sound penetrated the red haze of Ben's anger. Panting, he blinked his eyes clear of sweat and realized that Sebastian, equally winded, lay on his back beneath him. The other man had the beginnings of a spectacular black eye, the one that was already puffy from the mosquito bites. Blood trickled out of a nose that was probably broken.

Ben didn't imagine he looked much better, and that second blow had broken a tooth clear down to the nerve. With an effort, he seized control of his temper, but the pain did not abate. "Yield?"

Sebastian nodded.

Ben heaved himself to his feet and offered Sebastian his hand so that he, too, could rise.

Everyone in the hotel seemed to have gathered while they were engaged in fisticuffs. Ben dusted off his trousers, uncomfortably aware of being watched by Mrs. Ellington and Mrs. Curran, Mercy, Myron, Howd, both Lyseths, and Diana. Only Belle Saugus was missing.

Mercy stood beside Myron, speaking to him in low, urgent tones, undoubtedly informing him of Sebastian's perfidy. Once Ben saw that she was uninjured, he lost interest in her. His gaze shifted to Diana.

"You're safe," he said when she'd made her way down the steps to his side.

"Why wouldn't I be?"

He just gave her a look. She flushed.

He started to say more, but the intense pain in his jaw stopped him. His hand went to his cheek. The blow that had damaged his tooth had, not surprisingly, broken the skin, as well. His face was already swelling. "Damnation."

"What's wrong?"

"Tooth. Fractured."

It hurt to talk, and he realized he was speaking with a lisp. That tooth was going to have to come out. There was no help for it. He caught Howd's attention as the other man took hold of Sebastian.

"Is there a dentist nearby?"

Howd turned his mild gaze on Ben and Diana. "In Liberty. If you leave right away you should be able to drive there, have your tooth extracted, and still be back before dark."

"Just barely." Myron seized Sebastian's free arm but addressed Ben. "Want me to pull it for you?"

Diana stepped into the breach to decline the well-meant offer. "No doubt you could draw the tooth, but without proper dental implements, the risk of infection is much too great. Bad enough what a trained dentist will do."

While Tressa Ellington fetched ice, Howd provided directions to find the dentist's office. "It's right on the main street in Liberty," he said, eyes twinkling with what Ben took to be sympathy. "You can't miss it."

CHAPTER THIRTEEN

Diana drove the surrey from the livery stable, moving along at a good clip that should bring them to their destination in half the time it had taken Floyd Lyseth to drive from the depot to Lenape Springs that first day.

Ben wanted to ask her what she'd said to Belle Saugus, but talking just now was a torment he chose to forego. Obviously, she'd come to no harm.

After the first mile, she volunteered a brief summary of their meeting. If he could have spoken, he'd have been swearing. If he could have borne the pain, he'd have been gnashing his teeth.

"She seems to have taken what I said to mean only lesser crimes," Diana concluded. "She confessed to nothing worse than theft. She put the blame for everything else on her late husband. She's lying, of course. Well, it's only to be expected. She doesn't want to be executed for murder."

Ben grunted. New York had a death penalty. Maine did not. It had been abolished the previous year. And that was neither here nor there. If the woman was a killer, as Diana seemed convinced she was, then the last thing they wanted was for Belle to think Diana was a threat to her.

The surrey hit a rut and a new jolt of pain shot through Ben's jaw. Ruefully, he acknowledged that it hadn't been any more sensible for him to fight with Sebastian than for Diana to confront Belle. He didn't often lose his temper like that. Hadn't in years. The last time had been a knock-down, drag-out fight with his brother. Thank God there had been no serious injuries this time. When all was said and done, he deserved a little pain and the loss of a tooth for so far forgetting himself as to engage in fisticuffs.

He slanted a sideways glance at Diana. A lesser man would shift the blame to her. It all came back to Diana. Her family's feuds. Her family's greed. Her editor's need for scandal to sell newspapers.

"What was Sebastian's plan?" Diana asked abruptly. "To take over a hotel on the brink of bankruptcy?"

Guessing she'd caught part of Mercy's explanation to Myron, Ben nodded.

"Not very clever of him."

Greed, Ben thought, made people do strange things.

"I'll send a telegram to my mother while you're at the dentist's office," she continued, "and tell her to call off Ed Leeves."

So, she'd heard that too. She could save him the trouble of contacting Leeves. Just as well. He was having difficulty thinking straight through the pain in his jaw. Composing a coherent telegram was probably out of the question.

They made the rest of the trip in silence, although Ben found reassuring the fact that Diana shot frequent worried glances his way. When they'd passed the depot, Diana guided Old Jessie down a steep hill and into the business district, turning left at the intersection. The directions Howd had given them led, as promised, straight to a small house with a large tooth painted on a sign by the side door.

They were shown into a tidy little waiting room furnished with several chairs and a selection of magazines. From the inner office came an ominous moan. If his jaw hadn't been so swollen, Ben might have considered walking out. Instead he went to inspect the framed diploma displayed on one wall.

He was encouraged by the fact that the man had a proper dental education. There were far too many old-fashioned tooth-drawers around, quacks whose limited skills did more harm than good. He'd heard horror stories of men who'd lost large pieces of bone along with a tooth, or had their jaws broken during an extraction.

"Oh, my." Diana, standing beside him, was looking not at the name of the medical college, but at the name of the dentist— Arthur P. Buckley. "You don't suppose—"

"Dr. Northcote," said the familiar voice of the coroner. "I understand you have a tooth that needs extracting."

"Go send the telegram," Ben lisped. It had to be pulled but he preferred not to chance disgracing himself in front of the woman he loved.

When both Buckley's previous patient and Diana had left, Ben squared his shoulders and followed the dentist into his inner room. It was clean and well organized, with neatly arranged supplies of gutta percha, amalgam, gold foil, and porcelain on shelves and a collection of anesthetics that included nitrous oxide and cocaine as well as Letheon. Next to a drill with a treadle engine, given pride of place, was a pump-type hydraulic dental chair.

"Have a seat," Buckley said, indicating the chair. "Let's have a look."

"It's broken off too close to the gum to save," Ben told him. He'd taken a look in the mirror before leaving the hotel. The stub would have to come out. When the hole healed, he'd see about being fitted with a porcelain tooth.

"Who's the dentist here?" Buckley asked.

Reluctantly, Ben settled into the chair. He tensed when it was moved into a reclining position. He did not like feeling this vulnerable.

"Open up. Hmm. Well, you're right. Extraction is the only option. Anesthetic?"

"No." There was no way to judge how much gas to give and dangerous overdoses were far too common. Besides, he hated losing consciousness even more than he disliked enduring pain.

"This won't take but a moment, and I assure you you'll feel much better when I'm done," Buckley said. "I find the pelican the most useful tool for extractions because it takes out the tooth more promptly than the gum lancet or the punch, or the pinchers, or the lever. Hold still, now."

There were times when medical training was not a blessing. Ben knew that the pelican was also the most dangerous of the instruments used in drawing teeth. True to his word, however, Buckley completed the task quickly. When Ben had finished washing the blood out of his mouth, the dentist presented him with a glass of whiskey.

"Antiseptic *and* good for pain."

Ben had to agree. His jaw was still swollen, since he'd bitten the inside of his cheek and had the skin on the outside broken by Sebastian's fist, but the pain was manageable now, reduced to a dull throb. The ache in his hand was greater.

Glancing down at his scraped knuckles, Ben recalled Diana cleaning him up and putting his clothing to rights before they'd left Lenape Springs. He'd been so fixated on his tooth that he'd paid no attention to the other cuts, scrapes, and bruises. When he got back to the hotel, he decided, he'd mix up a sleeping powder from his medical supplies. Rest was the best cure for all his injuries.

"It's obvious you've been in a fight," Buckley said. "Did it have anything to do with Mr. Saugus's murder?"

"No. As it turns out, this matter was completely unrelated. A pity."

"I agree. Mr. Howard Grant came to see me this morning. His deposition doesn't clear his brother, but with nothing more to go on, I'll not be ordering Myron's arrest, either. Not yet, at any rate."

"That's good to hear, since he didn't kill Saugus."

"How can you be so sure?"

"Instinct?"

Buckley frowned. "I'm not certain I agree with you, and certainly some of the villagers do not. If I were you, I'd think about cutting short your stay at the Hotel Grant. Things could get ugly out there."

Ben thanked him for the warning, wishing he could follow the advice. He'd like nothing better than to take Diana and head for Maine.

A few minutes later, he heard the surrey pull up in front of the dentist's office and went out.

"Better now?" she asked, as he clambered onto the front seat beside her.

"Improving by the minute. Did you send the telegram?"

She nodded, but he could tell by the hesitation in her manner that something was bothering her.

"What's the matter, Diana?" He caught her hand as she was about to lift the reins. They could sit here in front of the dentist's office a few minutes longer. Even with a comfortable bed and a soporific waiting at the other end, he wasn't anxious to begin the long, rough ride back to Lenape Springs.

"While I was at the telegraph office, the operator gave Scorcher a telegram to deliver here in Liberty. He said to take it to the place two doors past Old Man Torrence's. Do you suppose I have family in town? My father's relatives?"

Had he been in better shape, Ben supposed he might have tried to counterfeit a reaction in keeping with his supposed ignorance of such a possibility, but he was not at his best.

Diana noticed the lack of surprise in his expression and leapt to the obvious conclusion. "You already knew!"

Warily, he nodded.

"How could you keep something like this from me?"

"I intended to tell you."

"When?"

Good question, he thought. "There hasn't been much opportunity. We've been here less than a week and a great deal has happened."

"But you *knew* I had Torrence kin here in town. Who are they? How are they related to me?"

They were still sitting in the surrey in front of the dentist's office. Ben glanced at the sky. The afternoon was on the wane, but there were probably two hours of daylight left. A full moon had already risen and wouldn't set until midnight. They wouldn't have any difficulty making the drive back to Lenape Springs after dark.

"Isaac Torrence is your grandfather. He lives with his daughter, your aunt Janette, who is a widow. We can go see them now, if you like."

"But . . . but I can't just walk in on them."

Time to confess all, Ben decided. "They want to meet you. Howd talked to them and—"

"*Howd* knows I'm his niece?"

"So does Mrs. Ellington. She overheard us talking that first night and told Howd. No one else knows, though, except Mr. Torrence and his daughter."

"How could you keep this from me? You *can't* claim it was for my own good. Not if they want to see me." Then she frowned. "They don't know about my father, do they? No, they couldn't. Oh, Lord—how am I to tell them? Maybe this isn't a good idea. I'll meet them another day."

The pulse in Ben's forehead began to twitch. Why should he feel guilty for keeping secrets when Diana kept changing her mind? Asserting himself, he took the reins away from her and set Old Jessie in motion.

"I just don't know what to do." Diana scarcely seemed aware that they'd left Dr. Buckley's office, nor did she notice when Ben turned down a side street.

"Yes, you do," he said, bringing the surrey to a stop in front of a plain, white clapboard building. "We're here. This is your grandfather's house."

Diana stared in panic at the structure. An angular woman in faded pink calico was giving the wrap-around porch a vigorous sweeping. "I can't. I'm not ready. I-I-I . . . ."

Her voice trailed off as the woman caught sight of them, read Castine's sign on the side of the surrey, and abruptly abandoned her broom. A moment later, she was standing at Diana's side. "You're her, aren't you? You're my niece. Howd said you were staying in Lenape Springs."

The intense emotions swamping Diana prevented speech, but she was able to nod. Then she couldn't say a word because she was engulfed in a smothering embrace.

The traces of family resemblance she'd sought in vain in the Grants were found with a vengeance in the Torrences. Diana's aunt, who introduced herself as Janette Farquhar, had William Torrence's eyes and chin. Or rather, Diana corrected herself when she was taken inside the house and got her first look at her grandfather, both of Isaac Torrence's children looked eerily like him. If her father had lived to the same age as her grandfather, Diana realized, his face would have taken on all the same planes and angles.

Isaac Torrence's shoulders stooped. His hands were gnarled and liver spots disfigured his skin. But he carried himself with pride, and his Torrence eyes went misty at his first sight of his only grandchild. "Diana. At last," he said, and wrapped his arms around her in a hug every bit as welcoming as his daughter's.

"You'll stay and have supper with us," Aunt Janette called over her shoulder as she headed for the kitchen.

"We don't want to impose. I didn't realize it was so close to supper time. I—"

But her aunt was already gone and her grandfather's choked voice drew her attention back to him. "Let me look at you." He stood her at a little distance and studied first her face, then the simple blue costume she wore.

Diana flushed. She hadn't taken time to change her clothes

before rushing Ben to the dentist, only fetched her hat and gloves and a shawl. The plain dress with its small bustle was appropriate for visiting a sheriff and interviewing a murderer, but she'd have put on something with a bit more flair if she'd known she was going to be meeting her father's kin.

Seizing her hand, Isaac Torrence led her to a sofa and sat beside her. He couldn't seem to take his eyes off her. "Family's important," he said. "The older you get, the more you realize that."

"Yes, it is," she agreed, and stopped worrying about what she was wearing.

Belatedly, he turned his attention upon Ben. "Dr. Northcote, I presume." Then he frowned, taking note of Ben's bruised and swollen jaw. "Are you all right?"

"Better now," Ben told him. "And pleased to meet you, sir. But I'm sure you have more important matters to discuss with Diana than the condition of my face."

Instead of the smile Diana expected, Ben's comment made her grandfather look indescribably sad. Again he took her hands in his. When she looked into his sorrowful eyes, she knew what an effort it took for him to get his next words out.

"Is your father still alive?" he asked.

"No, sir."

He didn't try to stop the tears that leaked from his eyes. "A man shouldn't have to outlive his children."

Ben stepped forward to offer his handkerchief, then faded into the woodwork once more. Diana patted Isaac Torrences's blue-veined hand. After a moment, recovering himself, her grandfather blew his nose with a loud honk and tucked the handkerchief into a pocket.

"I've so many questions. About Will. About you." He gave a raspy laugh. "About what's been going on out in Lenape Springs. Howd didn't seem to know much when he came to tell me about you."

Diana wasn't sure if he meant Uncle Howd hadn't known much

about her or hadn't known much about Elly's murder, but it didn't matter. She would do her best to answer all her grandfather's questions . . . within reason. She saw no point in disillusioning the old man.

For the next few hours, she told story after story of her childhood. There had been many good years with her father, things she willingly shared with his father and sister. She had no qualms, either, about admitting that she'd made a bad mistake in eloping with an actor, and expressed her regret that she'd been estranged from her parents afterwards.

"I was reconciled with my mother only recently," she said, "but by then, Father had already passed on to his reward."

The euphemism made her wince inwardly, but she was determined that her grandfather should not know what a thoroughgoing villain his son had become.

"I told Will he was no son of mine if he put going off adventuring ahead of taking his rightful place at home. I had a nice little carpentry business until my hands got too bad to hold my tools. Anyway, he took me at my word. Up and left and never a word from him afterward. I should have known he had a head full of stories about the Forty-Niners and wouldn't be content without trying to make a fortune on his own."

"He did succeed, though not in California. He was one of the Fifty-Niners in Colorado and eventually struck silver."

"Yet he didn't care enough to let me know."

"Maybe he meant to."

"He never told you about me, did he? Or any of your family?"

"Only one story of a long ago ancestor who was an expert on the uses of herbs."

"Probably figured I was dead. I'm ninety-two, you know." He preened when she assured him he didn't look it. "Howd said you didn't tell him who you were. Do the rest of them know yet?"

"No, and I'd appreciate it if you wouldn't say anything. I keep hoping to find the right time to tell Uncle Myron and Mercy, but as you've no doubt heard, things have been a bit hectic at the hotel since we arrived."

Diana knew she had to stop keeping secrets. Lies, even lies of omission, only led to more problems. Not even good intentions were an acceptable excuse.

She glanced at Ben, feeling momentary pity for him because he had not been able to eat much of Aunt Janette's excellent meal. His injuries continued to cause him considerable pain. But the fact that he'd put off sharing the information that she had a grandfather and aunt living in Liberty had created a new rift between them. She did not know yet how they could bridge it.

The matter of everyone thinking she and Ben were already married was another problem. How did she explain that bit of deceit to her new-found grandfather? She'd had to grit her teeth and force a smile earlier, when her aunt had admired the tourmaline wedding ring.

"We couldn't help but hear about them finding Elly Lyseth's bones," Aunt Janette said now. "I would have sworn on a stack of Bibles that she ran off with Racy Darden. My, he was a handsome fella."

"Racy . . . Darden?" Diana echoed, startled. "Is that the drummer's name?"

"Well, Horace, really, but everyone called him Racy."

"So, you knew him?"

"Well, of course. My late husband worked in Kilbourne's store here in Liberty. The same jobbers who stop at Castine's place stop there. We even had Mr. Darden to dinner once or twice."

"Then you know the name of the company he worked for?"

Janette did, but Diana's question sparked one of her own. "Why so much interest? It isn't your job to find out what happened. That's up to the law."

"Uncle Howd didn't tell you?" Perhaps he hadn't yet known when he'd talked to the Torrences. "I earn my living as a journalist."

Diana's tale of eloping with an actor, now deceased, had raised nary an eyebrow. Her stories of life in the mining camps of Colorado as a child had been accepted without comment. But this news had her grandfather pursing his lips and her aunt tut-tutting.

"Surely it isn't necessary for you to work," Aunt Janette said, shooting a critical look at Ben.

"As a widow, I had no choice."

"But now, surely—"

Ben cut in, attempting to assure her newfound relatives: "I'm hoping she'll try her hand at writing novels instead, now that we're married."

Diana just stared at him. His words infuriated her, but she did not contradict him. Later, she vowed. Later they were going to have a very serious discussion about their future.

℘℃ℛ

You're very quiet," Ben remarked when they'd driven half the return distance to Lenape Springs.

It was a clear, mild night, and the full moon above provided adequate illumination to see the road. The carriage duster he'd placed across Diana's knees kept any chill at bay but a certain coldness emanated from her that had nothing to do with the weather.

"I'm upset with you." The words were clipped, and she didn't look at him. "There are a number of things we need to clarify, and I suppose there's no time like the present."

That sounded ominous, and since his face still hurt, he was not in the best shape to field questions. He said nothing.

"Just how long have you known I had kin in Liberty?"

Confession was good for the soul, Ben told himself. "Since the first night. When Myron was carrying on about Elmira deserting him and Howd, he mentioned that Will Torrence was a Liberty boy."

"You should have told me at once."

"I wanted to wait. To find out if the Torrences were likely to be any more forgiving than the Grants. I was trying to protect you, Diana."

"Protect me?" Her voice rose.

"From more disappointments."

"What about honesty, Ben? Doesn't that count for anything?"

"You weren't exactly forthcoming with your grandfather. Your father was—"

"I know what he was! That frail old man doesn't need to."

"And you accuse me of—"

"You patronize me! Grandfather Torrence never needs to know what his son became. You'd have had to tell me about him sometime." She drew breath sharply and turned, at last, to glare at him. "You *would* have told me, wouldn't you?"

"Yes. Eventually. And I don't patronize you."

"You do! *I'm hoping she'll try her hand at writing novels now that we're married.* As if that's so much more respectable than journalism!"

"You may write what you please." The condescension Ben heard in his own voice made him wince.

"I intend to." Diana's back was ramrod stiff. "I hardly need your permission."

"Diana, this is ridiculous. You know I'd never try to restrict your choices."

"Hah! You've never made any secret of the fact that you don't want me working for Horatio Foxe."

"That's true, but it's because I don't like or trust Foxe. I've no objection to having a wife who is a journalist, but Foxe's actions when we first met put you in mortal danger. And now—well that was his philosophy you were spouting after Saugus was killed, the concept of playing fast and loose with the truth just to create a good story."

Diana started to speak, no doubt in defense of her employer, but subsided under the weight of Ben's scowl. Folding her hands primly in her lap, she refused to utter another word.

When they arrived back at the Hotel Grant it was very late and Ben still had to return the horse and buggy to the livery stable. By the time he joined Diana in their suite, she was already asleep—or pretending to be. She'd made a cocoon of the blankets and turned her back on his side of the bed.

Ben was in no mood to apologize, beg, or cajole. He retreated into the parlor and opened his medical bag, searching for something to relieve the ache in his jaw. At least she hadn't left a pillow and quilt on the couch for him. He took what comfort he could from that. When he'd dosed himself with a sleeping draught, he climbed into bed beside Diana.

He was too smart to touch her. Instead, he beat his pillow into a more comfortable shape and closed his eyes, determined to get a good night's sleep.

First thing in the morning, he decided, he'd pursue the lead Diana's Aunt Janette had given them. A handsome jobber named Horace "Racy" Darden had been linked to Elly Lyseth ten years earlier. Once and for all, Ben would rule out any connection between the drummer and Elly's death. Then he'd work his way through the other suspects, eliminating them one by one. Diana still thought Belle Saugus was their murderer. Perhaps she was. He was only certain of one thing—the sooner he and Diana figured out what had really happened to Elly, and to Norman Saugus, the sooner they could leave here, go back to Maine, be married, and live happily ever after.

He smiled to himself as he started to drift off. Perhaps it was only the narcotic making him feel so optimistic, but he was convinced that by this time tomorrow everything would be made right.

CHAPTER FOURTEEN

ဆာ

Diana did not want to think about her relationship with Ben. That focused her mind wonderfully on finishing the crime articles for Horatio Foxe. First thing in the morning, suitably attired in rationals and uncorseted, she picked her way through the rubble of the west wing to the spot where Elly Lyseth's bones had been found.

The scene had been disturbed by the workers who'd made the discovery and by the members of the coroner's jury, but demolition had been stopped. The construction crew—those who hadn't decided they'd rather earn their living elsewhere—were now engaged in giving the entire hotel a fresh coat of white paint.

There had been considerable debate over the color scheme. Mrs. Ellington had argued for pale yellow with white trim and green shutters, Mercy for Pompeian red, and Howd for various shades of green. Myron's vote being the only one that counted, the hotel was being painted cream white with light yellow window trimmings. It would go well with the ruddy brown shingles, Diana thought, glancing up at the pyramidal roofs that topped the towers.

She clambered over debris to reach the hole in the floor with little difficulty. She had no intention of climbing down into it.

There was nothing left to find there. What she hoped to gain was a sense of the place as it had been when Elly Lyseth was alive. Turning in a slow circle, head tipped slightly back so that she could look up, Diana tried to imagine the hotel with an intact west wing. It was not terribly difficult. She had the extant east wing to build upon. What was hard was understanding how Elly Lyseth had come to be here. She'd met Uncle Howd somewhere, but the hotel had already been closed for the season. And yet, Norman and Belle Saugus had still been in residence.

She hadn't asked nearly enough questions, Diana decided. Or, rather, she hadn't asked the correct questions.

She jumped when she heard footsteps approaching, but it was only her Uncle Howd. She started to say good morning to him, then realized she wasn't sure how to greet him. He'd known who she was for days and never said a word.

Howd solved the problem for her. "How is your mother, Diana? Is she well?"

"Fit as a fiddle," Diana replied, then winced when she realized she should have chosen her words with more care.

Howd didn't seem to notice. "Good. Good. She deserved her own life, you know. Myron was wrong to expect her to stay here. Is she . . . happy?"

That was harder to answer. "I think so. She's content with the choices she's made." Diana didn't know how much Ben had told Uncle Howd, but trusted her "husband" had been discreet. There was one thing, though, that her uncle should know. "She received a marriage proposal from Ed Leeves a while back."

Her uncle's brows lifted in surprise. "The same Ed Leeves who's been conspiring with young Sebastian? Well, well."

"I've telegraphed Mother. She'll put a stop to it."

"Will she? As I recall, Elmira could hold a grudge every bit as well as Myron does. And Ed . . . well, I wouldn't put it past Ed Leeves to think a bit of revenge on the Grant brothers was a suitable present to bring to a bride."

"Well, he's not going to. I promise you." Although Diana had been obliged to be careful what she'd said in the telegram she'd sent to Denver, she'd made what she hoped was a potent threat— to expose details of their respective businesses to the readers of the *Independent Intelligencer*—to keep both Elmira Torrence and Ed Leeves in line. That it was also an empty threat was irrelevant. Her mother didn't know her well enough to be certain she wouldn't carry it out.

Uncle Howd took her arm to help her back out of the west wing. "What were you looking for in there?"

"Inspiration. How did she get there, Uncle Howd? Where was she that day? Who saw her? Who talked to her? You said you gave her the locket. Where did you go to be private?"

A dull red color crept up his neck and into his face. "We went into the woods, mostly. Well, she lived at home with her parents, and my room is right next to Myron's . . . "

"And that day?"

"That day we took a couple of the lunch boxes Tressa packs for departing guests for their return home trips." A fond smile softened his expression. "You'll not have seen any yet this year, but they're made of very thin, light wood, dovetailed, and attractively tied. Guests call for the Pullman car porter to bring one of those little tables when they're ready to eat. You know the sort? They hook into the wall between the chairs and have a support on the other end that drops to the floor. Anyway, each box contains two sandwiches, a hard boiled egg, a wrapped pickle or olives, fruit, an attractive napkin, and a little salt and pepper shaker."

Since some response seemed called for, Diana said, "They sound lovely."

"Tressa's idea. So were the etched glass carafes we use to serve water in the dining rooms. 'Fragile but elegant,' she said, with pictures of the hotel on the sides, and she got just what she wanted. Of course it was Myron who insisted on putting Tremont's likeness on the top of the stopper."

"Tremont? The *goat?*"

"Hasn't anyone told you the story? It was a sick goat that led my grandfather, Matthew Grant, to discover the healing properties of the spring. Local Indians told him he should take the goat there to drink. He did, the goat recovered, and the Grants promptly laid claim to the land. That's the legend, anyway."

"Do you believe the waters are medicinal?"

"I think they stink, but as far as I know drinking from the spring has never hurt anyone."

They had been following the boardwalk that led to the spring while Howd talked but were only part way there when he stepped off and offered Diana his hand for balance. Once on the ground, he escorted her across a pretty glade, its beauty marred only by a pair of fallen trees.

"They came down in the blizzard," Howd said, noting the direction of her gaze. "Uprooted. We haven't had time to cut them up for firewood yet."

"As a child, I'd have loved finding something like that," Diana said. "I'd have crawled inside—it's something like a cave, you see, only open to the light—and imagined myself defending a fortress."

"That's quite an imagination you've got," Howd said.

A nearly invisible path led away from the glade on the opposite side. A few minutes of rough walking brought them to another small clearing, this one containing a dilapidated gazebo.

"This is where Elly and I used to, er, meet." Howd's face crumpled. "I haven't been here for ten years. I hadn't realized it had gotten so run down."

White paint had peeled away. The roof had partially collapsed and one section of railing was broken. The bench that ran around three quarters of the inside was covered with leaves and other natural debris. Uncle Howd brushed off a section so that Diana could sit but was too restless himself to roost.

"How long were you here that day?" she asked him.

"Only a short time—less than an hour. There was a strain

between us. I had been hoping . . . well, she didn't exactly throw herself into my arms and agree to marry me, did she?"

"Do you remember what time of day it was when you parted?"

His brown furrowed as he tried to recall details of that long-ago afternoon. "It must have been right around noon when we came out here. She was gone by one."

"Did you return to the hotel separately or together?"

"I stayed here awhile after she left. Thinking." I got back to the hotel around two and caught hell from Myron for disappearing like that. There was a lot of work to be done. We were closing up for the season."

"You didn't see her again?"

Howd started to lean against a section of sagging railing but thought better of it. "No. I was working outside. She should have been inside. I . . . I don't know if she was or not. The next day, after we knew she was gone, Tressa said something about her chores not being done, but that didn't mean much. I am loath to speak ill of the dead, especially of a girl I was thinking of marrying, but Elly was, well, a slacker." He raked his fingers through his hair. "I was a damned fool, Diana. I look back now, and I can't think what I saw in her. She wasn't half the woman Tressa is."

He'd seen a pretty young woman paying flattering attention to an older man, Diana thought, but she wouldn't hurt him for the world by saying so aloud. "It's time I started asking more questions," she said instead. "Someone must have seen Elly after she left here. Are you certain no one knew about the two of you?"

"We were careful. Unless she said something or—" He broke off, his face going a shade paler. "The locket. It's distinctive. And it has my picture in it."

"Uncle Howd, you're talking as if knowing you'd given her a gift would be reason enough for someone to kill her. That doesn't make sense."

He just looked miserable.

"Who would have recognized the locket?" she prodded.

His voice was so low she almost missed it. "Tressa."

Outraged, Diana was on her feet and across the gazebo in an instant. "Howard Grant, you're a bigger fool than you think if you can suspect, for even an instant, that Tressa Ellington would kill someone." That she'd added Mrs. Ellington to her list of suspects early on was irrelevent, Diana decided. She'd never seriously considered the older woman capable of murder.

"I knew she was in love with me back then," he confessed. "But Elly . . . Elly took my breath away."

"Tressa Ellington is *still* in love with you," Diana said. She was quite certain she was correct. All the signs were there, particularly the way Tressa referred to Howd as an "old fool." "And I think you've been in love with her for a long time now. Why don't you tell her, Uncle Howd? There's no reason for either one of you to be alone any more."

A few minutes later, Diana left him alone in the gazebo, at his request, so that he could think about what she'd said. She returned to the hotel, mulling over her uncle's revelations. Tressa wasn't the only one who'd have recognized that locket. Mercy would have. And Myron. It was even possible someone who had been at the hotel all that summer might have seen it in Howd's possession and recognized it when Elly wore it. Belle, perhaps?

Belle, who had suspected Elly was also carrying on with her husband?

Diana frowned. But had she? There was no doubt Belle was a criminal, but the more Diana reviewed her interview with the woman, the less likely she thought it was that she was a killer.

The elusive memory she'd been unable to recall a few days earlier had been the exact sequence of words she and Ben had overheard that first night. The exchange was still open to interpretation. Belle had shouted "that girl." Elly? Saugus had bellowed "whore!" Elly? Or Belle herself? Then Belle again, with a long speech out of which only two words—scoundrel and crimes—had been recognizable. That, at least, was clear. Saugus was both scoundrel and criminal.

The last part of the argument had been conducted in low tones once more, and the word "stage," which Diana had first taken to mean Belle had been an actress, now had a different interpretation. He could have been referring to the stage his plan for the hotel had reached. That made more sense if she assumed he was upset because the discovery of the bones was a setback for his schemes. An unexpected setback . . . because he hadn't known they were there?

It had been Saugus who'd used the word "murderer." Should he, more accurately, have said "murderess?" That question nagged at Diana as she returned to the hotel. She must speak to Belle again. Soon. But first, since she'd set out this morning to find out where everyone had been when Elly Lyseth died, she would complete that task.

Squaring her shoulders, she marched into the kitchen and confronted Tressa Ellington.

"I've been thinking about that ever since they found her bones," Mrs. Ellington said. "I saw her slip out of the hotel around four in the afternoon. She was supposed to be sweeping out the bedrooms. I remember I almost went after her, but I decided she wasn't worth the bother."

"Did you speak to her at all that afternoon? See her close up?"

"I think not. Likely I didn't want to. She was a disagreeable young woman. As a rule, I had as little to do with her as possible."

"But you were the housekeeper then, as you are now. Weren't you the one that hired her?"

"To get her parents, we had to take Elly, too."

"And are they such rare prizes?"

"They're hard workers, both of them. A pity they didn't pass that trait on to their daughter."

Neither Uncle Myron nor Cousin Mercy remembered seeing Elly Lyseth at all that afternoon. Celia Lyseth agreed to talk to Diana only after Myron Grant exerted his authority as her employer and insisted she cooperate.

"Your husband said you sat up all night waiting for Elly to come home. That she'd said terrible things to you before she left. But when did she leave, Mrs. Lyseth? Do you remember?"

"She went off to work that morning and I never saw her again. She didn't come home for supper. Lord knows what she was up to."

Diana recorded this version of the story in her notebook, filling the last page. She sighed, beset by the suspicion that she was just wasting paper.

"Anything else?" Mrs. Lyseth asked, seeming slightly less hostile. "I have work to do."

"What do you think happened to your daughter?" Diana asked.

"The Lord called her to His bosom. It was her time."

Diana, we need to talk."

"I haven't time. I only came back to the suite for a fresh notebook." Then she looked at him and her eyes widened. He had donned trousers and a percale shirt that fastened down the front, but he hadn't bothered to button it, nor had he yet attached his collar or tied his cravat. His shoes were still in the closet, rather than on his feet. "Are you ill?"

"My jaw aches like the very devil," he informed her. His bruises had turned a variety of interesting colors.

Diana seated herself in the cream colored chair. He'd have preferred it if she'd chosen the sofa, at his side, but she was close enough to touch. That was all that mattered.

Carefully keeping his hands occupied with the coffee Mrs. Ellington had brought up earlier, he watched for Diana's reactions as he spoke. This impasse between them had gone on long enough. It was time to get a thing or two settled. "I've been thinking," he said, deliberately choosing to make a suggestion that would annoy her, "that your family's story of the lost Indian mine might make an excellent basis for a fictional tale."

Yes, he'd been right. He saw the temper flare in her eyes. She didn't think she had any talent for writing fiction. He wasn't so sure about that, but he wasn't prepared to risk their future by arguing about it. What he was prepared to do was listen—really listen, this time—to what *she* wanted to do.

"I am a journalist, not a novelist," she informed him.

"Are you happy delving into murder? Can you really mean to follow Horatio Foxe's lead and put anything in print that will sell newspapers? Casting suspicion on innocent people ruins lives, Diana. I thought you knew that."

The appalled expression on her face reassured him. "I never meant . . . I don't want to invent stories, Ben, those that pass as news *or* fiction. And I shouldn't like to write about nothing but crime. But there are other newsworthy issues and events that interest me. In Colorado, for example, women have the vote. Why isn't that the case in other states?"

"No doubt because their husbands object."

She made a face at him.

"Never fear, Diana. I will not try to control you in any way."

"I wish I could be certain of that. You keep trying to steer me away from what I do best." When he tried to protest, she held up a hand. "You do. First you tried to convince me to write humor. Do you recall? I can sometimes inject humor into an article, but it is not so easy to be funny, Ben. I could not make a living at it."

"You've no need to make a living at all. You'll be married to me. I'll take care of you."

He knew as soon as the words were out that he'd made a mistake. She'd learned the hard way not to depend on anyone but herself.

"I don't want to take away your independence," he said as he reached out and took both her hands in his. "I love you, Diana. I want you to be happy."

"Then let me find my own way through this dilemma. I won't give up earning my own money, and writing articles for the news-paper is the way I do that. The only real question is what kind of reporting I will pursue in the future. I enjoyed the few weeks I spent writing about crime in New York City. They weren't all stories of murder. There were other interesting cases, too."

"I worry about you, that's all."

"I know." She patted his sore hand, and he tried not to wince.

Ben realized now what the problem was. Diana saw his confidence in her as a failure to pay attention to what she'd been trying to tell him. Perhaps she was right, but it was hard not to want the best for the one you loved. He started to suggest, again, that she apply for a position at the local Bangor newspaper, then repressed the impulse. The *Whig and Courier* was small compared to the New York dailies. He wasn't even sure they would hire a woman, let alone allow her to write anything of importance.

"I quit my job before I left New York for Colorado," Diana reminded him. "I let Horatio Foxe hire me back because he did me a favor. I'm still in his employ, and I have an obligation to complete my current assignment."

Ben repressed a growl. "What about later? Are you going to be at his beck and call all your life? Will Foxe send you away from home to cover stories *after* we're married?"

"He may want to. That doesn't mean I'll go."

Ben released Diana, picked up his cup, and took a sip of cold coffee. He wished now that he'd insisted she marry him before they'd left Denver, but he hadn't wanted their wedding to be rushed—that was too similar to what she'd had with Evan Spaulding.

"We spent some time on the journey here planning a June wedding," he said when he felt a bit calmer, "but we haven't talked about what will happen after the ceremony. Do you want to live with my mother and brother?"

Startled by the change of subject, she just stared at him.

"Diana?"

"It's your home. I guess I . . . I don't know what I thought. I hadn't looked that far ahead."

"We could live above my office instead, although the living quarters there are rather small."

This seemed to fluster her even more. He was about to suggest they build a house when she stood and headed for the door. "I can't talk about this now. I have people to question."

"Who?"

"Floyd Lyseth. Emma Cas—"

"I'll take Lyseth. He was on my list."

"I'd rather you go into the village. You know the people there better than I do. You helped young Freddy." She was gone before he could object and he had no idea what had made her run away.

Fifteen minutes later, Ben entered Castine's store. Myron was already there, trying to get his money back on the casket he'd bought for Norman Saugus. "The widow's going to be paying for it," he insisted.

"But you already did," Emma Castine reminded him. "Cash. And I don't extend credit to the likes of her. When she comes in and lays her money on the counter, I'll refund what you gave me, but not a moment before." She crossed her arms over her bosom, tucking her hands into her armpits, as if to give him a visual demonstration of how difficult it would be to get her to part with a cent.

Disgusted, Myron stormed out.

Immediately, Mrs. Castine relaxed. "What can I do for you, Dr. Northcote? After the way you took care of young Freddy, the whole family owes you."

"Just information, Mrs. Castine. Do you recall if you saw Elly Lyseth the day she disappeared?"

"Can't say I do. It *was* ten years ago."

"What about Horace Darden? Did you ever see him again after that?"

She frowned. "Curious you should ask. I did think I saw him

once, but it couldn't have been."

"Why's that?"

"Well, it was at a camp meeting."

"I thought sinners went to such things to be saved?"

"Well, yes, but you see, this man was already saved. He was one of the fellows working with the ministers."

"Working?"

"As a helper—bringing people forward to say their piece; finding those who came in hope of being cured of something."

"When was this, Mrs. Castine?"

"Oh, it must have been three or four years ago." She looked a trifle embarrassed. "I used to go to camp meetings quite a bit when I was younger. For the socializing, you know."

"So this wasn't the meeting at which Pastor Riker met his future wife?"

"Oh, no. This was at least a year or two earlier."

Ben stopped at the post office, asking the same questions, and then went to the livery stable. By then a vague idea had begun to form, and he asked Luke to harness Old Jessie to the surrey.

It had been barely ten in the morning when he'd reached Lenape Springs, and it was still well short of eleven. He had plenty of time for what he had in mind, especially if he didn't return to the hotel first to tell Diana where he was going. The sooner he went, he reasoned, the sooner he'd be back.

⁂

Diana was unable to locate Floyd Lyseth. Secretly, she felt relieved. She hadn't relished another conversation with the taciturn handyman. He obviously didn't like to talk about his daughter, and he wasn't going to appreciate her questions, which revolved around discrepancies in what he and his wife had told her previously.

Her other self-appointed task was almost as unappealing. She'd left Belle to go through her late husband's effects, particularly the proofs of his criminal activities. To save her own skin, Belle would cooperate. Diana had been certain of it when she'd left the other woman's suite the previous day, but she'd also intended to check on her before now. The longer she put off another meeting, the harder it became to face a potential murderess.

But was she? Belle's attitude after she'd told her story, Diana recalled, had been that of a child who'd gotten away with something. She'd made up at least part of the tale, but which part? Diana was certain Belle had lied to her, but about killing Elly? About her husband's death? Of that she was no longer so certain.

If Belle was a killer, then Ben was right. Diana had been foolish to confront the woman alone. But she *had* met with Belle and, aside from a profane rant denigrating Diana's ancestry and suggesting she try impossible physical feats, the actress/hotel thief had done nothing overtly threatening when she'd lost her temper.

Diana considered waiting until Ben returned before she interviewed Belle a second time. She considered it for about five minutes. Then she realized that if she left Belle to her own devices any longer, the woman was likely to refuse to cooperate further. Belle was still in a position to cause trouble for Myron, even if it led to her own incarceration. She struck Diana as the sort who wanted instant gratification. Diana had promised her a reward— her freedom and enough jewelry for a nest egg. It didn't seem likely that Belle would wait much longer for her to pay up. Besides, if Belle had too much time to think about it, she'd realize that Diana thought she was guilty of more than fraud.

"She could be a cold-blooded murderer," Diana muttered under her breath, but this last-ditch effort to talk herself out of confronting Belle alone had little effect.

"Talking to yourself now, are you?"

"Mrs. Curran!" Diana felt her pursed lips stretch into a smile as she looked up and recognized her landlady.

"Isn't this a delightful place?" Spry as a woman half her age,

Mrs. Curran's bright little eyes snapped with enthusiasm. "I've been out walking. Met a goat."

"Her name is Tremont, after the hotel in Boston, I presume." Built almost a hundred years earlier, that landmark had been the first hostelry to call itself a hotel—someone had told Diana that the word meant palace for the people—and boasted that it had offered the first bellboys, the first inside water closet, the first hotel clerk, the first French cuisine on a Yankee menu, the first menu cards, the first annunciators in rooms, the first room keys, and the first Reading Room.

"Where are you off to?" Mrs. Curran asked.

"To see Belle." She studied the smaller woman for a moment. If the two of them went . . . . "You said yesterday that you wanted to talk to Belle. If you still do, you—" Diana broke off in the middle of asking her landlady to come with her. She'd never seen the woman look so guilty as she did at this moment. "What have you done?"

"I suppose I'd best confess. I had a little chat with Belle already, last night after you and Dr. Northcote went into town. I had a few words I wanted to say to her. Leftover business, as it were."

And Ben thought *she* was impulsive. "Even knowing she might be a murderess, you visited her alone?"

"The day I can't handle myself with the likes of Belle Rhymer—"

"What if she'd had a gun?"

"She doesn't."

Diana didn't think she did, either. Wouldn't she have gone for it the night Myron attacked Saugus if she had? But Diana took a moment to consider the possibility. Was that what Ben had feared? If it was, it was no wonder he'd been so worried about her.

"Since she knows already that you're here, you may as well come with me now." Diana headed for the elevator. "Did she mention her husband's murder? Or the bones we found under the floor?"

"Those things may have come up, yes, but I was more interested in getting my good emerald earbobs back if she still had them, which of course she didn't."

The door to Belle's suite was cracked open.

"Stay back," Diana told Mrs. Curran. Then she stood to one side herself and cautiously gave the portal a shove. When nothing happened, she peered around the door frame into the parlor. "Belle?"

The place had an empty feel to it when Diana stepped inside, and it was chilly, as if the fire had gone out hours earlier. She glanced towards the fireplace and gasped. Belle had been burning papers. Even the boxes they'd been kept in had gone into the flames.

She checked the bedroom to be certain, but there were no documents left. Nor was there any sign of Belle.

"No body?" Mrs. Curran asked from the doorway.

Diana hadn't even considered that possibility. Belle was not the sort to take her own life. "She's flown the coop."

Why had Belle left? Diana didn't think the questions she'd asked the previous day could have frightened the woman off. On the contrary, they'd been designed to keep her here. Had she known more than she'd said when Diana had interviewed her? Or had she found something in Saugus's possessions after Diana had left the suite?

Mrs. Curran plopped down in the chair in front of the fireplace. She could see the evidence of what Belle had done as plainly as Diana could, though she probably didn't understand its significance. "Was it something I said?"

Diana pulled up a second chair and sat. "You tell me. Can you recall your conversation?"

"I always remember dialogue," Mrs. Curran assured her. She took a moment to gather her thoughts, then launched into an almost verbatim account. She even changed her voice when she spoke Belle's lines.

Most of it was irrelevant to the murders. Belle had stolen Mrs. Curran's earbobs years before, and Diana's landlady had wanted them back. She'd settled for an apology and a glass of Norman

Saugus's whiskey, after which the two of them had engaged in a surprisingly amiable chat about shared theatrical acquaintances.

"Did she say anything about her husband?" Diana interrupted.

"Only that he'd been too smart for his own good."

What did that mean? Diana wondered. That he'd thought he'd gotten away with murder? Or something else entirely?

"She was nervous. I could see that," Mrs. Curran said. "She wasn't *that* good an actress."

"Had she been packing? Her clothes are gone from the bedroom."

"The door to the other room was closed. There were several boxes of papers stacked by the fireplace, though. I suppose that's what she burned."

"Had she gone through them, do you think? Or was she going to burn them unread?"

"How would I know?" Mrs. Curran sounded a trifle irritated.

"You couldn't, of course," Diana said in a soothing voice. "And it wasn't your fault that she fled. I just wish I knew why. Does this mean she *is* the killer?"

"It might mean she's afraid she'll be his next victim," Mrs. Curran suggested.

"What makes you think that?"

"The way she answered the door to my knock, for one thing. She was startled when I identified myself, but relieved to have company, too. And she said something about people trying to get at her. Perhaps she meant you, my dear, but what if there was someone else? Someone who meant her harm?"

"Who?"

"I don't know, but she'd shoved the sofa in front of the door to the corridor to block it and had to move it aside to let me in."

Diana opened her mouth and closed it again. There was no point in chastising Mrs. Curran for holding back this pertinent detail. She'd had her own agenda when she'd gone to call on Belle.

"What Belle told me," Diana said, "was that her husband killed

Elly because Elly found out about the scheme to burn down the hotel. Then, after her bones were found, someone figured out he'd killed her and killed him to avenge her death. If that's true, the same person might have wanted to kill Belle, if he believed she was equally responsible for Elly's death and the fire."

But something about that theory didn't quite mesh. *How* had someone deduced Saugus's guilt after all this time? True, Diana herself had suspected him of the crime, but she'd had no proof. Not of murder.

"That's odd," Mrs. Curran said.

"What is?"

"If she really thought he killed that girl, why tell you and no one else? She could have convinced some simple country coroner of that story without a bit of trouble."

"And if she'd murdered her husband, she'd have wanted to cast blame on someone else."

"She would, yes, but I don't think she did. Belle's sneaky, but she's not vicious. Besides, the only reason she'd kill him was if he was a threat to her."

"If he realized she'd killed Elly Lyseth—"

"Why would she?"

"Jealousy?"

Mrs. Curran snorted. "If Belle had been jealous—and I doubt she was—she'd have taken it out on her husband, not the girl."

"An accident during an argument?"

But Mrs. Curran shook her head. "You saw them together. Was Saugus afraid of his wife? He'd have had reason to be if he believed she'd killed the girl, even if it was an accident."

"He was rattled by something. That's why he was drinking so heavily. And if it wasn't Belle he suspected, then—"

"He must have figured out who really killed that girl," Mrs. Curran finished for her. "That's why he was killed. The murderer had to silence him. And that's why Belle was afraid. She thought the murderer might be planning to get rid of her, too."

"But how did Saugus guess who it was? How did Belle?"

"Perhaps that's what frightened her most. She didn't know the killer's identity any more than you do."

Diana sighed. It made sense. Belle had certainly been afraid of something or she'd not have left without the reward Diana had promised her. Either she was guilty, or she was running for her life.

"I wonder how she managed to leave the hotel without anyone noticing? And she must have had transportation. She took all her trunks and boxes with her."

"There was plenty of confusion here last night. Even Belle heard the ruckus outside. She asked me about it when I first got here."

"It must have calmed down after Ben and I left."

"Hah! When I went back downstairs after talking to Belle, the entire family was still closeted in their parlor, deciding what to do with that dreadful young man. You could hear the 'discussion' clear out in the lobby."

"What did they decide?"

"He's being shipped back to his parents later today. His uncles are going to take him to the train station and send him on his way. In the meantime, he's being kept locked in his room."

"You heard all that from the lobby?" Diana asked with a wry smile.

"I did, yes." She looked a trifle uncomfortable. "That is, I heard raised voices. Is it my fault I had reason to go a bit closer while they were still debating the lad's future?"

The smile turned into a grin. Like Mrs. Ellington, Mrs. Curran was not above a bit of eavesdropping. What a pity no one had overheard pertinent conversations between Belle Saugus and her late husband!

CHAPTER FIFTEEN

໑໐໙

Have you seen Dr. Northcote?" Diana asked Mercy.

She wasn't sure what to do about Belle's disappearance. In her heart, she no longer believed Belle guilty of murder. Not after what Mrs. Curran had said. She wanted to talk it all over with Ben, to use him as a sounding board and get his reaction to what she'd learned. She couldn't imagine he was still in Lenape Springs. He'd had time to question everyone in the village by now.

The young woman didn't seem to hear her.

"Mercy? Are you all right?" She had a bruise on her cheek where Sebastian had struck her, but Diana didn't think she'd suffered any other injuries in the skirmish.

"What? Oh, I'm sorry. Did you want something?"

"I want to know what the matter is."

Mercy promptly burst into tears. It took some time for Diana to get a coherent explanation out of her, but when she did, she shed a few happy tears herself. "So," she said. "Your father asked Mrs. Ellington to marry him."

Mercy nodded, smiling as she dashed the moisture from her cheeks. "And he told me what he intended first. This time."

"I take it you approve."

"Aunt Tressa all but raised me. How could I not be happy for them?"

"She accepted, then?"

"She's loved him for years. And this is perfect timing. She was so upset about that wretch, Sebastian."

"Has he left yet?"

"He'll be gone in another hour."

"I'd like to speak to him."

"Why?" Mercy asked.

"Because I want him to know that he never had a chance of success. He would never have gotten Elmira Torrence's support, even if he had destroyed the document he was trying to steal last night."

"Your husband said he could call off Mr. Leeves. Was he able to contact him this quickly?"

"We didn't try to reach Ed Leeves." Diana took a deep breath. The deception had gone on long enough. "I sent a telegram directly to my mother. I'm your cousin, Mercy, and Sebastian's. I'm Elmira's daughter."

"Oh, my," Mercy said.

"I'm sorry I didn't tell you right away, but I wasn't sure I'd be welcome here if I did and I wanted to meet my family. I grew up thinking I had no one but my parents. I—"

"You can't tell Uncle Myron! He gets furious at the very mention of Aunt Elmira's name. I thought he was going to have an apoplectic fit last night when Sebastian kept saying she was behind his scheme."

"What?"

"That's what he said. I didn't believe him. It was obvious he'd changed his story because he'd thought better of bragging about it being all his own idea. What Dr. Northcote did to him would have been nothing compared to the thrashing he'd have gotten from Uncle Myron."

Diana's heart sank. She couldn't even deny her mother's role in this latest fiasco. The way Elmira had been treated by her family had inspired Ed Leeves to take this petty revenge. Even if she were totally ignorant of his plan, she had to bear some responsibility for it.

"Diana?" Mercy's sounded tentative. "You won't tell him, will you?"

"What are you afraid of, Mercy?"

"He's got a terrible temper."

"Surely you don't think Uncle Myron would lash out at me?"

"He throttled Mr. Saugus. Maybe he even—"

"You can't believe he killed him."

"I don't want to, but Sebastian . . . well, right after you found the body, Sebastian said Uncle Myron must have done it. He seemed certain he was right, and that we must be prepared for the worst." She frowned, reassessing this statement in light of Sebastian's perfidy.

"I expect he was quite pleased by the prospect, but that doesn't mean he was right. Let's go talk to Sebastian, shall we?" More than ever, Diana wanted a word with her bounder of a cousin.

But Sebastian was no longer locked in his room. A glance inside told them he was long gone.

Sebastian's room was no more than eight by ten feet with a narrow bed, a wardrobe, and a commode. The wardrobe doors hung open, revealing an interior empty of personal possessions. Only the wash basin and pitcher remained on the commode—no razor or soap, no tooth powder or hair oil. Mercy lifted the counterpane to peer under the bed. There was no sign of gripsack or Gladstone bag, only an accumulation of dust.

"It looks as if he took himself off, before he could be sent home in disgrace. What have you got there?" Diana asked when Mercy stooped to pick something up from the floor.

It was the corner of a telegram. The color and texture of the paper were too distinctive to be anything else.

"He couldn't have gone out the window," Mercy said. "It's too high up to jump."

"No, but someone handy at picking locks might have released him. During the night, I think. Late. After Ben and I returned and everyone was asleep."

"I don't understand."

"Belle Saugus is gone, too."

"You think she left with Sebastian?"

"She'd have wanted someone to help with her luggage, and to drive the hotel wagon into Liberty to catch the first train out of town. And she knew something of Sebastian's disgrace from Mrs. Curran."

Diana was about to say more when a commotion outside drew her to Sebastian's window. A small drama was being played out on the expanse of lawn below. Myron, backing away from Coroner Buckley, had both hands raised as if to ward off blows. Flanking him were two other men, strangers to Diana, who seemed intent upon seizing him. As she watched, they grabbed his arms. Myron grappled with them for a moment, then subsided, allowing them to lead him away.

Closely followed by her cousin, Diana sped down the back stairs and through the lobby, reaching the veranda in time to see her uncle being loaded into a wagon. "What's going on here?" she cried, although she could see perfectly well that Mr. Buckley had arrested Myron.

"Mrs. Northcote," Buckley said, tipping his hat. "New evidence has come to light."

"What evidence? Something Belle Saugus said? If so, there are things you should know about her." She proceeded to tell him, and had just finished when Mrs. Curran came puffing up behind her, carrying the heavy book that contained Belle's photograph. Mercy had taken one look at the restraints being put on her uncle and had fled back into the hotel for reinforcements.

"It isn't evidence from Mrs. Saugus," Coroner Buckley said, handing the book back to her unopened. "I have incriminating statements from Pastor Riker and Mrs. Lyseth. Each of them came forward, separately, to say they saw Myron Grant behaving suspiciously between the time Norman Saugus was killed and the time you discovered his body."

Howd Grant, accompanied by Mrs. Ellington and Mercy, had by now joined Mrs. Curran and Diana beside the coroner's wagon. The Lyseths were nowhere in sight but the painters were watching the goings on with great interest from their ladders.

"What statements?" Diana demanded.

For a moment she didn't think Mr. Buckley would answer. Then he shrugged. "Mr. Riker saw the hotel buckboard after midnight. It was stopped by the field. A man he identifies as Myron Grant was standing beside it. At that point, the scarecrow was still a scarecrow. The preacher was on his way back from an emergency visit to a parishioner at the time. He was tired and disinclined to stop."

"What parishioner?"

"He didn't say." Buckley held up a hand to forestall her protest. "As he reminded me, what a man says to a lawyer or a priest must be treated as confidential. Individuals have a right to privacy, especially when matters of a sensitive nature are involved. Mr. Riker cannot in good conscience bandy names about."

"He regularly exhorts his parishioners to air their dirty laundry in public," she reminded the coroner. "In church, at any rate."

"I will press for a name if I must. At the moment I'm willing to accept the word of a man of God."

"And Mrs. Lyseth? What kind of claim is she making?"

"Mrs. Lyseth saw Mr. Grant at the crack of dawn, coming from the direction of the field where the body was found. She was on her way to work at the time. She was still half-asleep and didn't pay any attention to the scarecrow when she passed it, but she followed Grant up the drive leading to the hotel. She is certain of her identification."

"Sunrise is around 4:30 in the morning at this time of year.

Surely even the farmers don't go to work that early. And don't you think it odd that Mr. Grant took so long to dispose of the body? If Mr. Riker saw him just past midnight and he was only just returning to the hotel at dawn, that's some four hours spent replacing the scarecrow with the body. It is not a task one would ordinarily linger over. They're lying, Mr. Buckley," Diana said with all the conviction she could muster. "Both of them. Myron Grant never even left the building that night."

"So he says, but his brother wasn't with him after midnight." He glanced at Howd for confirmation but received only a tight-lipped glower in response. "No one can verify that he stayed put. That means it will be up to a jury to decide who's telling the truth. In the meantime, I've no choice but to arrest Mr. Grant."

He climbed into the wagon with his prisoner and the two constables. Myron sat with head bowed in defeat, shackled and broken. If he'd heard her passionate defense or was aware of his family gathered around, he gave no sign of it.

As the wagon started to move, Diana reached out and touched his arm. "Don't despair," she said. "You have been unjustly accused and I will prove it."

He looked up then, meeting Diana's eyes. He must have recognized her sincerity, because he nodded his head and almost managed a smile.

"Thank you," he said gruffly.

෨෬

Ben made the trip by road from Lenape Springs to Monticello in good time. He stopped in Liberty only long enough to send a telegram.

Once he reached the county seat, he went directly to the jail. It was part of the courthouse, a substantial stone edifice with a bell tower. Together with a one-story clerk's office and the Presbyterian church, the three buildings formed one side of a pleasant park.

Sheriff Walter Vail Irvine received Ben warmly enough. He'd heard his name from Arthur Buckley.

"I hope you'll excuse the presumption, but I've asked that the reply to a telegram I sent earlier be delivered to me here."

"That depends on what the telegram says." The sheriff kept a straight face, but Ben caught the glimmer of amusement in his eyes.

"I won't know until it gets here," Ben replied. "In the meantime, you might be interested in this." He handed over the blank but signed and sealed document Diana had liberated from Norman Saugus's suite.

Irvine's bushy brows lifted in surprise. "Where did you get this?"

Ben explained, and waited while the sheriff sent a deputy for the county clerk. It was his signature, as registrar of deeds, on the blank right of way, a paper with the power to transfer land along a road between the parties whose names were yet to be filled in. It would look legal. By the time lawsuits were filed by the property owners who'd been defrauded, Saugus would have been long gone. The plan, Ben was certain, had been to sell the right of ways to some unsuspecting entrepreneur who'd think he was about to make a fortune by putting in a telegraph line for which the groundwork had already been laid. Ben wasn't sure exactly how the confidence game would have worked, but he knew it was one.

"I'm sending someone to confiscate the rest of these forms," Irvine announced when he finished talking to the clerk.

"You may want to send someone for Mrs. Saugus, as well." And he told Irvine about Belle's criminal record. And the arson. And the possibility that she might have murdered both Elly Lyseth and her own husband. "If you have her in custody for fraud, it will prevent her from absconding before more serious charges can be brought."

"I always thought Lenape Springs was just a nice quiet little town. Anything else going on there I should know about?"

"I'll answer that after I get the reply to my telegram."

A knock interrupted them. "Dr. Dickinson is here again, sheriff," a deputy announced. "Wants to see Jack."

Irvine grimaced. He thought about the request for a moment, drumming his fingers on the top of his desk. "Let him in, but keep an eye on them. Don't let Jack persuade the good reverend to take any written messages out."

"That would be Sailor Jack?" Ben asked.

Irvine nodded. "Dickinson is rector of St. John's Episcopal Church here in Monticello. He offers spiritual aid and comfort to prisoners. After one such visit, middle of last month, Jack Allen wrote him a letter. Somehow it ended up printed in the local paper. Then it got picked up by the New York City scandal sheets. Allen's trying to convince people he's found religion. Before he came up with that ploy, he made several tries at escape. Caught him digging a tunnel one time. Then he tried acting crazy. Trying to get sent to a lunatic asylum instead of the gallows."

Irvine grinned. Ben did not.

"Your prisoner attracts a great deal of attention," Ben remarked.

"Confounded newspapers are responsible for that. They keep printing stories about him."

"From what your deputy just said, I take it that more information than you like gets out to the public."

"Seems to."

"Could be you have someone on your staff who's earning a bit of extra income."

"You know something about this, Doc, or are you just guessing?"

"An . . . acquaintance of mine is the editor of a newspaper. I have reason to believe he has a contact here in Monticello. Someone who's been sending him information about Jack Allen."

The sheriff's feet hit the floor with a resounding thump. A thunderous expression on his face, he glared at Ben. "Who?"

"Sorry. I've no idea."

"I don't like information getting out through unofficial channels. All kinds of crazy rumors get started that way. And Jack

Allen . . . ." He shook his head. "The man's got respectable women writing to him. One even proposed marriage! Can you believe that? Man's good looking, I'll grant you, but he's a cold-blooded killer."

Ben gave the sheriff a considering look. "Ever think a sympathetic reporter might show you and your deputies in a positive light? Could be good public relations to grant an interview."

"No interviews. Not with me. Not with Jack Allen."

"It might stop some of the wilder stories."

Irvine scratched his chin and gave it some thought. "What newspaper?"

"The *Independent Intelligencer.*"

"It'll be a cold day in hell before a newspaperman employed by that scandal sheet sets foot in my jail."

Ben's response was cut short by a knock on the door. The telegram he'd been expecting had arrived. He read it eagerly. Horatio Foxe's resources had not failed him.

It seemed that Mrs. Castine had been mistaken about seeing Racy Darden at a camp meeting. The fellow still worked for the same employer, but he'd transferred to another part of the state . . . and married the boss's daughter. One loose end cleared up, Ben thought.

The rest of the information in the telegram was even more helpful.

"You asked if there was anything else going on in Lenape Springs that you should know about, Sheriff. Looks like there may be another case of fraud."

"Connected to Saugus?"

"Not that I can see from this. No, this confidence man is Jonas Riker, the pastor. Seems he ran into a little trouble with the law a few years back. He was making a name for himself at camp meetings by healing folks who weren't really sick. Spent time in jail for it. He'd just gone back on the camp meeting circuit when he met his future wife."

It might not have been Darden Mrs. Castine saw at a camp meeting, working as a helper, but the reminder that there were such men had made Ben wonder about the scandal in Riker's past. It hadn't taken Foxe long to come up with details. Fake healers were hardly new or original. The helpers made sure the right people were selected for the cure. Thus were the lame able to walk and the blind to see.

Ben supposed it was possible Riker had been rehabilitated by his time in jail and the love of a good woman, but it seemed more likely that he'd taken advantage of Lida Rose Leeves and her inheritance to settle down in one place for a while. What else had he been up to? Ben had to wonder now why Riker had been quarreling with Sebastian Ellington. Had Riker found out about Sebastian's connection to Ed Leeves? Not necessarily, he decided. From what he'd seen, Riker quarreled with everyone associated with Hotel Grant.

Ben glanced at the telegram again. "Jonas Riker's not listed as a graduate of any theological seminary." Those lists were published and Foxe had access to them. "If he's not ordained, any marriages he's performed aren't valid."

"Don't have to be ordained to perform wedding ceremonies, but you do need the civil authority. I'll pursue the matter, Dr. Northcote. If he's been breaking the law, I'll deal with him." After he'd sent an underling to check county records, he gave Ben a hard look. "What else does that telegram of yours say? And who is it from? Your friend the editor?"

"Good guess, though I'd hardly call him a friend. In fact, there is more. It seems his contact here has been busy. My . . . acquaintance asks me to confirm that Sailor Jack's been keeping a diary. He says it contains some pretty serious accusations. Jack claims you've framed him for murder in an effort to garner votes for your re-election."

"Son of a—"

"I suspect any editor worth his salt would kill that story if his reporter were granted interviews with both you and Jack Allen. And I can guarantee that the reporter in question will be fair-minded in what she writes."

"She?"

"My wife."

"You'd let your wife spend time with a killer?"

"I've given up trying to dictate how she earns a living. She has a job to do and she's very good at it. You can ask the police in Manhattan about her if you want references."

Irvine drummed on the desk some more. "All right. I'll talk to her. And she can speak with Sailor Jack. For an hour. With two of my deputies in the room with them—and him shackled."

Ben hid the elation he felt. With any luck, this would prove to Diana that he had no objections to her career. He sure hoped so. He couldn't think of anything more he could do to convince her.

"Getting back to Jonas Riker," he said. "If he has been pulling the wool over the eyes of the good people of Lenape Springs, then it seems to me that might make him a suspect in Norman Saugus's murder. A better one, in fact, than Saugus's wife."

"How do you figure that?"

"What if Norman Saugus knew Riker's history? Who better to spot a confidence man than one of his own kind? If that happened, Riker might have killed Saugust to keep him quiet about his past."

"Kind of a long shot."

"I keep coming back to the way the body was displayed. It was, to all intents and purposes, hanging on a cross."

"If your minister, phony or not, is the murderer, wouldn't he want to avoid calling attention to himself that way? Besides, putting Saugus there sends the wrong message. The man was no martyr."

"Originally, crucifixion was just another means of executing criminals," Ben reminded him.

"Seems a stretch to me. And I can't say I'm convinced of your theory about Mrs. Saugus, either. Not if it depends on there being a connection between Elly Lyseth's death and Saugus's murder. I'd be surprised if the two cases are related. The only thing they seem to have in common is that both deaths took place in Lenape Springs. Coroner says he can't even tell if the girl was murdered or not."

"It could be coincidence," Ben conceded. He hated coincidences. But he could not for the life of him figure out how Pastor Riker could have killed Elly Lyseth more than eight years before he arrived in Lenape Springs.

The man Irvine had dispatched a short time earlier returned to hand the sheriff a slip of paper. "Well, that's one question answered," Irvine said. "Looks like Mr. Riker, ordained or not, took the trouble to get himself the authority to perform civil ceremonies."

Rule out one more, Ben thought. It was progress of a sort.

He had just thanked the sheriff for his time and for the promised interview and was about to take his leave when another telegram arrived. With a word of apology, Irvine ripped it open and read the message it contained. He gave a low whistle and called Ben back.

"Looks like you've been barking up *all* the wrong trees, Dr. Northcote. This is from Coroner Buckley. He's arrested Myron Grant for Norman Saugus's murder. Wants me to send deputies to Liberty to transport him here to jail."

Ben swore under his breath. He had to get back to Lenape Springs. Diana would move heaven and earth to free her uncle. And she'd stand a good chance of putting herself in mortal danger from the real killer in the process . . . especially since she didn't have a clue who that person was!

Unfortunately, neither did he.

❧❧❧

Diana closeted herself in the writing room, alone with her lists and her thoughts, determined to discover the truth. She was suspicious of Pastor Riker. Obviously he'd lied about seeing Uncle Myron.

But so had Celia Lyseth.

Why would Mrs. Lyseth lie about Myron? To support the minister's claim? But then why the discrepancy in the time?

She shook her head, trying to order her thoughts. Celia Lyseth had never been consistent in her statements. Nor was she quite rational about her daughter or her religious fervor. Diana tried reversing the circumstances. Would Pastor Riker lie to support his parishioner's claim? He'd have been happy to cause trouble for the Grants. Then Mrs. Lyseth could have confused the agreed upon time.

But why would Celia make such a statement at all . . . unless she'd killed Norman Saugus and was trying to shift the blame. It made a perverted kind of sense . . . if Celia Lyseth had also killed her own daughter.

What if she'd struck Elly down during a quarrel and had hidden the body in a panic? The fire might have been a stroke of luck, covering up the crime. Then Celia'd had to dispose of Norman Saugus because Saugus, after the recovery of Elly's bones, had figured out what had happened. Had he seen something ten years ago, perhaps Celia and Elly together on the night she disappeared? The last verified sighting of Elly Lyseth had been around four in the afternoon in the orchard. Tressa Ellington had remembered because the girl was supposed to be working.

It had undoubtedly been Celia Lyseth who'd come up with the story about her daughter running off with a peddler. She was the one who'd said Elly's belongings were missing, too.

There was one person, Diana realized, who might have the answers she sought. Floyd Lyseth had thought for ten years that his only daughter had run away from home. Now he knew better. Surely he could be persuaded to help bring Elly's killer to justice.

CHAPTER SIXTEEN

℘℘

Mr. Lyseth, may I have a word with you?"

"I got work to do, Mrs. Northcote." He carried a carpenter's tool box and several pieces of wood.

"It's late afternoon. The painters have already quit for the day."

"Don't mean my work's done."

"Then I'll just tag along, shall I? I've only a few questions to ask."

He scowled at her. "Boss said I was supposed to cooperate with you. Then again, he's in jail for killing Mr. Saugus. No mortal reason I got to put up with foolish questions."

"I know how your daughter died."

That seemed to startle him. Eyes narrowing, he studied her for a long moment, then shrugged. "Come on, then. Talk while I work."

Taciturn as ever, he led the way to the gazebo Howd had shown her and started repairs. Diana settled herself on one of the benches. She sat and watched him for a moment, uncertain how to begin. How did one tell a man that his wife had probably killed their daughter?

A section of the old railing gave a shriek as Lyseth wrenched it free. At the sound, Diana felt a chill pierce her heart. She stared at the broken wood, suddenly as certain of what had happened as if she'd been a witness to Elly's death herself.

The young woman had come here that day with Howd. Tressa Ellington had seen her after that, so he hadn't murdered her. But Elly had come back.

Why? With whom? Diana didn't have all the answers, but she was sure now that Elly had been shoved or thrown into that railing with so much force that she'd broken it. Either the wood, as it splintered, or a rock on the hard ground below, had dealt her death blow.

"This is where it happened," she whispered.

Slowly, Floyd Lyseth turned, hands fisted at his sides, the usual glower on his face. "So, you did figure it out." Thin and stoop-shouldered he might be, but in the confines of the gazebo, he seemed to loom over her.

Diana blinked at him in confusion. How long had he known that his wife had killed Elly? "I—"

"Guess that means I have to kill you, too."

For a moment, Diana couldn't take in what she'd heard. *Lyseth* was the murderer? She swallowed hard and thought fast. It would only take a moment for him to reach out with those strong, work-hardened hands and strangle her. Her back was against the railing. She couldn't bolt from a sitting position. That left her no choice but to survive by her wits.

"It's traditional to grant a dying prisoner one last request."

"That's a last *meal,*" he corrected with a rough laugh.

With all the false bravado she could muster, she said, "I'm a newspaper reporter, Mr. Lyseth. I gather information, not nuts and berries." And if she could keep him talking long enough, she might think of a way to escape his clutches. At least she hadn't been knocked out or tied up and Mr. Lyseth didn't have a weapon.

On the other hand, he didn't need one. Anyone who could effortlessly cart heavy trunks up several flights of stairs was stronger than he looked. And they were well off the beaten path here. Was Ben back from wherever he'd gone? Did it matter? He wouldn't have a clue where to look for her.

"I thought your wife killed her." She really should have been clearer about that from the beginning.

Lyseth snorted. "That silly cow wouldn't have had the sense to hide what she'd done."

"I don't suppose she'd have known about Saugus's plans to burn down the hotel, either."

It was a guess, but the deepening of Lyseth's scowl told Diana she'd hit the nail on the head.

"Did Elly find out? Is that why you killed her?"

Lyseth glared at Diana. "You want to know what happened? Fine. I'll tell you what happened. Makes me mad all over again just thinkin' about it. Elly asked me to meet her here that day. Meant to taunt me. Told me what she'd been up to in this here gazebo with Howd Grant. Said she was goin' to marry him and lord it over me and her mother at the hotel. She'd be my boss, she said. Little slut."

With a snarl, Lyseth flung off his hat and stomped on it. Diana hadn't dared move during his tirade, and was terrified of his temper, but she took heart from the fact that, in his agitation, he had moved farther away from her.

"Wasn't about to stand for that," Lyseth muttered, raking dirt-stained fingers through his greasy hair. "Told her I'd tell Howd how she'd been carryin' on with Racy Darden. I seen the two of them sneak off together more than once. I knew what they'd got up to. That's when she attacked me. Tried to dig up my face with her fingernails, but I pushed her away before she could do any damage. She went right through that railin'." He turned and pointed. "Hit her head when she landed."

"A tragic accident, " Diana murmured.

When he didn't look her way, she slowly rose from the bench and inched towards the opening at the side of the gazebo.

"Think so?" His head whipped around and she froze. "Maybe. Maybe not." He shrugged. "She deserved what she got, and I wasn't about to chance a jury deciding I'd wanted her dead."

There'd been no guarantee he'd have been believed if he'd confessed to accidentally causing her death during a quarrel, Diana supposed. He might have been spared execution, but found guilty of manslaughter and been sentenced to a long term in prison.

They stood in silence, watching each other as she pieced together the rest of what must have happened. He'd have waited until after dark, then put Elly under the floor in the west wing of the hotel, knowing the building was going to be set on fire. He must have thought the blaze would destroy the body.

Diana's desire to know the truth momentarily overwhelmed her sense of caution. "Did Norman Saugus hire you to burn down the hotel?"

For a moment she thought he'd refuse to answer. He became downright loquacious instead.

"Saugus was payin' me to help him. I knew what he had planned. Him and the missus." His eyes looked unfocussed, but Diana did not dare move so long as he faced her. "Came to my house," he continued. "Woke me up. Said to come with him. He'd been drinkin'. Brought whiskey with him and we both had some. Been a long time since I tasted whiskey. Damn woman won't have it in the house. Saugus said he knew I killed Elly, but he'd forget all about that if I'd set fire to the hotel again."

Diana shivered. He wasn't talking about the day he killed Elly anymore. He was remembering the night he murdered Norman Saugus.

She understood now. After the bones were found, Saugus must have realized how Lyseth had taken advantage of the arson scheme to hide his own crime. Saugus couldn't tell the authorities what he suspected without incriminating himself. At first he must have had sense enough to be afraid of Floyd Lyseth. Had indulging in whiskey changed that? Or had it been the fight with Myron? She

wondered, too, if he'd confided in Belle. He might have let on
that he knew who'd killed Elly without giving Belle a name. That
would have given her a reason to run.

"Meant to kill him," Lyseth muttered, "but I didn't think it
through. Should have realized I'd have to get rid of his wife, too.
She'll be next. After you."

Keep him talking! Diana thought in desperation. "What made
you put him on that pole in place of the scarecrow?"

"Didn't start out to do that. Meant to bury him in the field.
Figured nobody'd notice fresh diggin' there. Got him out there,
then polished off the rest of the whiskey Saugus brought. Mighty
good whisky. I was looking at the scarecrow while I drank and all
of a sudden it seemed like a good idea—funny, you know?—to
dress Saugus up in those rags instead of the fancy duds he favored.
Buried the clothes, though. Just like I buried Elly's stuff all those
years ago."

Cautiously, Diana crept a few steps closer to the opening. Her
hand, sliding along the railing, touched a piece of the shattered
section and she caught hold of it to keep it from falling and alerting
Lyseth to her movements.

He jerked at the tiny sound and his eyes came back into focus,
finding her an instant later. "Hold it right there."

Diana bolted, taking the piece of wood with her. It was a poor
excuse for a weapon, little more than a pointy stick, but it had
jagged ends and was better than nothing. She fled back along the
overgrown path. By the time she broke into the next clearing,
Lyseth was only a few steps behind her.

She knew she'd never make it up onto the boardwalk and back
to the hotel without being caught. Instead she sprinted towards
the two fallen trees at the far side of the glade, grateful that she'd
worn a divided skirt. The tangled roots and branches promised
protection if she could just squirm in among them ahead of her
pursuer.

She reached her goal with only inches to spare and flung herself forward. Twigs scratched her face and arms as she crawled deeper into cover. Her hands and knees collected bruises. She felt a jerk as her skirt caught on a tree limb but a moment later it tore with a rustle of branches and a rip of fabric, setting her free.

As she tumbled into a gap in the foliage, Diana could hear Lyseth panting and smell his sweat. He was right behind her. Frantic, she wriggled and contorted her body until she was turned around. She used the broken board to ward him off, poking at him when he tried to crawl in after her.

Thank goodness he wasn't armed.

Thank goodness she'd left off her corset this morning.

But Lyseth was less than three feet away from her. She could see his eyes, full of unreasoning rage. The sound coming from his throat didn't sound human.

Diana scuttled backwards. She wanted to scream, but all that came out was a squeak. He was bent over at the waist, tearing at the fragile barrier between them. And then he charged . . . or seemed to.

Floyd Lyseth flew forward. Diana threw herself sideways just in time to avoid a collision. Then she stared, stunned, at the limp form beside her. Lyseth had struck his head on one of the larger branches and knocked himself unconscious.

An odd sound drew Diana's gaze to the open space beyond the trees. If a goat could be said to have a belligerent stance and a satisfied expression on its face, Tremont did. As if to make sure Diana knew what had happened, the little animal backed off and butted Lyseth again. This time all she could reach was his foot, but a few moments earlier, Diana realized, Lyseth had presented her with a much bigger target.

Diana didn't know whether to laugh or cry. Relief flooded through her. However absurd her rescue, she was safe now. With less grace than speed, she extricated herself from the maze of branches and roots, flung her arms around Tremont, and planted a smacking kiss right on top of the goat's head.

Ben arrived back at the hotel, together with the sheriff and Myron Grant, just as Diana came into view on the boardwalk. Her hair and clothing were disheveled, her face scratched and streaked with tears . . . and she was accompanied by the hotel goat.

"Are you all right?" Ben asked. And then, when he could see for himself that she was, demanded, "Where's Lyseth?"

"You *know* he's the killer?"

"We only just figured it out." He kept an arm around her as they joined the group gathered on the lawn—Sheriff Irvine and his deputies, Myron, Howd, Tressa, Mercy, and Mrs. Curran.

"He's in the glade between the boardwalk and the gazebo," Diana said. "Unconscious."

"That goat never did like Floyd Lyseth," Myron said after Diana explained how she'd escaped Lyseth's murderous clutches.

Ben felt as if he'd aged ten years in the telling, but he had her safe now. He sat with her on the veranda steps and surreptitiously checked her for injuries.

"I'm unhurt," she assured him. "Just bumps and bruises and scrapes. Stop fussing and tell me how you knew Lyseth was guilty."

"Pastor Riker turns out to be a reformed sinner. Much as he dislikes this hotel and despairs of the Grant brothers finding salvation, he couldn't let his accusation stand against an innocent man."

"He lied about seeing the hotel wagon in the field?"

"No, but he was mistaken about who was driving it. He only saw the man at a distance, bundled up in a heavy coat, stooped over on the seat. He was too far away to tell who it was. In fact, he saw Floyd Lyseth, but when Celia claimed it was Myron Grant out with the wagon that night, Riker decided he must have seen Myron, too."

"Then Celia lied."

"She did, but not with malice aforethought. She repeated what her husband told her to say, but what Lyseth didn't take into account was how easily she gets things muddled. The time of day, for example. When Riker heard that her story had changed between the time she confided in him and the time, at his urging, that she gave a statement to the coroner, he talked to Celia again, really listened to her for a change. Then they both went to Liberty to retract what they'd said."

"But she couldn't have known it was her husband in the wagon. That he was a killer. She——"

"She didn't. She didn't see anyone. But she confessed that her husband was the one who convinced her she *had* seen Myron. That was enough to make the sheriff and Coroner Buckley suspicious."

"And the sheriff is here because . . . ?"

"I went to Monticello to see him. I'll tell you about that later."

The men who'd gone to fetch Lyseth had come out of the woods. Lyseth was conscious but he staggered and would have fallen if the two deputies hadn't been holding him upright. When he'd been loaded into a wagon for the trip to jail, the sheriff approached Ben and Diana.

"Ma'am," he said to Diana, tipping his hat. "It's a pleasure to meet you. I'm looking forward to that interview, and if you want more than an hour with Sailor Jack, you've got it."

She stammered her thanks but then seemed bereft of speech until the wagon disappeared around the bend in the drive. When only a trail of dust remained, she turned to Ben.

"You arranged that?"

"That was one reason I went to Monticello. I had thought to convince the sheriff to arrest Belle Saugus, for fraud if nothing else, but I understand she ran off during the night with Sebastian Ellington. I can't think of any two people who deserve each other more."

Diana reached up, placed one hand on each side of his face, pulled his head towards her, and kissed him full on the mouth. "I love you, Ben Northcote."

Then her stomach growled.

"Come on," Ben said, grinning. "Let's see if Mrs. Ellington can find you something to eat."

By the time Diana had washed up and changed into clean clothing, Tressa Ellington had indeed produced the evening meal. There was a festive air in the small dining room as they gathered to break bread together. A killer had been captured.

Diana had another reason to feel relief as well. Even before he'd arranged the interview with Sailor Jack for her, she'd realized that her love for Ben was too strong to let fear stand in the way of making a life together. When she'd fled from him rather than talk about where they would live after they wed, she'd come to the conclusion that it was not just whether or not she'd be allowed to work that worried her. Marriage vows contained the promise to "obey" but they also bound two people together "till death." Suddenly the permanence of Ben's plans for them had overwhelmed her—a house of their own was more than a place to live, it was a place to raise children and grow old together. Was she capable of a lifetime commitment? How could she be sure she wasn't acting impetuously, as she had when she'd married Evan? It wasn't Ben she'd feared to trust. It had been herself.

Had been, she repeated silently, and sent a radiant smile in Ben's direction. She no longer had any doubts about marrying him.

They'd just finished eating and exchanging stories when Scorcher turned up. "Telegram for you, Mrs. Spaulding."

The glint in his eyes told her he already knew what it said, and that reminded her that she had a question for him. She took the message but put off opening it.

"Did you deliver a telegram to Sebastian Ellington in the last few days?"

"Yes, ma'am. Late yesterday afternoon. Didn't he get it? There was no one around but that lady—" He pointed to Mrs. Curran. "She said she'd give it to him."

"And she did," Diana said hastily. Of course she'd taken it to Sebastian. That would have given her an excuse to linger near the family parlor, where she could eavesdrop so much better than from the lobby. Exactly when she'd turned over the telegram hardly mattered. Sebastian had received it and read it before he'd decamped. "Do you remember what it said?" she asked Scorcher.

"Yes, ma'am." He closed his eyes and recited: "Not buying hotel. Stop sabotage. Leave town or forfeit fee." With a grin, he added, "It was signed Ed Leeves. He's mentioned in your telegram, too."

The paper in Diana's hand suddenly seemed ten times bigger than it was. She had a bad feeling about its contents, but forced herself to open it and read what it said.

"It's from my mother," she announced when she'd skimmed the contents. There was no point in putting this off any longer. "She has married Ed Leeves. They plan a wedding journey that includes a visit to Maine."

"I didn't realize your mother knew that scoundrel," Myron said. "Is that who you were visiting in Colorado? Your mother?"

"Yes," Diana said, and then quickly added, before she could lose her courage. "My name before my marriage to Evan Spaulding was Diana Torrence, Uncle Myron. My mother is your sister Elmira."

No one at the table dared breathe. Myron stared, speechless, color rising into his face. Then he looked, really looked, at Diana, and gave a rueful laugh. "Should have seen it. You're just as stubborn as she always was."

"You're not angry?"

The red hue that now stained his cheeks was clearly embarrassment rather than rage. "Been through a lot lately. You jumped in to help. I owe you."

She remembered his quiet "thank you" when the coroner had taken him away. Rising, she crossed to his chair and kissed him on the cheek. "I'm so glad. I've missed having family."

"Not forgiving Elmira," he muttered. "Just don't hold you responsible for what she did."

"That could make things difficult," Diana told him. "I want you all to come to our wedding."

Uncle Myron's mild expression darkened into a scowl. "Thought you were already married."

Diana shot a quick look at Ben, then blurted. "I was married by a justice of the peace the first time." That was true—of her marriage to Evan Spaulding. "Now Ben and I are planning a proper church wedding. It will take place in Maine on the thirtieth of June and I want everyone in my family to be there. All the Grants and all the Torrences. Including my mother and her new husband."

Uncle Myron grumbled a bit, but in the end he allowed as how he could stand to be in the same room with his sister long enough to celebrate with Diana and Ben.

Later that night, Diana and Ben took advantage of the small balcony in their suite to sit out under the full moon.

"You were right," she told him. "I rush in without thinking. I get myself into trouble. I almost got myself killed today. I will never complain that you are over-protective or high-handed again."

"Apparently you didn't need my protection. Not with Tremont around." He tried to keep his tone light, but did not quite succeed. She'd frightened him badly today.

If their situations had been reversed, Diana knew how she'd feel. Still, she tried to match his lightness. "I did have a pointy stick."

He pulled her into his arms, as if he had to hold her to be sure she was safe.

"I'll always need you," she confessed, rubbing her cheek against his breast. "And I vow I've had enough of murder. Three killers in three months is sufficient to last a lifetime."

"Don't make promises you can't keep, Diana. I understand that—"

"I don't want to be involved with crimes or criminals ever again—not to write about, not to read about, and definitely not to encounter in person."

He studied her face in the moonlight. "You really mean that."

"I do. The interview with the sheriff and Sailor Jack will be the last story of that sort I'll write. If Horatio Foxe fires me over my refusal to do anything but society interviews and travel pieces and stories on woman suffrage, so be it."

"He'll keep you on, Diana. He isn't going to lose a journalist of your caliber just because you've changed your mind about the sort of news you want to report." He frowned. "I suppose we'll have to invite him to the wedding."

"Yes, and the members of Toddy's Touring Thespains, too. I want all our friends and family to share our joy."

Ben chuckled.

"What's so funny?"

"I was just anticipating an event that will soon take place."

Puzzled, she gave him a questioning look. "You expect our marriage to be a source of amusement?"

"No doubt it will be, and full of surprises, too, but what made me smile was the thought of your mother's first meeting with mine."

THE END

AUTHOR'S NOTE

A great many people helped out with research on this book. I am particularly indebted to N. Fred Fries for information gleaned from local 1888 newspapers and to John Conway, Sullivan County Historian, who was able to confirm some of my guesses about people and places in 1888. I also want to thank Bill, Bette, Maggie, Geoff, and other members of LibertyNY@yahoogroups for providing wonderful little tidbits to incorporate into the novel. Also invaluable is a book by Manville Wakefield titled *To the Mountains by Rail.*

Sailor Jack was a real person, as were Coroner Buckley and Sheriff Irvine. What I say of them is based on newspaper accounts, but has been fictionalized. All books and newspapers I mention, except for the *Independent Intelligencer,* are also real. Any errors in portraying actual people, places, and events are mine.

Lenape Springs is my invention, although it incorporates bits and pieces of several villages in Sullivan County. I chose the name Grant because it is one of my family names. A real Mercy Grant married Samuel Gorton and their son John was one of the first settlers in Liberty, New York.

I grew up in Liberty and my family on both sides lived in

Sullivan County for a number of generations before that. A great many of the details in this book came directly from the memoirs of my grandfather, Fred Gorton, who was born in 1878. Stories told to me by my mother, Theresa Marie Coburg Gorton, also contributed. Her maternal ancestors, the Hornbecks, were among the first settlers in the area. Prior to coming to Sullivan County, Matthew Hornbeck had a store in Samsonville where he traded with the Indians. It was said they told him the location of a lead mine near Sundown. A map to this mine existed for many years, kept in "the blue trunk" at the Hornbecks' farm-boarding house in Hurleyville, New York. However, an attempt to follow the map, made in the 1920s by my mother's uncles, was a failure. Not only did they not find any trace of a mine, but the locals took one look at their big black car and Sunday suits and decided they must be gangsters.

It may seem to readers that Myron Grant is unrealistic in his plans to create a resort hotel. In fact, he's just a little ahead of his time. There never was a second Saratoga Springs in the area, but Sullivan County was well known as a thriving tourist area from the late nineteenth century until the last quarter of the twentieth.